ACCIDENTAL GETAWAY

MOLLY GRAY

To all those who have been made to feel less than: may you find your voice and someone who cherishes it.

Author's Note

While *Accidental Getaway* is a fun, sweet romance, the story does touch on serious topics. Within these pages, you'll find mention of past emotional and psychological abuse, on-page manipulative behavior (but not between our two main characters), and a brief mention of death due to domestic violence.

If you are in an unsafe situation with a domestic partner please know that there is help available. To access the National Domestic Violence Hotline, call 1-800-799-7233 or text BEGIN to 88788.

In addition, this book is a closed-door romance. There is heavy attraction between our main character, but all explicit intimacy occurs off the page.

Playlist

---

hate myself by Tate McRae
Trustfall by Ashley Kutcher
The Smallest Man Who Ever Lived by Taylor Swift
Narcissist by Avery Anna
Mean (Taylor's Version) by Taylor Swift
Who You Are by Jessie J
Scars to Your Beautiful by Alessia Cara
Butterflies by Kasey Musgraves
The Middle of Starting Over by Sabrina Carpenter
Begin Again (Taylor's Version) by Taylor Swift
Glad You Exist by Dan + Shay
Work of Art by Benson Boone
Lucky to Love You by Brynn Cartelli
SunKissing by Hailee Steinfeld
Sunshine by One Republic
Gimme That Sunshine by Animal Island
Brighter Than the Sun by Colbie Caillat
dancing in the kitchen by LANY

Chapter 1

For the second time that day, I accidentally graze the gum stuck to the edge of my library table and a gagging sound escapes me. I really need to just cover it with a tissue—but I don't, because it's a pretty fitting metaphor for my life as is. I have a marketing degree from a prestigious university; I shouldn't be desk-squatting in close proximity to a stranger's dried saliva. And yet, here I am: the chewed-up and discarded form of my prior self. I can't even really complain because it's all my own fault.

I'm not sure what's worse—the wad of Big League Chew or the fact that my job currently consists of copying and pasting someone else's slogan into an ad manager for them instead of running my own campaigns and client portfolios.

The couple that soaks together stays together.

Copy. And paste.

I find the corresponding image of two gorgeous thirty-somethings perched in an open-air hot springs pool while sipping champagne.

Upload. Schedule.

I guess this is what happens when you self-implode at

Chicago's biggest marketing agency and set every single bridge ablaze on your way out.

I move on to the next ad that Amber, my boss at Aspen Sky Marketing, has in the queue. Instead of an account manager, I'm an administrative assistant, with all of the prestige, and the crappy pay that goes with it. A fact I'm reminded of every time I get my student loan statements.

If I can focus and get these ads scheduled, I'll be able to get out of here on time. My schedule is going to be tight today, but if I leave in the next hour, I should have plenty of time to beat traffic and make it to Denver by 3:00 p.m.

I would rather be working at home than the library, but the problem is that I live with my parents—I am a bona fide twenty-four-year-old failure to launch—and today is Tuesday. Mom's knitting circle will be at the house until sometime in the late afternoon, when they will simultaneously complain about going home to make dinner. I avoid them like the plague. I would rather chew on the discarded gum in front of me than talk to another knitting lady about my nonexistent love life or about my job that they never seem to understand.

It wasn't supposed to be this way. This isn't what I planned for my life. After college, I was living in the big city with a fancy job and a successful boyfriend.

I wasn't allowed to call him my boyfriend in public, but that's another story.

I had a tiny, yet trendy, apartment and ate at the best restaurants. It was everything I had worked for throughout high school and college. My dad bragged to everyone he knew, and I was happy. I might have been worked to the bone and constantly stressed, but I had dreamed of getting out of Pineview Springs since I was twelve years old, and I had made it happen.

But then I threw it all away during one stupid meeting where I couldn't keep my mouth shut. I got too confident and upset a client by sharing my opinion. That super successful boyfriend took the client's side and fired me on the spot. I could have stayed and fought for that life, but instead, I fled. I left that night and never returned a single phone call or email from anyone I worked with.

I glance up from my laptop to the rowdy sight of a story time getting started. And while the jubilant toddlers piling onto colorful cushions is kind of adorable, it's nothing compared to the skyline views from my old desk in the bullpen of Chicago's largest luxury marketing firm. By now, I would have been a second-year associate—working on massive accounts, eating Chinese takeout around a conference table—and would have the paycheck to go along with it.

My phone vibrates on the table, and I go to silence it out of habit, but it's Amber. I answer, hoping it's a quick question so I can finish my work. I told her I would be away from my phone for a few hours this afternoon, but she doesn't know it's for a job interview.

"Jenni, I'm so glad I caught you," Amber says, as if I have ever not answered one of her calls. That's one habit I still have from my big firm days: I'm constantly available to my boss, day and night. "I need you to look at the Telluride Fourth of July event proposal before we send it to the client tonight. It's a bit of a mess and I'm running late for a doctor's appointment. Do you have time?"

I take a deep breath and check my watch. That document is at least fifty pages long. It will take me more than an hour to go through it, maybe two.

"Oh, the entire document?" I ask, stalling for a reason to back out. I don't have time for this.

"Yes, the whole thing. I need you to double-check all the figures to make sure they are accurate—oh, and can you take a look at the formatting? It's gone super wonky."

"Well, I'm working on the hot springs ads, but maybe I can…"

"Thank you, thank you. You're a lifesaver. Okay, I need to run. Send it over when you're done."

The line goes dead. Great. This is exactly what I didn't need today.

It's 11:30 a.m. and I haven't eaten all day. I guess I can put these ads on hold until tonight since none of them are scheduled to go live for a few days. If I take the proposal over to Bobby's Café and beat the lunch rush, I can eat while I look it over. If I speed through it, maybe I can still get out of here on time.

I shut my laptop to pack up.

Like most of the streets in Pineview Springs, this one is lined with black vintage-looking light posts adorned with hanging flower baskets and miniature Colorado state flags. Growing up, those little flags filled me with a sense of patriotism and belonging. But now? All I can see is where they are faded and ripped. Just like my life.

Once across the street, I step up into the restaurant and a bell chimes above the door. Bobby, the owner, smiles and calls out, "Iced caramel latte, coming right up!"

Some days, I feel like I live in Stars Hollow or some other romanticized little town where everyone knows your name and coffee order. It seems great on TV, but sometimes it can be downright suffocating. What if I wanted an Americano today?

Even if I did want something different, I wouldn't ask for it because Bobby takes pride in knowing the regulars and I would hate to deprive him of that joy.

"I'll take a BLT too, please. Keep the change," I say and set some cash by the register. Bobby is already drizzling caramel inside of a medium cup with my name on it. "Thanks!"

I'm just settling into a little table near the back when the bell above the door chimes behind me.

"Jenni Swanson, as I live and breathe. What are you doing here?"

Crap. I sigh. Not today. I don't want to see anyone or feel like I have to explain myself and why I'm here for the hundredth time. I just want to eat my lunch and get this proofread done. But I turn around anyway, with a stiff smile on my face, to see which part of my past has walked through the door.

"Mrs. Harper! Oh, my gosh!" My surprise is genuine. I haven't seen her since I moved home six months ago. "It's so good to see you!"

Mrs. Harper was my high school history teacher. My favorite teacher. I've heard she was still teaching, but I haven't made the effort to stop by and see her. Secretly, I've been waiting for my life to turn around before doing so. I didn't want to disappoint her. But I'd be surprised if the gossip train hasn't already blown my cover.

"My dear! It's so good to see you, too. Are you in town for a visit? Last I heard, you were in Chicago. Oh, I remember that was all you used to talk about. Getting away from Pineview Springs and seeing the world."

The way I see it, I have two options here. I can tell Mrs. Harper the truth and disappoint her, or I can stretch the truth a tiny bit to let her keep her believing I achieved all the goals she helped me set back in the classroom. The kind thing to do, really, would be to tell her what she wants to hear, right? I wouldn't want to ruin her day with my tales of woe.

I keep a smile plastered to my face. "Oh, you know, not much has changed for me! Working at a marketing firm, spending as much time outdoors as possible. I'm in town to see my parents. Piper and Sarah are also coming for a visit in a few days, and I wanted to be here for that."

None of that was too much of a lie, right? I do *see* my parents every day. And Piper and Sarah *might* be coming to visit soon. I never know with those two.

Seeing Mrs. Harper here, in town, brings back so many memories. Not only was she my teacher, but I used to work for Mrs. Harper and her husband. They owned the Pineview Inn —an adorable old-school bed-and-breakfast in town. My best friend, Piper, and I both worked there all throughout high school. I got the job first and then recommended her.

I don't allow myself to dwell on the irony that almost ten years later, Piper is the one who got me this job at Aspen Sky after I left Chicago.

"That's wonderful. I'm so glad that the two of you are still in touch. That girl has always been so unapologetically herself. It's one of my favorite things to see in a high schooler. These days, all the kids are so worried about social media that I can barely get them to tell me anything about themselves. They have to check if it's on-trend or canceled before they'll tell me."

I nod. Piper is pretty amazing like that. When she came out, the first thing she did was ask a girl to homecoming. She wasn't going to let anyone at school tell her she couldn't. Even when her parents struggled with her identity and she stayed with me for a while, she was confident they would come around.

Bobby sets my drink and sandwich down on the table.

"Well, it was so nice to see you, Mrs. Harper, but I have to catch up on some work, actually," I say, fighting not to let my paper-thin veil of confidence waver. "I'll stop by the school next time I'm in town."

"No use in that." She chuckles. "I'm retired! Had my last day in the classroom a few weeks ago. Jerry is needing a lot more help these days, and I just couldn't do that and keep teaching. He keeps me on my toes, though."

Jerry Harper's stroke forced them to close the bed-and-breakfast since he had been the one running the inn's day-to-day operations. They've been trying to sell the inn, but haven't had much luck finding a buyer they like. Still, I hadn't realized

Jerry was needing so much care. I should really check in on him.

Mrs. Harper always talked about the two of them traveling the world once they both retired. That must be so hard on them.

"I'm sorry retirement isn't going the way you planned," I say. "Do you think you still might take that round-the-world trip?"

"I don't think so, honey. Not for a long time anyway, but that's okay. Dreams change. And our job is to adjust and make new dreams. I get to spend lots of time with the man I love. I also get to go for long walks whenever I want and I'm reading more than I ever thought possible. Life is good."

Bobby returns again, this time handing Mrs. Harper a to-go cup.

"I'll let you get back to work," she says. We hug and she waves as she exits the restaurant, turning toward the lake. I take a deep breath.

All of that about making new dreams? That might work for retirement plans, but not for careers. I can't just sit here and say, "Never mind. I'd rather just give up."

I've seen how that plays out. My mom was supposed to be a dancer. She had trained her whole life and was apparently incredible. She had dreams of going to New York City and being on stage. But then, she met my dad—a schoolteacher with a job already lined up. She settled. And though she would probably deny it, I know she regrets her choices. Growing up, I would catch her longingly looking at magazines in the grocery store, or tearing up at Christmas when we watched *The Nutcracker*. Sure, she threw herself into her life here: homesteading, camping, and supporting her family as much as possible. But I think she secretly always wished it had happened for her.

I frown at the food on my plate, suddenly not feeling quite

so hungry. I do not want to be stuck here like my mom, wishing I had ended up somewhere else. With a sigh, I grab my phone and text Piper.

> Jenni: You'll never guess who I just ran into…
> Mrs. Harper!

> Piper: Wow! What did she say about you
> moving home?

I should have known she would ask. I'm tempted to change the subject, but Piper's the only person I don't have to pretend with. She's known me too long and can see through all my BS nine times out of ten anyway.

> Jenni: I might have let her believe that I was still
> living in Chicago…

> Piper: The teacher's pet LIED? That's some
> piping hot tea. Why?

Is she really going to make me say it? It's embarrassing. I set out to do all these big things, and I made sure everyone knew it. I tell Piper as much, and she sends back an exasperated emoji. It's her way of telling me she can't have this conversation with me, again. Which is fair. I'm definitely a broken record lately.

> Jenni: I also might have told her you and Sarah
> were coming up and that's why I am here ;)

> Piper: Ha! Well, we are in New Mexico, so just a
> few hours south, but we're heading to
> California next.

> Jenni: I know, I know. Wishful thinking.

What I wouldn't give to have a girls' night. My social

calendar involves watching *Wheel of Fortune* and *Jeopardy* with my parents every week night at 6:00 p.m. on the dot.

> Piper: Are you heading to your interview?

> Jenni: Not yet. Amber just asked me to proofread the Telluride proposal and it's going to take forever. I'm not sure I'll get out of here on time.

I probably shouldn't bother going through another interview anyway. It will be my tenth interview in the last few months and none of them have amounted to anything.

> Piper: Send me half and I'll help you.

> Jenni: Seriously? You're the best. Thank you!

> Piper: You owe me. LOVEYOUSOMUCH

Forty minutes later, we're both done, and I'm heading down to Denver.

Chapter 2

I cruise down the mountain toward Denver in my trusty little Subaru wondering where six months have gone and how the heck I'm still so stuck. When I first moved home, I thought a few weeks would be all I needed to get back on my feet. I thought I would sleep, eat mom's homemade mac 'n' cheese, go hiking with my dad, and then get my butt in gear. My focus would turn to finding a new job and moving on. But the longer I laid in bed and the more I put off my job search, the harder it got to want to do anything. I would sit around and play games on my phone or tag along on all of my mom's errands. And the longer I went not looking for jobs, the further I dropped into depression—unable to see a way out. It was a vicious cycle.

Finally, after a couple months of doing nothing, Piper begged me to apply to be an assistant at the same start-up marketing agency she worked at. The agency is entirely remote, so I didn't have to move or start over in a new place with new people, which would have terrified me. And because I was applying to be an assistant, I hoped to avoid talking about my job in Chicago and what happened. As it turned out, I didn't even have to interview; Piper's recommendation was enough to get me the job.

And for a while, things felt better. I had a reason to get up in the morning again. Though, I'm starting to dread that same routine that gave me so much security in the beginning.

I yearn for something exciting to happen, but at the same time, my chest feels tight any time I think about taking steps toward the future I want. It's easy here. I don't have to worry that I'm going to mess everything up again or humiliate myself in front a client. I don't have much of a life, but I also don't have much to lose either. It feels safe. Most days, that is good enough for me, but every once in a while, I wonder if things might be different if I try again. And those rare days are the ones where I get my hopes up and fill out job applications.

Forty-five minutes later, after cursing downtown parking for being so impossible, I walk through the doors to the marketing agency on the eighteenth floor of a high-rise overlooking the city. After checking in at the front desk, take a seat on a plush leather chair in the waiting area. Though, the moment I do, I notice my mouth feels like sandpaper, and I can't ignore it thanks to my nerves. I grab a cup of water from the water dispenser in the corner. With a tight grip on the cold cup in one hand and my portfolio in the other, I close my eyes and inhale a deep breath.

"Miss Swanson? Dan can see you now." A woman in a little black dress beckons me.

"Great, thank you!"

I look around for a trash can to toss my cup. My eyes go wide when the water inside it splashes up as the cup hits the bottom of the can, but the woman pretends not to notice. She escorts me into a sleek office overlooking the baseball stadium. My dad would be so jealous.

A man with a perfectly-tailored blue suit and tie stands to greet me. "Hi, Jenni, my name is Dan. Come on in."

I know Dan is the hiring manager from stalking the company online after sending in my application. He went to Stanford and has worked here in the seven years since. He loves to ski and he has two Dobermans, according to his company bio.

"Have a seat. Tell me a little bit about yourself."

I try not to cringe at this question. Even after so many interviews, I still haven't figured out a satisfactory way to answer it.

"Sure." I paste a smile on my face. "I'm a Colorado native, and love hiking, and camping." I picked these details to share because I know the firm represents a major recreational clothing company. "If you take a look in my portfolio, I did my senior project on marketing principles for the outdoors enthusiast."

He flips through the folder I gave him when I sat down. "Excellent. Your portfolio is very impressive."

"Thank you. I really strive for excellence with every project, no matter how big or small."

"I can see that," he says, looking at a magazine ad for a mommy blogger's cutesy first-aid kit brand that has been taking off. Most of my portfolio is made up of assignments I did in school or spreads I have created in my own time. One Aspen Sky campaign made its way in there, too, because I did 90 percent of the work. But I didn't include anything from my days in Chicago. "Tell me, why you are pursuing a career in marketing?"

"I have always been inspired by the challenge of creatively meeting the needs of two groups of people at once. I love when a campaign not only helps the client increase their business but also when it helps get the right product or service in the hands of people who need it. I think it's a beautiful synergy that often gets overlooked when people see marketing as an extension of consumerism."

He nods. I believe every word of what I just said, but I also read an article from one of the firm's partners who basically said the same thing, so I'm hoping it's the right answer.

After a few more questions, I'm sitting taller in my chair and the tightness in my chest has eased. I haven't hesitated or talked in circles. And when he asked me to name a recent marketing book I've read, he said he was currently reading the same one. I have been right on point for the whole interview.

"Jenni, I have to say, your portfolio and the way you carry yourself is very impressive. I love everything I'm seeing. However, this position requires at least a year of experience and I just don't have any wiggle room on that. According to your résumé, you haven't done much since graduation, outside of your current position as an administrative assistant. I don't even see any internships. Can you help me understand the gap? Have you held a marketing job before?"

And there it is—the sound of the other shoe dropping.

I have experience. I have a ton of experience. But I can't put that experience on my résumé without having to explain why I left Prewitt Luxury Marketing after two internships and nearly two years of building my career. But I can't do that. Nor do I want anyone calling the firm to check for references. I left in such a messy way and in such a hurry that even the people who liked me probably wouldn't be able to recommend me.

Well, we liked her, but she basically disappeared overnight, and no one ever knew why. I don't think that would go over well.

"I had a personal situation that disrupted my career path," I finally explain. "I know it's far from ideal, but I have stayed up on trends and done work for friends. I know I have the skills and ability to handle the workload. In my job as an assistant, I have my hands on a very wide range of projects."

He looks over portfolio once again. Does he realize he holds my future in his hands? That he can make or break me? All I need is one person to overlook my lack of "on paper" experience and give me a chance. I can prove them all wrong…I only need a chance.

Dan sits up straight and wrings his hands.

With that simple body language, I deflate. He is bracing himself to tell me something I don't want to hear.

"I sympathize with your situation. I really do," he says. And I wait for the "but."

"I think you have a ton of potential, but we really aren't in a position to hire someone without experience for this role. There are HR mandates I have to follow. You might have better luck at smaller firms. We also have a robust internship program you can look into next summer."

I rise from my chair, ready to get as far away as possible before the self-loathing kicks in. "I understand. Thank you for your time."

"Please come back when you have some more experience. I think you've got a lot of talent."

Is that supposed to make me feel better? Because it doesn't. It feels like I'm up against a brick wall and the only option I have is to turn around. Do not pass Go, do not collect $200.

And it's not as if that would be easy, either. As humiliating as it is, I've looked at internships. That's how desperate I am. But they all want students. I even looked into grad school, but I already have a mountain of student debt that I can't add to in good conscience.

As I head back to my car, I can already hear the conversation over breakfast tomorrow morning. Mom will offer me a steaming mug of black coffee she knows I hate and when I refuse it, she'll ask me how I'm doing with "you know… with everything." She is always vague, as if naming my depression will make it contagious. Then, Dad will ask about my "job situation" and I'll have nothing to report. Mom will smack him because she's perfectly happy with me being home adding in a "You shouldn't be so hard on her."

Then, one of them will inevitably bring up my younger brother, Jeremy, who is off in Seattle working for a tech company that's paying his college tuition because he started designing video games for them while still in high school. He saw his dreams and never looked back.

This same conversation happens once a week, like clockwork. I can practically set my watch by it.

It makes me want to scream.

Don't get me wrong. I'm so grateful that they took me in because I don't make enough money to afford my own place, even in Pineview Springs. But that fateful night I left Chicago and drove through the night to get here, I never thought I would still be here. I don't know where else to go.

More experience. It's always about more experience. But how can I magically get myself more experience if no one will hire me because I lack it?

Chapter 3

The next morning, I settle at my desk with a cozy blanket and power up my computer, just in time to join our weekly staff meeting.

Amber started Aspen Sky Marketing three years ago as a start-up agency with a focus on independent boutique hotels, resorts, and small visitors' bureaus like the one in Telluride. Though she started as a one-woman show, she has hired four associates, including Piper, and then me as her full-time assistant.

My job consists of proofreading, admin work, taking meeting notes, setting up new clients, billing, and helping out when a project is more than an associate can handle on their own. But right now, my biggest duty is making sure everything is set for Amber's maternity leave next month.

To start the meeting, Amber announces that she has a few scheduling conflicts to discuss with the team.

"As some of you know, I've been in communication with a hotel in Greece I am very excited about. But we haven't signed on the dotted line yet because the board of investors have decided they want to hear all proposals at a board meeting before the general manager can sign a contract."

Greece. Wouldn't that just be a dream. Too bad for Amber that all of our client meetings are held virtually these days. I'm sure this will involve joining the board meeting via webcam.

Amber continues to discuss the needs of the hotel, which is being rebranded after a change in ownership.

I think one of the hardest things about this job is holding my tongue; I'm just supposed to be taking notes. When I was at Prewitt Luxury, I worked on quite a few hotel rebrands. They were all big chains, rather than independent properties, but there can be a lot of overlap, particularly in target audiences and performance metrics.

On a particularly challenging project I worked on with a resort in Mexico that had experienced a few unfortunate incidents involving spring breakers, they were trying to reposition themselves as a family hotel. When travelers were not biting, we ended up procuring a commercial spot during a nationally televised sporting event showcasing families having the time of their life. Bookings skyrocketed. We celebrated at Chicago's nicest steak house after that one.

"I am looking for someone who would be able to take this on next week," Amber goes on.

I jump, ready to take notes again. I need to pay attention to who gets this assignment so I can make the necessary scheduling allocations.

"The board convenes quarterly, and the next meeting is on the fifteenth. You'll being working closely with the general manager to plan the proposal. He wants to be heavily involved in preparations."

No one on the call says anything. Most are looking down, not wanting to make eye contact.

"Does anyone have the availability? It would really help me out."

Still, silence. What is going on? Did I miss something? This is a big deal assignment. I would kill for it.

Wait. Could I … Maybe this is what I've been waiting for. If no one will hire me because of my lack of experience, maybe getting experience here at Aspen Sky is what I need. A simple presentation over video. I can handle that. I could even rent a co-working space to make it more official-looking than my bedroom or the library. If I nail this, Amber will have no choice but to hire me as an associate, right? And once I put that on my résumé, I could finally get a new job and get out of my parents' house after a year or two.

My knee starts bouncing. In a moment of pure adrenaline and little bit of recklessness, I slam down the spacebar to unmute.

"I could do it!" I spit the words out before I can stop myself, speaking over Amber, who is, at the exact same time, saying, "I would do it if I could, but of course, the pregnancy."

She shrugs and what she said registers in my brain. What does being pregnant have to do with negotiating a contract? Her maternity leave isn't scheduled to start until after the meeting.

"Jenni? Was that you? You can do what?"

I frantically scan the other faces on my screen for a hint at what Amber might have meant. I come up empty.

"Um, I could take over preparing the proposal? I know I'm just an assistant, but I have experience. Only if no one else can do it, of course … just trying to be helpful." I clench my jaw to keep myself from continuing to backpedal before Amber responds.

Amber's face lights up and I can practically see the wheels turning in her mind.

"That's not a bad idea," she comments, and then mutters to herself for a moment. "Are you sure? It's kind of a lot to take on for a first timer."

Am I sure? Absolutely not. The only thing I'm sure about is that it feels like every single person on the meeting is now staring at me. They're all expecting me to say yes, so I do.

"Absolutely," I reply. I can't back out now, even though my surge of confidence is waning at a rapid pace. "I'll get to work right away."

Amber seems to be considering me. I don't know if it's because she can tell I'm desperate or if she's trying to decide whether I can actually pull it off.

"That's fantastic, Jenni." She smiles. "I'm sure the GM won't mind if you go to Greece in my place. I'll touch base with him after our meeting and get the ball rolling." Then, after a beat, she says, "Great initiative! Everyone, take note. I love to support people who ask for opportunities."

I'm frozen. Stiff as a board. In fact, I might be DOA.

Go.

To.

Greece.

That's what pregnancy had to do with it? She couldn't *travel* to Greece for the board meeting because she's too far along in her pregnancy?

All the adrenaline and courage that was just coursing through my veins sinks to my feet and turns into lead, anchoring me to the floor. I want to crawl back into bed.

I know it's not the reaction one would expect when someone's boss wants to send them to a freaking Greek island. I should be elated. I should be jumping up and down. But the prospect of having to be in a room with the board of the hotel makes me feel like I'm going to throw up.

E-mail is one thing. Phone calls and video calls are even digestible. But my stomach flips and turns as I picture standing in front of a room of businessmen, desperately seeking their approval and knowing that I'll never get it. Knowing that one wrong word could have them turning on me just like what happened in Chicago. The helplessness fills me with terror.

Amber moves on to the next topic of discussion, but all I can focus on is determining how badly I have screwed up. This is bad. So, so bad. Thankfully my laptop camera is the epitome of low-def, and no one on the call can see the panic I'm sure is written all over my face. At least I hope not.

My computer pings and a chat box flashes open.

> Piper: O. M. G. JENNI!!!!! Holy cow! That was gutsy AF. You are going to GREECE! I bet you could extend your stay a bit. Island hop. You are going to be a total GODDESS!

My fingertips hover over the keyboard. My mind and body aren't connecting. I wouldn't be able to make my hands type out a message even if I knew what to say.

Why did I think this was a good idea? I can't do this. I should have recognized the risks. The last time I was in a meeting flashes to the surface—the heart palpitations and nausea as the client ripped me apart in front of my superior, my boyfriend.

Finally, I manage to connect the synapses in my brain and slowly type out a response.

> Jenni: Yeah. I did not realize it was a trip. I was distracted. I can't go. Do you think Amber is going to hate me?

> Piper: What?!? Why can't you go??

> Piper: Amber isn't going to hate you. Because unless there's a wedding or a funeral, you are going to rearrange your schedule and go to Greece.

A wedding or a funeral … there's an idea. I can fabricate a

cousin. A cousin who is more like a sister and she's getting married in California. But no, that will never work. Piper knows I don't have a cousin. She's the only person remotely close to being a sister to me.

I grab my water bottle just to have something to keep my hands from shaking. But instead, I knock it over with my fumbling, nervous energy. Water floods my notebook and gets dangerously close to my laptop. I toss the computer onto the couch and use the blanket in my lap to sop up the spill. So much for people not witnessing me freak out.

> Piper: Hello?! Where'd you go? Does this have anything to do with that stupid ex? You have to stop giving a crap about that guy and what he may or may not have thought about you.

I throw the wet blanket on the floor and pull my computer back onto my desk. I read Piper's message, and my stomach lurches at the mention of Malcolm. I can practically feel his cold eyes on me.

> Jenni: Ew. No. Of course not. I just can't go. It doesn't matter why. I'll talk to Amber. I'm sure it will be fine. Someone else would be way better for the job anyway.

I watch the chat, hoping she doesn't see right through me. The words *Piper is typing* … appear and disappear while I debate saying more.

I try not to think about Malcolm, but the way he looked at me when I spoke out of turn and pissed off that client has burned such a deep hole that it's impossible not to. Malcolm somehow manages to creep his way into every decision I make, even still. I can't get him out of my head. It feels like he's waiting around every corner and mocking my every move.

Last week, I got a card in the mail with no return address. I opened it and Malcolm's smug face smiled up at me from an engagement announcement. It was even personalized, letting me know that he's officially off the market—barely six months after we split.

It was like he knew I was having a particularly good week and wanted to pop that bubble before it could get too big.

I never intended to get back together with him, *ever*, so how dare he act as if I would need this information? And while it made me furious, it also freaked me out. He remembered where my parents lived. He was still keeping tabs on me.

Finally, the chat pings.

> Piper: Don't do anything stupid. Don't say anything to anyone. Especially not Amber. I'll call you as soon as this meeting is over.

Then ten seconds later…

> Piper: You deserve this, Jenni. Don't throw it away. This is your chance.

I minimize the chat, grab a new notepad, and intend to pay attention to the rest of the meeting. But then the engagement announcement pokes at my brain, urging me to pull it out of my desk drawer. I double-check that his new fiancée still looks just like me but better—smaller curves, longer dark wavy hair, and a prettier round face. It's unsettling.

Honestly, seeing him this way, all I feel is regret. I wonder if I would have even dated him if I hadn't been so desperate for approval in college. I was a brand-new intern and the dreamy, charismatic son of the head partner of my firm was interested in me. How could I say no to that? I thought it meant I was special—that I had what it takes to make it in that world. But looking back, it's clear he only saw someone desperate enough to let him walk all over them. He practically said as much when we broke up the third or fourth time. I lost count.

"You were so easy. You practically begged me to take you out. It was pathetic."

What if I hadn't ever said yes? What if I had never let him into my life to turn it upside down and rip it apart at the seams?

Chapter 4

Not even a minute passes between the end of the meeting and my phone buzzing. My eyes narrow as I glance at the screen. Piper's name, along with a picture of us paddle boarding on Pineview Lake, fills the screen. At least it's not Amber. I grab the phone and run up the stairs to my bedroom. I need privacy and to lie down for this conversation.

The phone keeps buzzing in my hand, and I briefly consider letting it go to voicemail. But I know she won't stop, so I swipe to answer.

"Ok. Tell me what is going on. What in the world could possibly keep you from accepting a trip to Greece *for free?*" Piper practically shouts as soon as I answer the call. She's talking a mile a minute. "Not to mention the career opportunity. This is huge for you! Have you lost your mind?"

"Hello to you too. So nice to hear from you," I respond, acting offended to buy myself some more time. I sit on the bed and start picking at the embroidery ties of a quilt I made in elementary school. "I don't know. I just don't think it's the right time to go. I've got my parents to consider. They are going camping next week, so I need to watch the house and animals. And I have some other plans."

"Sorry, friend. That isn't going to work with me. *You* know that *I* know you have no life. And since when do your parents need you? They can take care of themselves."

But the chickens can't.

"And chickens don't need tending while your parents are camping. They are also self-sufficient."

I groan. Dang it. She always reads my mind.

I put the phone on speaker and take three steps to the mini fridge I have tucked in my closet. My hands are still slightly shaking as I pull out a jug of cold brew and a bottle of creamer. I need some caffeine to have this conversation.

"I … I don't know what to tell you. I had a brief moment of insanity. I literally don't know what came over me. But it was a mistake."

I grab a mason jar off the top of the mini fridge and get to making myself an iced coffee.

"It wasn't a mistake. You are the perfect person to do this! Obviously. You have the experience, you have the talent—you just need the opportunity. And here you go."

The sincerity in Piper's voice has softened my anxiety. She's my best friend, so of course she supports me.

"Look, I'm not taking no for an answer. I got you this job and I want to see you thrive. If you don't do this for yourself, do it for me. Or tell me what is really going on."

I can't tell Piper what's wrong. I never told her how horrible that final meeting was. The way hot tears streaked down my face before I even stepped out of the elevator. The way I walked twenty blocks in the middle of a Chicago winter and bled into my heels. The way my head throbbed for hours. I have never told her how absolutely terrified I am of being in a meeting with a client again. I thought if this was just over video call I could fool myself into thinking it wasn't that bad, but every time I picture sitting in a boardroom in front of a bunch of men in suits, my blood runs cold. What if I say the wrong thing? I don't think I would be able to handle the looks on their faces. The looks I got back in Chicago.

Even with Piper, I can't talk about that. I have spent a year trying to forget that feeling of being so small. So insignificant. So annihilated by the opinions of a few men in suits. It keeps me up at night. So instead, I tell her the acceptable reason—the one that doesn't require me sinking to that low again.

"You know I don't travel."

While it's a secondary issue, it's true I have never left the country. My parents don't travel, and I've just never had the opportunity to do it on my own. I wouldn't know the first thing about managing my way to Greece for this project.

"And?"

"What if I get lost? Or make a cultural faux pas? Or hate the food?"

Okay, when I say it like that, it definitely sounds silly. But that doesn't make it any less anxiety-inducing on top of the other fears attempting to drown me.

I always wanted to travel. After taking an art history class during my freshman year of college, I dreamed of seeing Europe.

At the end of my sophomore year, I was accepted for a fall study abroad in London. It was extremely competitive to get a spot. I even convinced my mom that it would be safe. I got a passport and even researched all the shows and museums and cities I wanted to visit. I was so excited. But that summer was my first internship at Prewitt Luxury, where I met Malcolm. I dropped out of the program a couple of weeks after we started dating because he said he would miss me too much. *"Do you really expect me to stay here for months by myself? I could never do that. If you go to London, we have to break up. I just wouldn't be able to handle you being gone."* I was so inexperienced that I thought he was being sweet. I couldn't believe that this smart older guy cared so much about keeping me in his life. Not to mention I was already worried that if I broke up with him, my chances at the firm would be affected.

Piper finally clears her throat. When she speaks, her voice has softened, and she doesn't sound quite so confused or accusatory. "I see you. I get it. That's a lot. But I know you can handle it. So tell me, what could go right?"

I try to picture it. I volunteered to try and get promoted and fix all of my problems, but what else?

"I could prove him wrong." The words are out of my mouth before I even realize I'm thinking it. Crap.

"Malcolm? I thought you said—"

"No," I say immediately. I can't believe I said that out loud. "Not Malcolm—I told you this isn't about him. I meant the guy from my interview yesterday. He said something about me not having enough experience, and it bugged me."

I retreat into myself. Proving Malcolm wrong would be the best sort of vindication. Showing him I'm not as useless as he always made me feel.

"I know it's scary, but you can do this. You just have to say yes."

I can't shake the feeling that this might be my only chance.

"Wait," Piper says. "Do you have a passport?"

The little blue book came in the mail a week after I withdrew from the London program. Opening the envelope and holding it in my hands turned into a painful moment once I knew I wasn't going to use it. But I tucked it away, hoping I would one day.

"I think so … I mean, yes, I do. I just have to find it somewhere."

"Then there is no problem. You are going to kill this

presentation. Don't let your fear of travel stop you from finally taking control of your life."

If only it were that simple. Before I can respond, my phone rings with another incoming call.

"Ugh. I've got to go. Amber is calling."

"Please don't say anything—"

I hang up before Piper can finish and switch calls. Looks like I have to face the reality of this trip sooner than I hoped. I move to the window bench in my room, sit up tall and answer the phone with a happy-to-help voice, through a wave of nausea.

"Hi! Is now a good time to chat?"

"Sure, yeah. Happy to." Anything but, really. Delaying this conversation isn't going to change anything, though.

"The more I have thought about your involvement here, the more I think it's perfect," Amber says.

"Oh, really?" I grip my phone in surprise. "Because I was going to apologize for being so presumptuous. You can absolutely change your mind, and I would be happy to continue on with my work and forget I ever suggested it."

I can always find another opportunity. Somewhere down the line. When I feel more ready.

"I think taking this on will be a great experience for you. You've earned it, and I can't wait to see you succeed. I'll be here on the other end of a phone call or email the whole way through."

My nausea wanes knowing she will be involved the entire time. And the thought of waiting months or years for another opportunity or job interview to go my way is enough to make me second-guess myself.

"Are you sure I'm the right person? Maybe Piper or one of the other associates can rearrange their schedules." My voice wavers.

"When I hired you, Piper said you were an incredible

marketer, but that you needed to get back on your feet in a low-pressure job. I didn't ask any questions because I was happy to help. I would hate to lose you as my assistant, but we're going to need to expand if we land this client, and I would love to see you shine."

I'm going to kill Piper. She did *not* tell me that was how I got the job. "I… I don't know what to say."

"Say yes, of course! I know you can do this."

I bite my lip. How do I say no when she is being so kind and supportive? I am just going to have to figure out how not to mess it up. "Okay, I'll do it. Thank you, Amber. I really, really appreciate it."

"That's what I like to hear! I'll send you over all of the details, but for now all you need to know is that the Omorfiá Hotel is owned by a Greek conglomerate, but the general manger, Niko Psomas, is running the show. He's been modernizing the hotel and called us to help with the US market. The board simply wants to approve any partnerships before contracts are signed. They are pretty old school, so it should be easy to focus on facts and figures and show them we get results."

That sounds easy enough, I guess.

Leave it to you to screw up something easy, though. My stomach turns at the voice in my head. It's Malcolm's voice, still constantly beating me up.

I try not to let Amber hear me falter.

"Great! I'll familiarize myself with the property and create a portfolio of similar hotels and resorts we've worked with, showcasing ROI and year-over-year bookings and maybe look at demographic trends—" I stop, realizing that I'm rambling. "Does that sound right to you? I'll do whatever you think is best."

"That's exactly what I would be doing. I'm fully confident you can do this."

That makes one of us.

"This is such a dream come true moment for me," Amber continues. "When I started this company, Greece was the one of the places I dreamed of representing once we broke into the international market. There is just something so magical about it. I was devastated that I couldn't go to the meeting myself. I can't tell you how much it means that you volunteered."

Great, that doesn't sound high pressure at all. I was nervous enough already without knowing Amber's dreams hinge on me landing this client. I can't let her down. Not only because I need a promotion, like tomorrow, but because she wants this so badly. I don't think I will be able to return to work and meet her eyes if I fail.

My phone vibrates, and I pull it from my ear to take a peep at the notification.

Piper: Love you! You've got this!

Heat spreads across my cheeks. I guess I really don't have a choice, do I? But maybe Piper is right. Maybe I can do this. Maybe it could even be fun?

"When do you want me to go?" I ask.

"I'll get in touch with Niko and get you booked. I think he wants you to spend some time there before the meeting to get to know the place and so you can work together on the presentation. But sometime next week. I'll send you an email once everything is nailed down."

We say our goodbyes and I stare at my phone, trying to process what just happened.

Jenni: I hope you're right …

Piper: Eeeek! Does that mean you're doing it? You can SO do this! We're coming to help you get ready. Don't try to talk me out of it. We're already loading the RV, and we'll see you tomorrow!

What have I gotten myself into? How did I accidentally get myself a trip to Greece? This is either going to be the adventure of a lifetime, or it will crash and burn with the heat of a raging bonfire. I try not to think about which is a likelier outcome.

Chapter 5

By the time Piper and Sarah arrive late in the afternoon the day after my meeting, I am an anxious wreck. I have spent every free moment between work tasks searching for my passport without success. I've torn apart my room and am now sitting in a pile of random junk and clothes.

I have gotten myself in way over my head. Clearly, I have lost my mind. All I want to do is crawl into bed and forget any of this is happening, but I'm supposed to meet Piper and Sarah at a restaurant in thirty minutes, and I'm still in my ratty sweats. At least I showered this morning.

I go stand in front of my closet to find an outfit to wear. Piper and Sarah always look amazing with their funky, unique style that anything in my closet feels dull in comparison. I finally find a pair of old jeans and grab a vintage-looking black T-shirt from my favorite deep-dish pizza joint in Chicago. It used to be my lucky T-shirt, actually. I wore it anytime I had an exam. So maybe it will help me today. I grab a green bomber jacket and run downstairs.

The night is warm, and I decide to bike to the restaurant. At this point in the summer, traffic can be pretty bad with tourists making their way through town. Biking will be easier and faster. When I cycle into the restaurant parking lot, my friends are already there, looking like they walked over from where they parked their RV by the lake. The two women rush over and wrap me in a huge bear hug before I can even lock up my bike. Both of them look gorgeously relaxed and happy. Piper has gotten some sun and is wearing a collared shirt and chino shorts. Sarah's hair looks freshly braided and her black skin glistens in the afternoon sun. In their presence, the anxiety I have felt about our conversation melts away, and my heart feels like it's going to burst. I hadn't realized how much I missed them.

"You guys look amazing! I missed you so much."

"We missed you more," Sarah says. Sarah and Piper have been together for years, and she has become one of my dearest friends. "But also, I'm starving, so let's chat inside."

The restaurant is just so Colorado. Skis and hiking gear hang on the walls atop mountain murals, and the tables are painted like old state flags. Despite how cheesy it is, it does feel like home. I order my favorite item on the menu—BBQ pulled pork on a gourmet brioche bun with honey-tossed sweet potato fries.

We spend the first chunk of dinner talking all about the couple's RV adventures. I desperately want to ask them to save me from myself and help me get ready for this trip—it burns at the tip of my tongue. Instead, I shuffle my feet and listen to their stories.

They've recently been making their way west across the bottom of the United States.

"There we were on a boat in the swamp of Louisiana," Sarah goes on. "And the tour guide started bringing a baby alligator around. The second that little guy was in my hands, all I could picture was the momma alligator lurking in the waters outside the boat, ready to climb aboard and devour me. I nearly wet myself."

They both make eye contact before erupting into laughter. Their joy is intoxicating, and I wish for the millionth time that I could be as sure of myself as they are, instead of constantly second-guessing myself.

Finally, after we order dessert, Piper pulls a sheet of paper out of her shoulder bag. The time has finally come.

"And now the reason for our detour north," she proclaims. "Let's get you to Greece! Sarah drove today, so I could research everything we need to do. You have your passport, right?"

Sarah gives Piper a look and interjects. "Piper, she's not a child. Of course she has her passport."

Clearly, no self-respecting adult would lose their passport. I really am that pathetic. Both women look at me expectantly.

"Yep! I have my passport. Found it last night." I give them my most convincing smile, hoping they don't see right through me. They don't have to know I haven't found it yet. I will. I think. "But I'd love your advice on anything else." Like, do I need to learn Greek? Will my credit card work over there? There are probably a dozen other things I haven't even thought of yet.

Piper slides the paper she's been holding across the table toward me and I pick it up. It appears to be a long hand-written list of action items and things I need to buy and pack.

"Of course, we've got your standards—packing cubes, travel pillow, external battery packs—but with what we know of your travel history, we also took the liberty of making a list of clothing, accessories, travel hacks, et cetera."

My eyes make their way down the list.

"And you're getting a makeover."

My eyes spring from the list to Sarah, who is brimming with excitement. You've got to be kidding me. This isn't a rom-com. I don't want or need a makeover montage that is going to magically change my entire outlook.

"Like what, exactly?" I ask, hesitantly. Please don't—

"Well, we thought maybe a haircut, some new clothes, and makeup? You're going to need to look the part of a sexy international marketing exec," Sarah says.

I stare at her with pursed lips.

"We all know you are brilliant, capable, and beautiful, but I looked up this hotel, and it's the definition of luxury. We just want you to feel comfortable," Piper declares. "When was the last time you took those hiker's feet for a pedicure?"

I know she's right. I thought the same thing last night when I looked up the hotel. It's incredibly swanky—or at least, it was. I'm not sure how much the new owner has changed, but I'm guessing he hasn't downgraded it to an economy-level hotel. I won't fit in without major help.

Sarah feverishly swipes through her phone. "By the way, I looked up the general manager, and he is *hot*."

Piper and I both tilt our heads at her. She isn't usually one to ogle.

"Seriously! Look." Sarah reaches her phone across the table. "He's so dreamy. I can see it now. You're going to fall for him and never come back to us."

I take Sarah's phone and study the photo staring back at me. A dark-haired and olive-skinned man is smiling casually in a gray suit, posed outside of the Omorfiá Hotel. He doesn't look much older than us, maybe thirty at the absolute most. Sarah's not wrong; he is gorgeous—but in that untouchable, *too charming for his own good and knows it* kind of way. Definitely not my type.

"First of all, I do not need to date anyone right now, thank you. Second of all, do I need to remind you that he is going to be a client?"

Piper rolls her eyes. "Who said anything about dating? You

can hook up and not date. I mean, I wouldn't know, but that's what everyone says."

Piper and Sarah have been together since we were all seventeen. Sarah grew up a few cities over, and the two of them met while rock climbing. It was love at first sight, and they've never looked back. I'm only a *tiny* bit jealous.

"It's true," Sarah says as I hand back her phone. "Haven't you seen literally any television show in the last ten years? Everyone dates at work or through work. Half our couple friends met at work. How else are you supposed to meet people?"

I met Malcolm at work and *that* didn't turn out too well. I don't bring him up because they are both so happy, and I love hearing them laugh. Bringing it up would only bring down the mood.

"Well, it's not going to happen, either way. A guy like that would not be interested in me."

"Yeah right," Piper chimes in. "Of course he would. You're hot, you're brilliant, you're funny. I'm calling it. You're getting lucky on this trip."

I spit out my soda. "Piper!"

"What? Why not? It's been months since Malcolm, and you shouldn't have grieved that steaming pile of bear droppings anyway. It's time to get back out there. And you definitely aren't meeting anyone here in Pineview Springs. You deserve to have fun!"

As if I don't have enough on my plate with the work aspect of the trip. Now I have to have fun, too? They really don't get it.

"Girls, there is no way. I have too much riding on this trip professionally. I am absolutely not going to hook up with the client."

"Fine, it doesn't have to be this Niko guy, but someone. You need to find someone to have a little vacay fling."

They are still joking around, but suddenly, it's all just too much to handle. The makeover, the shopping list, the missing passport, talking about dating—it's too much. I will never succeed. I'm having flashbacks of freezing in conference rooms, being talked over, and pushed around. What makes me think this time will be any different?

Steaming hot tears brim my eyelids, threatening to over-flow. I squeeze my tongue to the roof of my mouth to prevent a sob from escaping.

I try to look away and buy myself a minute, but it doesn't work.

"Oh, Jenni! Don't cry!" Piper asks. "Forget we said anything. We were just messing around."

"I don't think I can do this." My voice comes out as a whisper, but inside, it's a scream. Everything is wrong. The tears are flowing now, and there is no stopping them. I can feel the dampness running down my hot, blotchy cheeks. I hate crying in public, but somehow being with my friends again makes it so I don't care all that much. I want their arms around me. I want them to tell me everything is going to be okay.

"Talk to me," Piper begs. "This is clearly about more than being nervous to travel."

"I just feel so inadequate." My voice cracks as I speak. "If I go on this assignment, I'm going to fail. I know it deep in my bones."

I know it, because I have spent years being told I'm not good enough. I know it, because Malcolm's voice is still in my head, making sure I remember my place. As much as I want to prove him wrong, what would be even worse would be to prove him right.

"I'm just broken. I don't fit in my life. And I can't figure out where I'm supposed to be."

Sarah gets up from her seat and joins me on my side of the

table. She gently rubs my back. "I think it makes perfect sense with everything you've been through."

"What do you mean?" They couldn't possibly know, could they? I've never told anybody about how weak I really was in that relationship. They would never look at me the same way again if I did.

Piper sits forward, taking over from Sarah. "We watched how much you struggled in Chicago. We saw you wither away and lose all of your light. I don't know if it was the job or Malcolm. You never really gave us details. But I'm guessing both. Then they all dropped you like a hot potato with no explanation or recourse."

The waitress saves me from having to respond by checking to make sure everything is okay. We haven't touched our chocolate cake. Sarah says something to her, but I'm not listening because I've buried my tear-streaked face in my hands.

"You don't understand. It was all my fault. I just wasn't good enough."

Piper puts her hands down on the table and leans toward me. "Listen, Jenni, I don't know exactly what happened, but I can promise you that it was never your fault. Malcolm was controlling and abusive and took advantage of you. That's all on him."

"I—" My lips quiver and the words get caught in my throat. Malcolm never hit me. Not really. He left fingerprint bruises on my arm a few times and I thought he pushed me when I was getting into the car once. He acted like I tripped and was so worried about me that I doubted my own perception of the event. I still struggle to call it abuse because it was always so confusing. I usually ended up being the one apologizing after every fight.

"We know," Sarah murmurs. "It's okay to not be okay. We're here."

I want to believe her. I don't want to feel broken anymore. I hate this. I don't want to be the girl living in her parents' house that everyone feels sorry for. I want to be the girl everyone is proud of. I just don't know how.

"So what do I do?" I ask in a quiet voice, afraid to admit it's time for a change.

"Let us help you get back out there. Career-wise," she adds when Sarah side-eyes her. "I know you can nail this and then, maybe, you'll find your spark again."

Could that really be it? Faking it until I make it to a new life? Maybe or maybe not. But surely, it's the only opportunity I have to fix my mistakes and prove him wrong.

"Okay ..." I finally say, giving Piper and Sarah the answer they want. "You're right. I'll do anything you tell me to. Except dye my hair."

Both women look at me with giddy expressions, like they are about to roll up their sleeves and get to work. I just hope their plan pays off.

Chapter 6

I should have known this shopping trip was going to be a disaster.

"What do you want your outfit to say about you?"

I raise an eyebrow and look questioningly at Sarah. We're at a thrift shop in Golden, working on my wardrobe for the trip. Unlike Piper, who mostly shops in the men's section, and me, who lives in hiking clothes, Sarah always looks fabulous. Her style is timeless and yet also so unique to her. I've always been envious of how she can throw together an outfit and look like a million bucks, even when living out of an RV. So it's good that she's taken me on as a project, but she is definitely enjoying it more than I am.

"What about 'I have no idea what I'm doing here; please don't mug me'?"

Sarah heaves out an exaggerated sigh. She's either amused or annoyed; I can't tell which. She grabs the neon orange jumpsuit that I picked up as a joke.

"Yikes."

Sarah returns the jumpsuit to the rack and moves on, blazing a trail through the colorful shop with racks upon racks of mismatched clothes. I follow behind, letting her take control of the shopping. It's easier that way.

I booked my flights last night while on the phone with Piper and Sarah and we all squealed and cheered. I'll need to find my passport soon so I can put in that info, but luckily, I was able to purchase the tickets without it.

As soon as we hung up, I crawled into bed and stared at the cracks on the ceiling, wishing I could anchor myself to the spot and never leave. I dreamed my suitcase broke open in Greece and clothes exploded all over the hotel lobby, and rich, beautiful guests jeered while I tried to stuff everything back into my bag. I woke up right before being swallowed whole by the mess.

Sleep was impossible after that and the girls were standing in my parents' driveway by 7:00 a.m., ready for me to drive us all down the mountain for the day.

"I'm serious, Jenni. What vibe do you want to put out there? Don't underestimate how much the right outfit can boost your confidence. I want you feeling comfortable and fabulous, but I can't do that if you don't tell me what you are looking for!"

Bzzz, bzzz, bzzz. I pull my phone out of my pocket and see my mom's name across the screen. I hold the phone for a second, debating whether I should answer.

"Hello?" Sarah's voice demands my attention. "Put the phone away! This is important."

I don't know, I want to scream as I shove the phone back in my pocket, choosing to ignore my mom. She probably just needs help with something.

I have no clue what I'm looking for. I'm too overwhelmed to think about any of it. Earlier this morning, a friend of Sarah's gave me my first professional haircut in years. The stylist gave me a center part with loose sweeping waves that feather out from my face. They also eventually convinced me to let them give me some highlights. By the time they had dried and styled my hair, I barely recognized myself in the mirror. I felt like I was pretending to be someone else—someone ten times more confident and successful. So I guess the makeover worked, if that was the objective.

"Whatever you think is best, Sarah. I trust you." I move around another rack that's full of colorful dresses. Piper is off gathering the electronics and other travel supplies I'll need.

"Then here, Try these on."

I turn toward Sarah, who has her arms full with a pile of clothing. She hands them over and pushes me toward the dressing room.

The first outfit I pull from the pile is a bright yellow dress with poofy sleeves, ruffles, and a tiered knee-length skirt. I look like a pineapple. This can't be what Sarah thinks will land me this hotel deal. I might be out of practice, but not so out of practice to think this dress looks good. I slowly pull back the curtains, preparing to be laughed at. Or worse, for Sarah to tell me she loves it.

"Oh, my gosh," Sarah gasps, putting her hand over her mouth. "That was not supposed to be in the pile. You look like a lemon drop!" She bursts into a fit of giggles and I join her, relieved.

"I'm sorry," she gasps out, trying to catch her breath from laughing. "It's not you, it's the dress." She shoos me back behind the velvet curtain.

I slip out of the dress and into the next outfit from Sarah's pile.

"I definitely don't want to look like a lemon drop," I call out. The comedic relief has broken through my nerves a bit.

"That's a start. But really, you need to decide what you *do* want to look like. Otherwise, none of this will feel right."

I pull on another dress. It's a flirty, floral cotton dress that feels like sunshine and fresh starts. Is that what I want? Maybe. I can picture myself strolling cute waterfronts and flower markets in this dress, wearing a wide-brimmed hat, and stopping for fresh fruit from a market stall. The image fills me with a sort of energy I'm not used to. A boost that maybe, just maybe, I can pull this off.

"I like this one," I tell Sarah as I emerge from the dressing room. "I think this is what I want. Bright, simple, and maybe a bit whimsical? Is that the right word?"

Sarah's face lights up. "It's perfect. I can work with that."

After three or four changes, I put on a pale blue linen pantsuit over a white tee. It is surprisingly comfortable. The pants make my butt look great and the jacket fits perfectly: not too tight around my shoulders or too short in the sleeves. And when I catch my reflection in the mirror with my new haircut and pale-pink gel manicure, I believe I look the part. I might barely recognize myself, and it's a far cry from the black skirts and tops I wore in Chicago, but it just feels right. I could rock this look at the board meeting.

"Jennnnniiii!" Sarah squeals as she peeks her head in through the curtain. "You look amazing! How do you feel?"

"Actually, I feel kind of—" I get cut off by my phone loudly vibrating against a discarded belt buckle.

"Your phone has been ringing off the hook. Who is it?"

"It's my mom." I groan. "She won't leave me alone." Although I'm starting to worry that something is wrong. "Maybe I should just answer it."

Sarah shrugs and retreats back into the shop. I call my mom back, and she picks up on the first ring.

"There you are! I need your help. I can't get the computer to connect to the printer, and I need to print out the new patterns for our knitting group. Are you going to be home soon?"

Of course, it's a tech emergency. I don't know how my mom functioned before I moved home.

"Sure, Mom. I'll take a look. I bet the Wi-Fi just got disconnected. I'll be home in a few hours, okay?"

"I really need to get these to the ladies this afternoon ..."

I sigh. I shouldn't complain. Helping with computers is the least I can do to repay my parents for taking me in when they really didn't need to, so I don't tell her that I'm busy or that it's important. I just tell her I'll be home as soon as I can.

Sarah and I filter through the clothes, but my excitement is more lackluster now because I'm realizing I'm actually going to have to tell my mom about the trip.

"OH, YOUR HAIR IS DIFFERENT," my mom comments, her hand on her chest. I had all but forgotten about the cut, highlight, and style when I walked into the den where my mom sits at the computer. This morning feels like ages ago.

"I just thought I would do something different," I say. I'm not ready to tell her about the trip. I know she's going to worry, and I don't know if I can handle her worry on top of my own. "Do you like it?"

I pull out my phone to check if it's connected to the Wi-Fi. Sure enough, it's not. The router probably just needs to be reset.

"It's different," is all she says about my hair before turning back to the printer. "I just don't know what happened. All I did was type the pattern into my computer and press print. I've pressed all the buttons on the printer. I put new paper in. I changed the ink cartridge. Nothing is working!"

And there goes an expensive printer cartridge that I can almost guarantee didn't need to be changed. "No worries. We'll fix it. I'm just going to go check the router."

Mom follows me to the living room.

"What is the haircut for? Did you meet someone?"

The only thing that might be worse than telling my anxious mother that I'm leaving the country is talking to her about my love life.

"No, I didn't meet anyone. I'm actually going on a trip … for work."

"Oh? Really?" She sounds skeptical.

"My boss had some meetings scheduled that she can't attend, so I'm going instead."

"Can't you just do that remotely? Where is the meeting?"

Mom was thrilled when I moved back home, even though she didn't know what to do about my depression. She never wanted to talk about that, but I think she secretly loves having someone other than my dad in the house. She is always inviting me to join her and making sure we eat together. I think she'd be happy if I never left.

"Mykonos."

"Mykonos? Where is that? California?"

Mom is tidying up, gathering coffee mugs and stray knitting needles.

"No, Mom. It's in Greece. Like, in Europe."

She drops her handful of knitting needles, and they clang on a glass side table. I am currently crawling behind my dad's armchair to inspect the router so I can't see her face. I can only imagine it's full of worry lines.

"Oh, wow. That is quite the trip."

"My boss is trying to sign a new hotel on Mykonos. The owner wanted her to fly out there, but she can't do it because she's pregnant. So I said I would. It's a really great opportunity and could finally get me back into a real marketing job."

The words tumble out of my mouth in an attempt to say as much as I can before she rebuts any of it.

"Aren't you a bit worried? I don't think I could ever …"

Of course I'm worried. At this point, though, that doesn't matter anymore. It's happening. I have to pretend like I know exactly what I am doing so that she doesn't worry more than she has to.

"It will be fine, Mom. I know what I'm doing," I say, and emerge from behind the armchair, having solved the problem. "Next time you want to plug in an extra lamp, try not to unplug the router. You shut off the internet, so the computer couldn't send the document to the printer."

I pick up the extra lamp she uses when she's knitting with black yarn and place it on a different table. She sheepishly apologizes before we head back to the den to make sure the printer does its thing.

"Are you sure about this trip, honey? You're feeling up to it?"

Oh, my gosh. Can she just stop meddling?

"Yes, Mom. It's going to be fine. It's not a big deal. All I have to do is go in, give a presentation, and answer any questions. I would barely consider it traveling. I'll probably be at the hotel the entire time working."

I don't believe most of that, but I'm trying to reassure her. As I'm doing so, the corner of a gray box catches my eye beneath a pile of papers—the fire-safe box. It's where Mom and Dad keep all our vital documents, like birth certificates and social security cards.

I pull off the pile of papers.

"Mom? What's the combo for the fire box?"

"Your brother's birthday. But what if something goes wrong? Will anyone be there to help you?"

I enter the six-digit number into the padlock and hear a click.

"Nothing is going to go wrong, Mom. And I'm sure the general manager will be able to help me if anything does."

It only takes me a second to flip through and find what I'm looking for—tucked in a manila folder with my name on it. My passport. "Finally. I've been looking everywhere for this." I let out a huge sigh of relief.

"You should have asked," Mom says. "I put it there that weekend you came home before junior year. Safe and sound."

I should have known. I close the box back up and replace the pile. Surely, this has to be a sign that I'm doing the right thing. It has to be. I slip the passport in my pocket.

I'm doing this.

Chapter 7

I feel lied to by every single movie ever made. Heroines arriving at their tropical destination with beautiful windblown hair, perfect makeup and a million-dollar smile ready to hit the ground running? Lies!

I don't know what magic those girls are dabbling in because when I hail a cab at the Mykonos airport, I've got matted hair, hot pink compression socks digging into my swollen legs, and a dozen new pimples across my face.

Well, here goes nothing! Neck pillow and all.

I'm not even sure what day it is. All I know is that I have been on three different airplanes and crossed nine time zones. With how exhausted I am, I cannot wait to get to the hotel. Once I'm there, I can figure out everything else. And while I wish I was talking about whether I'm going to sip cocktails by the pool or on the beach, I'm not. That isn't remotely on the schedule. I've got my first meeting with Niko Psomas tomorrow afternoon, and my brain has been running circles around it since I left Colorado, playing potential conversation topics over and over. I still don't feel entirely ready.

While in the cab, my phone pings with messages from

Piper and my mom, both equally as concerned about my welfare but for different reasons.

> Mom: Did you make it okay? How are you getting to the hotel? I keep telling your father we should cancel our camping trip so we're reachable. I don't want something to happen and for us not to know because we're in the middle of the desert in Utah.

> Jenni: I'm fine. I'm in a cab. The company is paying for it. Please, do not cancel your camping trip. Go, have fun.

> Piper: You made it! Woohoo! Okay, what's up first? The pool or the beach? And where are you going out tonight?

> Jenni: I'll be staying in, drinking water. Alone. I have a meeting to prep for.

> Piper: Ugh. Jenni. Live a little. Please!

> Jenni: Can I please just take a nap first?

> Piper: Fine. If you must. LOVEYOU.

WHEN WE PULL up to the Omorfiá Hotel, I'm struck by just how white everything is. I've seen pictures but these white walls are practically blinding in the afternoon sun. As we made our way here through windy roads, I couldn't help but stare at stark-white buildings of all shapes and sizes. It's breathtaking. I feel like I've been dropped down right into a magazine spread.

Inside the hotel, everything from the floors and walls to the furniture are white too. It's immaculate and sparkling—a far cry from the Pineview Inn, or any hotel I've ever stayed at, for that matter.

I immediately feel 100 times more self-conscious about my haphazard appearance and the neon-green zebra-print suitcase I borrowed from Piper. I didn't want to, but had no choice when she pointed out that my duffel bag wasn't going to cut it for an international trip.

There is nothing I want more than to get to my room, take a long hot shower, and collapse in bed. I smell like the airport, and I'm pretty sure I could sleep for twenty-four hours straight at this point.

As I approach the desk, a waterfall that seems to be running right out of the ceiling and down the wall at the far end of the lobby distracts me. The muted blue-green of the water is a striking contrast to the white stone walls as it falls into a colorful pile of marbled rocks. It barely makes a sound, just carries on, endlessly cascading.

"Checking in, miss?"

It takes me a second to register that the concierge is talking to me. I turn away from the waterfall and face the front desk.

"I'm sorry. Yes. My name is Jenni Swanson with Aspen Sky Marketing."

The man is about my age, maybe a bit younger, with a sincere smile. "Ah, yes! Welcome, welcome."

I set my backpack down on the counter and dig out my passport and a credit card to hand over. He taps away at his computer. "Mr. Psomas is very excited for your meetings tomorrow. Very excited."

I smile at the sweet way he repeats everything he says.

"Are you telling lies about me, Alexander?" A deep voice says from behind me.

My breath catches. I didn't realize anyone had walked up behind me. I spin around and come face-to-face with Niko Psomas. I recognize him from the photo on Sarah's phone. His tanned golden skin, deep eyes, perfectly messy hair—all of it, about six inches from my face.

Heat rushes to my cheeks and my legs suddenly feel like Jell-O. I cover my mouth, afraid he can smell my airplane breath or body odor—a sharp contrast, I'm sure, from his fresh sea air aroma. I stumble backward, trying to find the right distance of space between us.

I bump into my suitcase and then practically land on top of the front desk, sending a glass of pens flying in the process. Niko never breaks eye contact.

"Are you all right?"

I nod, so he turns to gather the pens scattered across the lobby floor. I notice a bit of dried salt on the curve of his jaw and wonder if he's just come from the beach. He's taller than me, but not towering, and he holds himself with an air of comfortable confidence, neither pretentious nor arrogant. His gray eyes and tousled hair are striking, giving off a sense of calmness, as if he doesn't have a care in the world. Which is probably true, looking that handsome.

As much as I hate myself for it, I am tongue-tied and stuttering in his presence. It must be the sleep deprivation and how intimidating it is to meet him this close up. Niko is dressed in white linen pants and an ocean-blue button-down shirt, which is only about half buttoned, showing off his muscular chest. Of course. My elbow slips off the front desk and I stumble again. I feel my pulse quicken as I move my suitcase and find a place to stand.

He grins at me, as if waiting to see what catastrophe I'll cause next.

Finally, I sidestep away from Niko, pulling down my sweatshirt in the process, hoping he can't see where I spilled my in-flight tomato juice during a bit of turbulence. I inhale a deep breath and crack a smile. What does one say after making a complete fool of herself?

Alexander saves me from having to figure it out.

"Mr. Psomas! So nice to see you. So nice. I didn't know you were in today! This,"—he gestures at me—"is Jenni Swanson. From Aspen Sky Marketing. She is very excited to meet you. Very excited."

"So you're the pinch hitter, huh?"

I'm thrown by his American accent. Amber told me his family is one of the richest in the country. They own a bunch of vineyards or distilleries, I think.

"Excuse me?"

"Sorry, it's a baseball metaphor. It's a person who is sent in to cover for someone who can't bat."

"Right, of course. Sorry, jet lag. My brain is mush." I twirl my fingers by my temples. "Yeah, that's me! Just call me good ol' Babe Ruth."

Oh my gosh. Did I really just tell him to call me Babe? I can't be any more awkward. And where did that bit of baseball trivia come from anyway? I guess my dad has rubbed off on me more than I realized. I swallow. "Or don't. Sorry, that was weird."

"I'm impressed. I didn't peg you for a Yankees fan."

"I'm not. More of a Rockies fan, but they are terrible. My parents joke that if the Rockies ever make the World Series, they'll sell the house and move to Morocco."

Why can't I stop talking? Shut your mouth, Jenni. Niko is staring at me, again, like I've lost my mind. And I'm staring at his insanely pretty eyes. On further inspection, they aren't just gray. Specks of green and blue swirl together in a moody haze. My heart flutters in my chest. I haven't felt this way in years, if ever, locking eyes with a man.

"You must be—"

And then, out of nowhere, I yawn. Are you freaking kidding me?

"—tired," Niko finishes, in that low gravelly voice. "I'll let you get checked in, but I'm really looking forward to working with you. I can't wait to see what you're planning for the proposal."

The reminder that Amber sent me with a pre-written sales pitch and slide deck hits me like a ton of bricks. I reviewed them on the plane, and it was painful. Everything seemed so out of touch and impersonal, like a telemarketer. I was bored out of my mind. If I'm not convinced from reading the materials over, how am I going to convince this has-it-all-together man?

"Yes, me too," I say, wanting to run and hide before I say or do anything else embarrassing. "Oh, and thanks again for hosting me."

Niko extends his hand. I take it and shake, trying desperately not to notice how soft and warm it is, like morning rays of light. Niko smiles and turns toward the front door of the hotel.

"Excuse me, Mr. Psomas?" Alexander asks, looking unsure of himself. "Before you go, I just wanted to let you know that there were more … you know … ducks in the elevator about an hour ago."

The tail end of his statement comes out as a whisper. Ducks? What is this place?

"I was afraid that might happen. Have you disposed of them?"

Disposed of them? Cute little ducks? My heart drops.

"I'm sorry." I throw up my hands. "What is going on? You can't just *dispose* of perfectly innocent ducks because they get stuck inside your elevator!"

I cover my mouth, shocked that my inside thoughts made it outside. The sleep deprivation really must be getting to me. Who knows what they can and can't do? This is Greece. This is his hotel.

But then Alexander and Niko are both laughing.

I stand speechless, looking between the two of them. What is funny about duck massacre?

"Not live ducks, Miss Swanson," Niko says, fighting off more laughter. "Small rubber ducks. *Someone* has been leaving them around the hotel for the last few days. I have asked Alexander to get to the bottom of it because I have watched all of the security footage twice and not seen a single sign of our culprit."

My cheeks burn hot with embarrassment.

"Don't worry, sir! You can count on me. We won't have any ducks, real or rubber, by the end of the day."

"Thank you, Alexander. I know you can quack the case."

Niko winks at me and then turns and disappears out the front door. Did he just drop a duck pun and then saunter off without another word? Who is this man? I turn my attention back to Alexander, and I can finally breathe normally again.

"Okay! I'm so sorry about that disruption," he says. "I have everything ready. Can I show you to your room? Let me grab your bags. Follow me to the elevator."

I insist on carrying my backpack myself while he takes the suitcase and leads the way around the waterfall to a tiny elevator.

On the second floor, we snake through the maze of a hallway. There are steps up and then down again without reason and so many twists and turns that I might get lost trying to find my way back to the lobby. Each corridor is full of light from open windows facing the sea, and I can feel the tension in my shoulders from the flight—or maybe my interaction with Niko—easing as we reach my room.

After thanking Alexander, I place my suitcase near the closet and head to the bathroom to freshen up.

I splash my face with frigid water from the tap. The cold against my face grounds me and uncoils the tension in my body. I take in the bathroom after blotting my face dry, taking in marble and gold fixtures, fancier than I've ever seen. There are little glass bottles of shampoo, conditioner, and perfume, with facial masks and makeup remover in turquoise sea glass bowls. I really, truly, don't belong here with my plastic dollar store travel toiletries.

I open a water bottle from a basket on the counter and take it to the window. I draw the curtains and open the windows, a wave of fresh sea air washing over me. My room has an ocean view. Every little detail continues to leave me stunned. To the left, I can see the deep blue of the Mediterranean lazily rising and retreating. The sun glimmers off little peaks in the water like diamonds floating in the tide. To the right, I can see the white-and-gray rooftop of what must be the front lobby of the hotel. Behind that, a rocky hillside slopes up to the sky, dotted with buildings, and filled with the faint noise of scooters and taxis vying for space on the winding roads.

The view is to die for. Maybe this trip wasn't such a bad idea after all. I could get used to this. As long as I don't think too much about Niko or next Monday's board meeting. So long as I don't fall into Niko's arms or send any more office supplies flying, I think I'll be okay.

I snap a picture and post it to my socials. I tag the hotel location and drop a song lyric in the caption.

After a few mesmerizing minutes, I pull myself away from the window to collapse on the bed and tell myself I'll rest my eyes for five minutes before jumping in the shower.

Chapter 8

The last thing I remember is thinking I would just rest my eyes. But when I open them again, the room is darker, and the fading light of the sunset bathes the view from the window. What time is it? I reach for my phone and find that it's a quarter to seven. No wonder I'm ravenous. I can't remember the last time I ate.

I rummage through my bag and throw on a pair of jeans and a light-blue, off-the-shoulder blouse. I twist my hair into a messy bun, cursing myself for falling asleep instead of showering, and go in search of food.

I navigate the hallway maze back to the elevator and notice stairs hiding behind it. My sandals clap on my heels as I descend, echoing in the white stairwell all the way down. The lobby is even more beautiful with the warm light of gold sconces mounted on the walls.

Alexander is standing at attention at the front desk. "Miss Jenni! Wonderful to see you. How are you settling in?"

"Good, thank you! I passed out. The bed is so comfortable! I'm starving, though. Can you point me in the direction of the hotel restaurant?"

"Ah yes, the best beds in Mykonos," he says with a wink. "Unfortunately, our restaurant is full at the moment. You could come back in an hour or so for a table, or you can walk down to the beach. There are a lot of restaurants along the water."

I let out a sigh, my shoulders slumping. I didn't think I'd have to leave the hotel just yet. I bite my lip, contemplating. My empty stomach does not want to wait over an hour just to be seated, but I also don't think my brain is quite ready to tackle venturing out. Alone. Nearing nightfall.

Alexander leans across the desk and attempts to whisper. "Honestly, you might enjoy the beach restaurants better if you are starving. They will have bigger portions. More food, yes?"

My stomach lets out a low growl. "How far of a walk is it?"

"Not far at all! Just follow the road downhill until you get to the beachfront resorts. You'll see a path to the water. Once you hit the sand, just head right. You can't get lost unless you start walking uphill!"

"Downhill, got it. Thank you, Alexander! Send a search party if I'm not back in a couple hours, okay?"

He laughs like he's supposed to, but in my gut, it wasn't entirely a joke. Please, travel gods, let me make it back to this hotel in one piece tonight.

The walk to the beach is delightfully pleasant. A light breeze mollifies the heat emanating from the asphalt road, and I can smell the sweet flowers hanging off buildings and crawling up the hillside. I stick to the far-right edge of the road in fear of cars and Vespas zooming around the turns. It would be just my luck to be pummeled in an accident before I even get started here. I'm nervous, but not quite that desperate to get out of my meetings.

I can feel the steepness of the road in my quads and wish I had worn tennis shoes instead of cute sandals. After only a few minutes, I find myself staring up at the beachfront resorts. Wow. If I thought the Omorfiá Hotel was swanky, I don't have a word to describe these resorts. They are all larger and flashier than the Omorfiá, with glittering walkways and huge spotlights casting a yellow glow on the signs and entrances.

Looking around, I see a small placard that reads "Beach Access" with an arrow pointed toward a walkway between the resorts. I follow the path and find myself out on the sand. I can feel the moisture in the air even more down here than up at my window, and the seascape takes my breath away.

I visited the ocean once as a little girl. I can't remember exactly, but we were somewhere in Southern California. Dad had been attending a convention, and all four of us had piled into the Subaru and taken a road trip. We hung out at the hotel most of the week. I think Mom was terrified of the traffic and massive freeways in California. But on the last day of the convention, Dad finished early and took us to the beach.

I must have been eight or nine, with Jeremy a bit younger. We dug giant holes in the sand and ran around right at the edge of the water. Little foamy waves tickled our toes amidst squeals and giggles. I remember scooping up big handfuls of the salty water and throwing it in the air, letting it rain down around me like confetti, glittering in the sun. We were carefree in that childlike way that feels terribly out of reach these days.

At one point, late in the afternoon, Jeremy decided he was going to be brave. He didn't stop when the water reached his ankles. He kept going, running and then wading further into the ocean. In an instant, I knew I wanted to be out there, too, so I started running after him.

But then, he just disappeared. He must have tripped or stepped in a hole, but all I remember is his head slipping under the surface. My dad was close and managed to reach Jeremy in seconds, but it felt longer. When Dad pulled him out of the water, Jeremy had the biggest smile on his face. Like he had just experienced the thrill of the lifetime. I figured it must not have been that scary after all and was about to start running again when my mom put her arms around my shoulders, hugging me to her stomach.

"I'm so glad you will never scare us like that, Jenni. I can always count on you to be the sensible one."

Her words float in my mind now as I watch the dark water churn. Sensible. Responsible. Reliable. Always doing exactly what my parents wanted and expected of me. I've always prided myself on being all those things. Which is part of the reason it hurt so much to lose my job and go back home. There's nothing sensible or responsible about that picture.

It's all just too much to think about. I shake my head and my stomach grumbles, reminding me why I'm down here. I slip my sandals off and walk in the sand toward a handful of restaurant patios alive with people and music.

I put my shoes back on and ask for a table at the first restaurant I come to. I don't even glance at the menu board, thinking only about satiating my hunger. The hostess sits me at a small table against the wrought-iron fence separating the dining area from the beachgoers. I look over a menu of traditional Greek fare. People pass by, holding hands and talking quietly, and I feel starkly alone. Eating by myself doesn't usually bother me, but there's just something about the setting, or maybe being so far from home, that feels particularly isolating.

I order a Greek salad and a gyro plate—grateful that the menu has pictures and some English. When the food comes, the salad is unlike any Greek salad I've had in the States. First, there isn't any lettuce. Instead, big juicy chunks of fresh tomato, cucumber, green olives, and red onion are drizzled in oil, salt, and spices. And in the middle of the bowl, on top of everything, is a solid block of feta cheese drizzled in golden olive oil.

The only problem is that I don't know how to eat it. What am I supposed to do with a giant block of cheese? I glance around the tables. Is anyone else eating a salad? Will I look like a dumb tourist if I pull out a knife and cut it? Ugh. This is what I was afraid of!

It's just a simple salad and already I'm going to embarrass myself.

I decide to jab at the cheese with my fork and it breaks off in a chunk, which I'm able to scoop up with a few of the veggies. As soon as it hits my mouth, I let out a tiny moan. Yes, I'm a walking cliché. Whatever. It's that amazing. I want more in my mouth, right this second.

After my second bite, I decide that's it. I'm never eating an Americanized Greek salad ever again.

The gyro plate is just as delicious. Lamb gyro sizzles on a bed of round-cut french fries that are the perfect combination of crispy and smooth. The outside is crispy, while the inside is steamy smooth. Next to that, a mound of hummus and chopped up cucumbers drizzled with more olive oil cover giant wedges of pita bread. Alexander wasn't kidding about the portion sizes. There is so much food on my plate right now.

However, in what feels like a matter of minutes, I have cleared both the plate and the bowl without a second glance around the restaurant.

My waitress returns, smiling.

"Looks like you enjoyed it! Is this your first time in Mykonos?"

"Oh, my gosh, it was amazing! Seriously so good. And yes, this is my first time in Greece, actually."

"In that case, let me bring you a dessert. Our specialty, on the house!"

She walks away before I can say I'm too stuffed for dessert and I lean back in my chair, taking in the vibrant ambiance of the evening—the warm air, the mood lighting, the relaxing sounds of the ocean. If this meal is any indication of what is to come, this trip might just be better than I thought.

I start to take a sip of water when my gaze lands on a familiar blue shirt, half-buttoned across a golden chest. Niko is walking my way along the sandy sidewalk between the beach and the restaurant. And of course, as if right out of a movie, there's a stunning and equally golden woman in a silky full-length dress dangling on his arm. *Crap.* I can't see him again today. We've already proven how terrible I am at small talk. I don't need any more reason to be embarrassed around him.

As they get closer, I panic and turn my entire body in toward the restaurant, pretending to look for my waitress in the hopes Niko won't see me. Once they pass and I go undetected, I turn and stare after them.

Of course he has a drop-dead, gorgeous girlfriend. I feel a pang of surprising jealousy. There's no way I'm interested in Niko. I've barely even met him. Regardless, I'm jealous of everything the image of the two of them represents. They both look so comfortable, confident, and exactly as society expects them to be: two beautiful, successful people in love. While I'm average at best, flailing in my career, and carrying around my terrible dating history like a ball and chain.

The waitress reappears with my dessert. She tells me what it's called, but I can't quite understand and I'm too embarrassed to ask her to repeat herself. So, I thank her and survey the small plate in front of me. It looks like some sort of pastry, covered in honey and sesame seeds. The waitress hands me a spoon before heading off.

A spoon? For a flaky pastry?

I glance around once more to make sure no one is watching me eat. I gently press my spoon into the corner of the pastry, only for it to crack. The amber-colored crust falls away and something gooey flows out, like a molten lava cake. But it's not chocolate; it's light-colored and creamy. I hesitantly bring the spoon to my mouth for a taste. It's more feta. And just like everything else, it's delicious.

I'm probably going to be sick from all this cheese, but I can't stop myself. Nothing compares to this meal. I finish the entire thing, scraping up the last bits of honey and sesame seeds with my spoon when the waitress brings me the bill.

I scrounge in my bag for my wallet and suddenly remember that all those euros I converted at the bank in are tucked safely away inside of a rolled-up sock in my backpack at the hotel. I never got them out. I hope they take credit. Otherwise, I'm going to look awful, coming in here and practically licking my plates clean and then trying to skip the bill.

"I'm so sorry, but do you take credit card? I left my cash at the hotel." Like an idiot.

"Of course! Let me go get the card terminal. Just a minute!"

Relief washes over me. For a moment, I imagined myself washing dishes to pay off my meal.

I quickly snap a picture of my empty dessert plate with the twinkling lights of other restaurants in the background, the beach having fallen under the shade of night and text it to Piper.

> Jenni: Just had an amazing dinner at the beach. I'll give you my promised nightly update when I get back to my room.

After a leisurely climb back up the hill, I find my way back to the hotel without getting lost. My first outing was a success. When the hotel comes into view, the white walls aren't quite as stark as they take on shadows and blue tones, as if someone has painted them in watercolor. I wander through the lobby, taking my time to notice all the details. It really is a beautiful hotel, which Aspen Sky would be lucky to represent.

The bubbling of the waterfall is the only discernible sound, making me feel like I'm in a spa rather than a hotel. I sit on one of the white lounge chairs to enjoy the space for a few minutes before turning in. Jet lag and my nap have me pretty awake anyway.

Just as I settle into my seat, the sound of a spirited debate pierces the quiet of the lobby. Niko and the woman I saw on the beach have just entered the hotel.

They breeze past the front desk with a nod toward the night concierge and make their way straight toward me. There's no hiding now. I sit up and brush off my top, in case any lingering crumbs decide to make themselves apparent at this very moment. I don't think the couple has noticed me, and I consider heading toward the stairs. But then Niko clears his throat.

"Good evening, Miss Swanson," he says, locking eyes with me. I expect him to introduce his date, but he doesn't. "Are you having a nice evening?"

"Hi, Mr. Psomas. It's so great to see you … again. I just had an amazing dinner and was about to head upstairs and get to work. I don't want to bother you outside of business hours, so I'll leave the two of you to enjoy your night."

I smile and practically curtsy, much to my own shock and embarrassment.

Niko puts his hands up and starts to speak. "She's—"

"Ooooh, are you the American?!" The woman squeals and slaps Niko on the arm, playfully. Her accent is much more how I expected Niko's to be. She's clearly from Greece. "You should have introduced us." She beams with excitement, and I'm more than a little confused. "Please, don't spend all of your time with Niko—he's such a bore. I must take you out tomorrow! Have you been to the beach yet?"

Um. What is happening? Should I know who this is? I glance at Niko and then back at the woman. I was planning on spending the morning preparing for our meeting, but the look on her face reminds me of a puppy hoping to go outside to play. How do you say no to that? And I don't want to offend either of them.

"Well, we have our meeting in the afternoon, but I guess I don't have any plans in the morning?" I look toward Niko, begging him to offer some sort of insight into what I should say or do.

The woman breaks into a smile so big it makes me smile uncomfortably too.

"Amazing! Meet me here at ten. Wear your bathing suit! We're going to have so much fun!" She grabs my hands in hers and practically jumps up and down. "Oh, I'm Ana, by the way! What's your name?"

The corner of Niko's mouth turns up, revealing a dimple in his cheek. He is loving this for some reason.

"I'm Jenni. It's so nice to meet you, Ana. And sure, I'd love to go to the beach. As long as that's okay with you, Mr. Psomas?"

He shrugs. "Of course, be my guest. As long as Ana has you back by three o'clock, it's not a problem with me." He gives her a pointed look, as if she's not to interfere with the more important things on the schedule.

I can't decide if he's happy about his girlfriend spending time with me or not.

"Well, in that case, I better go try to get some rest! Um, good night." I wave and start walking, only to realize I've turned in the wrong direction and have to spin around and walk past them to make it to the stairs. I hope they can't see my cheeks flushing crimson in the dim lighting.

"See you tomorrow! I can't wait!" Ana sings out, her velvety voice echoing in the quiet lobby.

~

Piper: Oooh, dreamy! That's so pretty. What's on schedule for tomorrow?

Jenni: I've somehow managed to get myself an invite to the beach with Niko's girlfriend. So that won't be weird at all.

Piper: Why would it be weird? Unless you're still considering hooking up with him? Just kidding. Have fun! You don't have to only work while you're there, you know?

Jenni: So you keep telling me.

Mom: Have you eaten dinner? Are you okay? Is the hotel safe?

Jenni: Yes. Yes. And yes. It's the nicest hotel I've ever been to. And I have a chain on the door. Please don't tell me you canceled camping?

Mom: No. We're leaving in the morning. But I'm going to find a way to check in with you.

Jenni: Not necessary. Go worry about Jeremy.

Chapter 9

My canvas tote bag is practically overflowing as I lug it down to the lobby the next morning. I wasn't sure what I needed, so I packed a towel from the hotel bathroom, a change of clothes, my water bottle, plenty of euros, sunscreen, granola bars, and dried fruit. After my unplanned nap, sleep was elusive, so I spent the night repeatedly going over the materials from Amber until I could recite every single word. I thought about canceling on Ana so I could continue working this morning and then remembered I didn't have her number. But maybe that's a good thing, because she could tell me more about Niko, for my meeting.

I'm fidgeting with the rope belt on my cream slip-on dress when she breezes down the stairs and into the lobby.

"Jenni! It's wonderful to see you!" Her voice, full of radiance and optimism, fills the white room as she air-kisses my cheeks. "Did you get some rest? Are you ready to go?"

Ana looks amazing in another flowing floor-length dress, with a Christian Dior straw hat, gold bangles up both her arms, and a touch of heavenly perfume.

Suddenly my thrift store find feels more like a flour sack. I am clearly underdressed and must have misunderstood what we would be doing. I thought she said we were going to the beach, not to wherever the dress code calls for gowns and gold jewelry.

I glance over at Alexander for help, but he's blushing and obviously hoping to get Ana's attention without outright asking for it. He's puffing up his chest, like a bird looking for a mate. I bite back a laugh.

"I—I think so," I reply. "To be honest, I wasn't sure what you had planned or what I needed. But I can go change if I need to." I gesture toward my outfit and wince in apology.

"No, no, you're perfect. As long as you're wearing a bathing suit, you'll find everything else you need where we're going."

She winks at me, and I give my best attempt at a casual laugh. It comes out strangled. I glance down at my overstuffed bag. I need to dump this thing. I pull out my water bottle and the small cross-body bag that holds my phone and wallet and then call to Alexander.

"I'm so sorry, but can you hold this for me? I don't think I need it after all. I'll pick it up first thing when I get back."

"Of course, Miss Jenni! Anything for you. I'll personally take it back to your room." He smiles and then turns his attention to Ana. "Good morning, Miss Ana. Is there anything I can get for you? Coffee? Tea?"

Ana air-kisses Alexander, causing his cheeks to flush.

"You're a gem, Alexander, but no. I'm dying to show Jenni a good time at the beach, and Niko already has us on a time crunch. We must be off!"

I smile sheepishly and give a little wave as Ana grabs my elbow and sweeps me to the front door and out onto the road.

The walk to the beach seems shorter now that I know where the little path I found last night is.

"Is your family from Mykonos?" I ask Ana.

"No, I'm just here visiting Niko for a few weeks. I grew up in Athens mostly. Though my family does own property on most of the islands, so I've spent a lot of time here."

Ah, Ana must be another wealthy heiress, kind of like Niko and his family. That must be how they met. I imagine a long-distance relationship is challenging, though. "That's great that you can take time off to be here with Niko. What do you do for work?"

"Oh, I'm in the family business, but that is boring!"

She says "boring" in a way that makes me think it's anything but. Her nonchalance does make me wonder, though, if I'll get any answers out of her about Niko. I'm still terrified about our meeting this afternoon. It might not be the board-room, and we're supposed to be on the same team, but my stomach somersaults anytime I think about it. That's why I've combed over the material backward and forward. I won't say anything other than what is written in Amber's material. I can't get myself in trouble that way.

Instead of turning right toward the restaurants like I did last night, we turn left and make our way toward a fleet of cabanas.

We approach an attendant, who is dressed in all white aside from the black sunglasses reflecting the morning light. He stands at a podium in front of a pile of beach chairs and a rack of towels. This confirms my earlier worries: I absolutely do not fit in here.

"Good morning, Ms. Psomas. Would you like a cabana today or just some lounge chairs?"

Ms. Psomas? Are Ana and Niko married? I glance at her hand but don't see a ring. So what's the deal?

"We'll take the cabana at the front. Only the best for my guest. Can you send some food and drinks?"

The attendant nods, and Ana says something in Greek, which I obviously don't understand. I think I hear my name, though. Did she say something about me that she didn't want me to hear? My cheeks prickle with embarrassment. I knew this was a bad idea. I don't belong here with these people. I should be back at the hotel working on my presentation.

Before I can think through what to do or introduce myself, Ana turns, and pulls me toward the navy cabana closest to the water. Its canvas sides sway in the gentle breeze. Two lounge chairs draped in plush white towels rest inside. There's an empty ice bucket and a small cart with sunscreens, oils, and lotions in a basket. A towel is even folded into a swan.

"Oh, my gosh!" I squeal as I point to it. "It's adorable!"

Ana looks at me, amused. "Do they not do these in America?"

I immediately realize my mistake. Of course I shouldn't have been surprised, pleasantly or not, that there was a cutely folded towel. This is a five-star resort. It's probably the most normal thing here. The last thing I want to do is give away that I've never actually been to a five-star resort. She'll tell Niko and he'll never trust me to market his hotel.

"Of course! I just meant that I usually see frogs or monkeys. I've never actually seen a swan. I thought no one did them anymore."

Ana looks at me with one perfectly manicured eyebrow lifted above her sunglasses, but a server arrives with a fresh ice bucket holding champagne and a tray of fruit and pastries. I try to thank him, but he vanishes just as quickly as he appeared. When I turn my attention to the goodies, I notice there's a small, folded card nestled among the fruits.

Welcome, Jenni! is handwritten in beautiful calligraphy. Who did this? Is that what Ana had been arranging with the attendant? A broad smile spreads across my cheeks. It's a thoughtful, if unnecessary, gesture.

"Thank you for this," I say, waving the card at her. I set it back on the tray, not knowing whether I should put it in my bag as a keepsake or throw it away. It feels too special for the trash, but surely someone in Ana's stratosphere wouldn't feel that way.

Not wanting to draw any more attention to the card or my lack of social sense, I pick up a triangle-shaped pastry and ask, "What's this one?"

"Spanakopita. It's filled with feta and greens. Not sure what it is called in America. Basil?"

The pastry is warm, and when I take a bite, the flaky dough crumbles in my mouth. Sure enough, feta and spinach light up my taste buds.

"Spinach!" I tell Ana. "It's delightful. Also, I'd be happy to pay for this. Just let me know what I owe you because I have cash."

"Don't worry about that! They will put it all on my family's account. We can get whatever you want!"

She pops the champagne and pours each of us a glass. I start to remind her that it's before noon and I have work meetings later, but she lifts her glass in a toast, and I stop myself from interrupting.

"To Jenni, may your time in Greece bring you everything you hope! And maybe a little bit more!" She winks as she clinks her glass with mine. The cold drink feels nice under the hot sun. Drops of moisture speckle the glasses, and my face glistens with sweat.

We both recline on the lounge chairs while we finish our bubbly and enjoy the views.

"Niko must have some great plans for the hotel. What are you most excited about?" I ask, hoping she'll divulge some insight into his vision. But she doesn't take the bait.

"You're not on the clock yet. You shouldn't be talking about work," she says, taking a sip. With her arm lifted, I notice a bracelet on her wrist with two interlocking hearts. The charms glisten in the sunlight. "I'm not involved with any of the planning anyway. I'm just a glorified guest."

I catch her smile drop, just slightly, before she plasters on a look of excitement.

"Okay, I need the warmth of the sun on my skin!" Ana declares and strips off her dress, hanging it on a hook near the cabana's entrance. "Let's test out the water."

I stand as well and turn around to remove my dress to lay it on my chair. For some reason, it hadn't really crossed my mind that we would actually get in the water. I thought we would mostly sunbathe. I lay the dress on my chair. My bathing suit is a pale-pink bikini with wide crisscross bands, and ruched, high-waisted bottoms. This bathing suit always gives me a decent boost of confidence. *So, why not? Let's swim.*

I take a deep breath and turn around. Ana is already walking toward the water.

Topless.

I freeze. That was not what I was expecting, at all. But while she struts down the beach, her black string bikini lies haphazardly across her lounge chair.

After a moment, she turns, realizing I'm not following her. "Are you coming?"

My hands instinctively cover my chest. I completely forgot that most European beaches are topless. I don't even know how I feel about it. In high school, we used to skinny-dip in the lake all the time. So it's not like I've never been swimming topless. Right now, though, I don't know how I feel about it.

I feel a need to maintain professionalism. I am here for work, after all. On the other hand, what if Ana ends up thinking I'm a prude, or that I don't understand the Greek way of life? She might tell Niko, and he'd hold that against me. I need to prove that I understand the lifestyle we're selling. This is what a Greek island vacation brings with it—the ability to let go. What's the worst that could happen?

Before I can second-guess myself, I strip off my bikini top, drop it on the chair, and catch up with Ana.

"Sorry, just needed a sip of water!"

My heart races as we jog to the water's edge. When my feet hit the shoreline, the cool water sends a tingle up my spine. We wade in up to our chest. The cool water feels divine. I take a deep breath and cock my head back into the waves with an exhale.

I can't remember the last time I felt so free. I have spent so long in the dark shadow of Chicago that being out here, with the sun sizzling on my skin, feels like a new beginning.

Ana wades over. "Nice, isn't it?"

I nod and spin around with my arms stretched out. I start to laugh, a rush of emotion bursting to the surface. Ana starts laughing with me, and we both lay back in the water to take in the sun.

"I'm sorry!" I call out. "I don't know why I'm laughing."

Ana says something in response, but I'm distracted by the music from a passing yacht.

I turn to ask her to repeat herself, but before I can, a sharp pain in my left calf stops me in my tracks. A white-hot sensation travels up my leg in seconds, making me forget everything and everyone around me.

Chapter 10

I yelp in pain, my vision blurring.

"Jenni, what's wrong?" She stares at me in confusion.

"I—I don't know. My leg feels like it's on fire! I must have stepped on a rock or something. It's nothing!" I spit the words out between sharp intakes of breath. I don't want her to make a big deal about this. No matter what I've done to my leg, I'm not going to let Ana or Niko see me as a clumsy amateur. They cannot see me as weak.

But it's not nothing. The pain is very quickly taking over. "I'm sure it's fine, but I'm just going to get out of the water to take a look."

I limp my way out of the water, starkly aware of how naked I am.

I hear Ana sloshing through the water behind me. "Let me help you!"

"It's okay! Don't worry." I try to wave her off while favoring my throbbing leg and covering my chest.

I don't have enough arms for this situation!

The thought of Ana following me to the cabana makes my

cheeks burn nearly as hot as my leg. She puts an arm around my waist anyway and grabs hold of my right arm.

When we reach the cabana, Ana makes space on my lounge chair and helps me sit, wrapping a towel around my shoulders. I pull it tightly around my chest. Of course this would happen to me. I decide to do something new and exciting and it explodes in my face. If Mom could see me now, I think she'd drop dead of a heart attack, and then rise again, to tell me she told me so. *"This never would have happened if you played it safe."*

I glance down to examine my throbbing leg. Instead of dripping blood and an open wound, I find an angry horse-shoe-shaped, red welt. Pain pulses through my nervous system.

"What in the world is that?" I gasp out.

"I think it's a jellyfish sting," she replies, leaning closely in to examine it further. "I'm so sorry!"

A freaking jellyfish? Are you kidding me? My *first day* in Greece and I get stung by a jellyfish?

"Please don't tell me I have to pee on myself." I crack a joke to keep from crying.

"You're so silly! Of course not! That's definitely a myth. On this fine island of Mykonos, we have first aid kits. I'll be right back."

Ana dons her bikini top and dress and runs off to the resort. Now that I'm finally alone and not fighting to hide it, I really register the pain. Holy crap. Who knew jelly fish stings hurt this much? And who did I piss off in the universe to deserve this?

Tears streak down my cheeks, but I'm not sure if they are from the excruciating pain or the humiliation.

I grab the towel from my shoulders and wipe my cheeks, thankful no one is around to see me looking like such a hot mess. I should also get my bikini top and dress on before she gets back. I attempt to stand, putting most of my weight on my un-stung leg.

I turn around and the lounge chair where I had set my bathing suit is completely empty other than a wet spot where I've been sitting.

My eyes dart around the cabana and I pull the towel even tighter around my upper body.

Think, Jenni. My clothes must have slipped to the ground when Ana grabbed the towel. I hobble over to look on the other side of the chair.

"She's just in the tent over here. I feel so terrible," Ana's voice reaches my ears. She is approaching with someone. Probably the attendant with the first-aid kit.

No bikini top behind the chair.

"Thanks for getting her stung by a jellyfish on her first day, Ana. That's exactly the first impression I was hoping for."

My stomach drops. It takes me half a second to realize she's not talking to the attendant. She's talking to Niko. Niko, the intimidating general manager of the Omorfiá Hotel. Niko, with whom I have a marketing meeting in a few hours.

My heart skips as I race the clock to find my clothing.

I pull out the lounge chair to check underneath it for either my top or cover-up. Even just one of them would do at this point.

"Just a minute," I call out, my voice a few octaves higher than it should be.

Still no clothes and now my right leg is aching from supporting my bodyweight in the uneven sand.

I can hear Ana and Niko just behind the canvas side of the cabana, and the realization that I'm not going to be able to get my top back on before they come around to the front is sinking in. I'm done for. I exhale a long breath at the ache shooting up my leg and thigh.

Just as I'm about to give up, a flash of pink catches my eye underneath the drink tray. I hobble over, but my ankle rolls in a divot of sand. Before I know it, I'm falling through the air. I knock over the tray with our expensive champagne and land sideways on Ana's lounge chair. I try to scramble to my feet, but I put too much weight on one side of the chair and it flips. Suddenly, I'm butt in the sand and feet in the air at the precise moment Ana and Niko come to the opening of the cabana.

"What was that? Are you all right, Jenni?"

The pair stand there, staring at me. At least, I assume so, because all I can see around the end of the lounge chair are their feet: a set of pedicured toes and another with cuffed khakis and tanned but slightly hairier feet.

"I'm okay," I announce, sounding as squeaky as a mouse. "Just took a little tumble trying to grab my dress. Probably should have just stayed put." I attempt a self-deprecating laugh.

Niko seems to take the hint that I might not be fully presentable and excuses himself while Ana comes to help me up. Thank goodness for that. I can only survive so much humiliation for one morning and Niko seeing me topless is far above that limit.

"I think you've made him blush." Ana giggles as she rightens the lounge chair and sits me down. She grabs my bikini top and dress, exchanging them for the towel that I somehow managed not to drop from my shoulders during all of the chaos. I guess I had a desperate grip.

As I get dressed, Ana tells me that she ran into Niko while getting the first aid kit and he had wanted to see if I was okay.

"Out for a walk, I guess," Ana finishes. Then she calls out to Niko. "Okay, we're all dressed! Can you bring me the kit?"

Niko saunters into the cabana, all smiles and charm as he hands over the kit and sets a few coffee cups on the cart.

"I can't begin to tell you how sorry I am, Miss Swanson." Niko locks eyes with me and I am momentarily stunned, distracted by the depth of his stare. I expect to find concealed amusement, annoyance, or even pity. But instead, all I find is genuine care in the soft expression on his face: his brows pulled together, the corners of his mouth turned down.

"Please put my cousin out of his misery and tell him you forgive him," Ana says.

Cousin? Oh! That makes so much more sense. That's why they have the same last name. They aren't married; they're related. No wonder they are both so beautiful.

"Miss Swanson?"

I snap to attention and realize Niko is waiting for me to respond. "Yes, I'm fine. And please, call me Jenni. It's really not a big deal. I can take care of myself—"

"This says we need to pluck out any spines," Ana reads from her phone. "Let me see your leg."

I lift my foot to rest it on the lounge chair. Ana leans in close to my leg. "I can't see anything, but I don't have my contacts in. Niko, can you see any spines?"

Reflexively, I pull my leg back. I am not—absolutely not—letting Niko Psomas, Greek god lookalike, pluck jellyfish spines out of my leg. Nope.

But then he gently cups the back of my calf and pulls it toward him. His hand is soft and warm, and I'm tempted to give in and let him do whatever he wants with me.

But not tempted enough.

"No, that's really unnecessary." I can handle this. I jerk my leg back and twist down to try and get a closer look. It's not as easy as I thought it would be, and I definitely can't get close enough to see anything.

"For what it's worth, I've seen stings before with my surfing buddies and this one doesn't look too bad. Why don't you rinse it and then we'll get you back to the hotel?"

I relax a bit, knowing that my leg is safe from any more surprising, though not totally unpleasant, physical contact.

"Can I get you a drink?" Ana asks, her voice sounding

desperate. I hate the fact that they are both hovering over me. I just want to disappear and deal with this on my own.

Niko jumps in before I can answer. "Why don't you go find a scooter to get Jenni back up the hill? I can help her get her leg cleaned up."

"I can walk. Please don't make a big fuss," I say, even as the pain in my leg continues to throb.

"Don't be silly. I can rent a scooter at the resort. I'll be right back."

With that, Ana gives Niko a look that says not to make anything worse before heading up the beach. Niko and I work in silence after Ana leaves. He hands me a cup with what smells like vinegar. "Here, rinse with this. It should prevent any lingering spines from releasing more venom."

"Thanks." I'm not sure what else to say. This is really not how I wanted my first impression to be. My first impression was supposed to be in a conference room with my presentation. Now he will forever think of me as the helpless tourist rather than as a smart marketer worthy of doing business with. I've ruined everything.

"May I?" he asks, while hovering the cup above my leg. This knight-in-shining-armor thing is equal parts arresting and annoying. He's so gentle, but I also want to scream *"I can take care of myself!"* I can feel my embarrassment turning into agitation that I am in this mess to begin with.

The only thing worse than being seen topless and stupidly injured would be lashing out at Niko when all he's trying to do is help.

"That would be great. Thank you." I finally respond, swallowing my pride yet again. Maybe he wants to be the hero. Maybe, I should just let him.

He slowly pours the vinegar on my leg, making sure to cover the entire horseshoe. I bite down on the inside of my cheek in anticipation of the sting, but it doesn't come. I don't know if that means it's working or not. But I'm relieved that it's not worsening the pain.

"How are you doing?" Niko asks. He is still gently holding my leg, his brow furrowed.

"I'm good, thanks," I reply. We let the vinegar sit for a minute, and then Niko pours the cup of warm water onto a towel and blots the sting.

I watch him work, lost in the movement of his shoulders— all muscle under his shirt. Okay, maybe I'm enjoying this a tiny bit because I don't even notice when Ana returns. Not until her voice breaks my focus, anyway.

"There's a scooter in front of the hotel with your name on it, Niko," she announces. He thanks her and hands me a clean, dry towel. "Are you ready?" Niko asks me.

I nod. I'm definitely ready to get back to the hotel and forget this whole thing ever happened. From taking my top off to being stung by a jellyfish—what a wild turn of events on a beach. Is the universe punishing me for leaving my bubble?

"We can reschedule our meeting this afternoon, if necessary," Niko offers.

I can't tell whether the right move is to take him up on his offer and postpone or forge on ahead, injuries be damned. Amber is expecting a report tonight, though. I'm supposed to call her after our meeting.

"No, no, it's fine," I respond. I'd rather just get this over with so I have one less thing to worry about on this nutty trip. I struggle to my feet, gathering my things.

"May I?" Niko approaches with his arm out.

"Only until we get on more solid ground. I'll be fine on the pavement," I say, handing him my shoulder bag, even though I know he meant to help me walk. I still have the tiniest bit of pride left, somewhere beneath the sand that's caked all over my body. I will walk on my own two feet to this scooter, even if it kills me.

A pale blue scooter sits perched on the sidewalk when we reach the front of the hotel. It has a cream-colored leather seat and two white helmets hanging from either side of the handle-bar. If I weren't in so much pain, I would think it was adorable.

Niko makes his way onto the bike, and Ana holds my hand as I swing my injured leg over the back of the scooter and climb up.

The scent of sea salt and pine overwhelms my senses. Niko smells amazing. And while I try not to inhale his scent, it's hard with how close he is.

Ana gives me a hug and tells me to feel better, saying she'll walk back to the hotel after she takes care of the cabana. Niko turns on the scooter.

"Well, well." I hear Malcolm's voice in my head. *"Aren't you just a damsel in distress. You never could keep upright on those two left feet."*

My jaw clenches. He always had a way of making me feel like everything was my fault.

"Hold on." Niko's voice breaks through—the contrast between the two voices is startling. His voice isn't cold or sharp. It's deep and warm.

Niko hits the gas and we speed off. Instinctively, I wrap my arms around his waist and try not to notice the ripples of muscle in his back.

Chapter 11

After cleaning my wound and my pride, I'm sitting in the
conference room waiting for Niko. I made my way to my room
to take a shower the moment we entered the hotel, and by the
time I was done, Alexander was knocking on the door with
steroid creams, bandages, and pain killers. Apparently sent by
Niko. He's either still trying to apologize or at least show the
full-service quality of his hotel. Either way, I want to run away
from the special attention.

I've been over and over the presentation Amber sent me
and can recite it word for word. I know every stat, every figure,
every marketing plan.

I'm wearing the dress I found at the thrift shop, the floral
cotton that rests just past my knees with a modest V-neck.

I start to flip through the materials again for the sake of
keeping my hands busy. There's a giant spread of fruits,
pastries, and cheeses on the conference room table, and it's
making me a little nervous. I know it's just supposed to be Niko
and I at this meeting, so who is all the food for?

"There she is."

Niko has entered the room and is striding toward me, a confident smile on his face. His sleeves are rolled up on his forearms, and he has one hand casually in his pocket. "How's your leg?"

"It's great!" My voice is loud and a bit too enthusiastic. I can still feel a bit of an ache, but it's definitely improved. "I mean, not great, obviously, but I'm doing much better." I fumble over my words. "Are we waiting for anyone else?"

Niko looks confused and I gesture to the all the food.

"Oh, that," he says with another smile. "No, I just thought I would have the kitchen provide us with a sampling for you. I'm trying to get the chef to embrace more traditional fare. It was a fusion kitchen under the previous owners."

This is all for us? My eyes almost bug out of my head.

Niko grabs two plates from the end of the table. "Let's dig in!"

Hesitantly, I grab a few pieces of fruit and some sort of pastry. I try not to overload my plate, for fear of looking greedy. But the food looks irresistible—like everything else on this island.

Niko piles his plate full before taking a seat at one corner of the oval table. He then pulls out the chair next to him for me. Not across. Not a few chairs down. Right next to him. I take the seat he offers, slowly, making sure I don't brush against him. I set my plate on the table and ignore it.

"I know you've spoken with Amber, but I wanted to first take some time to introduce Aspen Sky Marketing," I start. "We're a small boutique marketing firm based in Colorado and mostly focus on independently owned small-to-medium resorts and hotels."

My voice is unusually high and a bit twangy. I always sound like a sorority girl on helium when I'm nervous. My fingers are shaking, and I swear, I can feel sweat stains already permeating my dress. I should have worn a sweater.

Niko sucks on a piece of melon so I continue despite feeling out of breath already.

"I would love to learn more about your hotel and show you some recent campaigns that might match your needs in the US market."

I need to focus on what Amber would do. She said he wants to be hands-on, so I'm hoping he will guide the discussion.

Niko sits up in his chair and leans toward me, gesturing at my plate and picking up the pastry. "First, you need to eat. Here, try the baklava. It's the best you've ever had, I promise. You just need to try it."

I really don't want to eat in front of him—this close in front of him, especially—but if taking a bite of baklava will get him to move on, I'll do it.

I take a diamond-shaped pastry from Niko's outstretched hand. It's golden brown with little pistachio bits on the crust. I try to take a small, polite bite.

The warm pastry hits my tongue, lighting up about a thousand taste buds. It's gooey, slightly crunchy, and so sweet that it makes my eyes widen. I pull the remaining baklava away from my mouth, sending a cascade of flaky pastry all over my dress. I move to apologize, but the sticky liquid gold has my mouth glued shut. All I can do is mumble a "Mm-hmm" while brushing off crumbs. I should be embarrassed. I set aside any and all embarrassment to finish the baklava first. Like right now. Crumbs or no crumbs. It's that good.

"See! Was I right?" Niko asks when I shove the rest of it in my mouth.

I nod vigorously until I finish chewing. "It is, definitely."

I make a mental note to find more as soon as I'm out of this meeting. But I'm not here to eat, at least, not right now. I'm here to bring in a client. I leaf through my portfolio, ready to capitalize on the food conversation. "You know, I have a few campaigns here that center around food and restaurants."

I find the campaign we created for a hotel in Northern California last year; the chef would get fresh seafood from the docks every morning before setting the day's menu. But Niko waves me off.

"No, no business yet. You have to try these apricots. They are perfect this time of year," Niko says, passing me an apricot with one hand while biting into his own fruit with the other. I sit stunned holding the apricot. Is he serious right now? But the juice dribbling down his chin tells me that he is absolutely serious.

I have never had a meeting like this.

I take a small bite, holding my apricot in a napkin so it doesn't drip down my dress like the pastry flakes. I've only ever had dried apricots at my grandma's house. This is an entirely different experience. Rather than tough and leathery, fresh apricot tastes and feels more like a peach but with hints of cinnamon and honey. It might even be better than the baklava, if that's possible.

"Wasn't that good? Maybe not as good as the baklava, but delectable in its own right," Niko declares, reading my mind.

"It's so sweet and juicy," I respond. But can we *please* focus on the task at hand? I didn't rehearse this with Amber fifty times over the last week for nothing. "Why don't you tell me a bit more about the Omorfiá Hotel? I always find that getting to the heart of the business helps to create meaningful and successful campaigns."

Niko stands, carrying his plate. "Perfect idea! Let me take you on a tour of the property. I'll show you the changes I'm making to the hotel, and you can tell me about yourself. Bring your plate, but we'll come back for more food later."

Well, it's a start. I grab my plate and leave the materials on the table.

"Let's start downstairs." Niko leads me to the door, and we take the stairs down to the lobby. While we walk, Niko angles himself to face me.

"So, Jenni, tell me about yourself. What are your interests? How did you end up here?"

Me? Why me? I don't matter here. Niko matters. Aspen Sky matters. Amber matters. And I ended up here on accident after volunteering for what I thought was one thing and then ended up way over my head in something else. I don't unload that on him, though.

"Well, I'm from Colorado. I've worked at Aspen Sky for about a year. I had actually offered to step in when Amber couldn't travel, so here I am. That's probably all you need to know about me!"

My voice is getting dangerously high again. Let's just get to the tour, *please*. As I wring my hands together, I know I am a thousand times more comfortable talking about the hotel than I am talking about myself.

"I disagree." Niko smiles and cocks his head. "I know I look like a boring business guy, but numbers and portfolios are secondary to me. I want to make sure we connect on a value level—on what makes you, you."

Niko looks nothing like a boring business guy to me. He's too casual, relaxed, and tan. Way too tan.

There are a thousand ways I imagined this meeting going. A thousand ways for Niko to tell me I wasn't good enough or for Amber to say I failed her. But this—being forced to talk about myself—was not remotely on my radar. And values? That's how I got in trouble in Chicago. I stuck too strongly to my values when they clearly weren't shared by the client. I'm going to have to be very careful here.

"All that to say," Niko continues. "I'm sure your portfolio is great. I wouldn't have asked Amber to come if I didn't think Aspen Sky was a competitive marketing agency. I'm less concerned about that than making sure we understand each other and the hotel."

What if this is some sort of catch? Some sort of test or trap? Am I supposed to keep pushing the work stuff? Is he trying to make sure we will stay 100 percent focused for him? Nothing in my cramming prepared me for this.

"What else is there to know about you?" he asks with a smile, leading me into a large room off the lobby.

"Well, I like to hike. And camp. I spend as much of my free time outdoors as possible."

"I bet you love living in Colorado then. I hear the Rockies are amazing," Niko says, stopping once we're inside. "The mountains, not the baseball team—as we've already discussed."

His laugh puts me at ease. He isn't Malcolm. This isn't Chicago. I don't need to panic. Yet.

"This is our event space." Niko gestures to the room. "We can host small weddings, parties, banquets—you name it. My favorite thing about this space is that when we're not holding an event, my team partners with local artists to showcase their work. No gallery fee, of course."

I look around the room and notice the variety of artwork from landscape photography to still paintings. This would make such a cool thing to highlight in our marketing efforts. Local artisan work that you can't see or get anywhere else. People always a love a good "supporting locals" campaign.

"Wow, that's amazing. What a cool way to integrate into the community," I say. "Do you have a favorite piece?"

He wanders around the room for a moment until he stops in front of a canvas painting. It displays a rocky cliff side, somewhere here in Greece, I assume. But the entire thing is done in shades of blue, with the contrasting white canvas acting as negative space. It's simple and beautiful.

"I would say it has to be this one. The artist is incredible. She's in her nineties and she didn't start painting until she was, like, seventy-five. She says she found her fifth calling in life. How cool is that? To reinvent yourself over and over again?"

I don't know. I'm still trying to figure out where I fit for the first time. I can't imagine doing it more than once.

"It's really lovely," I say.

When we are done in the gallery, we exit through the lobby and wind up in a long outdoor corridor. To the right are the spa, gym, and pool. And to the left sits a rack of bikes, which Niko tells me are available for guests to get around the island.

"All you have to do is scan your key card on the locking mechanism on the rack. The bikes have been really popular since we incorporated them at the beginning of the summer."

Wow. Maybe this hotel isn't the out-of-touch luxury place I thought it was during my research. Niko is changing a lot.

"I love that. It's so down-to-earth," I tell Niko. "I bet guests feel like they can really experience a part of Greece here."

Maybe Niko isn't the out-of-touch upper-class elite I thought he was, either.

"Exactly! You get it. When we bought the property, it had previously been a very high-end luxury hotel, but that type of place is all over. I want the Omorfiá to be different. I want it to stand out and appeal to a different type of traveler who isn't looking for that pomp and circumstance."

I nod. It makes total sense, and I can see how passionate he is about the idea. "It's brilliant."

"I'm not sure the financial backers think so," he says. "They are worried it will flop and would rather just continue with the status quo. I'm slowly making changes and hoping they get on board eventually. That's why we'll stick with pretty traditional methods for our marketing pitch. I don't need to ruffle their feathers any more than I already have."

Really? That's so frustrating. Ideas on ways we could market these features have been popping up like popcorn since we started the tour. The bikes alone would make such a great video for socials.

"Sure, that makes sense," I tell Niko, not letting him see my disappointment. "Where are we headed next?"

"You'll see."

I laugh. He loves the mystery, doesn't he?

We reach the top of the stairs, and Niko opens the door onto the roof. We walk around the stair entry, and I see that the roof is covered in raised garden beds. I see tomatoes, peppers, cucumbers—so many cucumbers—basil, spinach, and more.

"You grow your own food too?" I am seriously impressed. The roof is like a tiny oasis. The garden beds are remarkably well kept and abundant. Niko smiles at my excitement.

"We use most of it in the restaurant, but we also donate anything that we can't use."

He looks so proud, like he is genuinely invested in all of this.

"Have you done a photoshoot up here?"

"We haven't," he responds, cocking his head. "What for?"

What for? He can't be serious. There's no way he's doing this out of the goodness of his heart. Businessmen don't think that way.

"Marketing, of course! People love this kind of stuff."

"Oh, maybe. That's not really why we do it, but I guess we could. Don't suggest that at the board meeting though. It won't go over well."

There are so many amazing things on the property, and Niko wants to hide all of them in our marketing pitch? We would be left to discuss thread count and spa packages, like every other cookie cutter resort. I'm confused.

As we make our way back to the conference room, Niko asks, "What fun things have you planned for your stay?"

Fun things? Like what, sitting by the pool?

"Oh, you know, I'll probably do some shopping. I plan to

visit the pool. I'm here at your beck and call to work on whatever you need most, though. My top goal is to help you promote this hotel."

He clutches his heart like he's just received the shock of a lifetime. "What? That's it? That simply will not do. I am going to have to change that. We'll have fun."

I laugh. "No, it's fine. I'm sure I'll find things to do."

Honestly, the thought of doing activities with this man for fun is terrifying. Intriguing but terrifying.

He clasps his hands together. "You have to let me take you around the island. Please. Playing tour guide is my favorite thing to do."

I roll my eyes. I guess I don't really have a choice, though it will give me more time to figure out how he ticks and what we can do to make our presentation amaze the board. Especially if he won't let me talk about all the things that make the hotel unique.

"Okay, if you insist. I'm all yours."

Goodbye, quiet afternoons at the pool. Hello, Niko. A wave of excitement fills my body.

"Fantastic! This is going to be so much fun. Let's go parasailing on Sunday. It's going to be great weather. You'll love it."

Oh, no. Para-what? That does not sound good.

Jenni: Have you ever been parasailing? Is it what I think it is? I'm too afraid to look it up.

Piper: Hahahaha! No, I bet you're thinking of paragliding. Parasailing is more like waterskiing, but in the air. Why?

Jenni: I'm going the day after tomorrow, apparently. With Niko.

Jenni: PS The girlfriend is actually his cousin. Not that it's important, but just thought you should know.

Piper: Yessssss. Get it, girl. That's going to be so much fun!

Chapter 12

It's not that I'm afraid of heights. I've hiked plenty of very tall mountains. But I'm not the biggest fan either. And I really don't like the feeling of my feet dangling around with nothing to grab hold of. Or the possibility of plummeting. On a mountain, at least I've got dirt and rock under my feet.

Okay, maybe I might be afraid of heights … I refuse to share this with Niko, though. No way. Not when this is a way for me to connect with him and figure out a plan to win him over to Aspen Sky.

I contemplate the implications of this new phobia as I pace back and forth in the lobby. I came downstairs way early because I didn't want to be late meeting Niko, but I think I think I came down too early because the waiting is making me even more nervous. I'm wearing my swimsuit, as instructed, with a pair of sandals, khaki shorts, and a green cotton tee.

I fire off a quick text to Piper and Sarah, letting them know they can have my camping gear if I don't survive this.

> Piper: Your camping gear is junk. We don't want it. ;) So you better survive. HAVE FUN!!!

I roll my eyes, even as a chuckle breaks through my nerves. Everything I have is secondhand and decades old. Still, I appreciate her sarcasm.

> Jenni: Fine. You can have my bike. Also, why are you awake? Go to bed!

> Piper: I told you I'd be here for you day or night. But yes, I should get some sleep. Love you!

> Jenni: Love you too. Even though this is all your fault.

> Piper: You'll thank me later.

I check the time and slide my phone into my pocket. Niko should be down any minute. My only goal today, in addition to surviving, is impressing Niko in order to convince him that we're a good fit.

"Good morning, Miss Swanson!" Alexander, who has just arrived at the front desk, smiles in greeting.

"Hi, Alexander! Please call me Jenni," I say. He and I are basically peers here, both either working for, or hoping to work for, Niko.

"Of course, Miss Swanson. I will. Mr. Psomas has instructed me to have you meet him in the hotel restaurant before your excursion today. Right this way."

I follow Alexander across the lobby toward the restaurant. Has Niko prepared even more food for us? My mouth salivates at the memory of the baklava. I could go for more of that. Although, I am feeling slightly queasy about this whole flying-through-the-air-while-tethered-to-the-back-of-a-boat thing.

"Niko is taking me parasailing today," I tell Alexander as we walk. "Have you been?"

"Me? Oh, no! I'm much too afraid of heights."

"Me neither. I'll let you know if I survive."

When we round the corner, I scan the room and find Niko off to the side, standing next to a table set for two. The sight of him tickles something inside me, like the first bubbly sip of cola on a hot, sunny day. Niko has replaced his suit with swim trunks and a black T-shirt, the sleeves tight around his biceps. He looks so friendly and fun, and I just know it'll be a great day. Then my brain catches up and sends a wave of nervous energy crashing through my veins. I need to focus. Last time I checked, being a good marketing team doesn't involve ogling the client.

"I hope you had a pleasant night," Niko tells me. "Are you getting adjusted to the time difference?"

"I think so. I only woke up twice last night—either confused about where I was or what year it is." I shrug while he laughs. The sound catches me off guard. I'm not used to people responding so well to my humor. Only Piper usually shares my frame of mind.

"What's all this? You have to stop feeding me!" I gesture to the table set in front of us, just as a woman in a chef's coat approaches and hands Niko a circular aluminum tray with a tall three-pronged handle. He thanks her before setting it down in the center of the table like a lantern.

"No, I do not need to stop feeding you. But alas, we aren't eating. I wanted you to try traditional Greek coffee." Niko pulls a chair out for me. *Hmm*, he's charming.

Niko takes a seat across from me and hands me a tall glass of water and a small white cup of coffee from the silver tray. "Drink the water first to clear your palate."

I do as he says.

The coffee has a thick layer of creamy foam on top, which smells nutty and sweet. Will this be the first thing I end up trying in Greece and hating? I drank enough warm gas station beer in college. I can get this down without letting on that I hate it. I normally can't stand coffee that isn't iced and loaded with sweetener.

I bring the cup to my mouth, taking a tiny sip of the hot, thick liquid. Barely enough to taste it.

"It's good, right? We boil our coffee grounds in water and sugar instead of just pouring hot water onto them. It's what gives Greek coffee the thick, creamy texture."

He dips his finger into his own cup and pulls it out. "This foam is called *kaimaki*. It's the best part. Make sure you get a bit of both when you drink it."

He's not going to let me wing it here, is he? I take a bigger sip to get both the foam and the coffee. Well, he might be on to something. It's the creamiest coffee I've ever had. And sweet too, in a subtle way. Way better than my parents' drip coffee at home.

"That's actually really good!" I say, wiping my mouth with a napkin.

He laughs. "I'll try not to be offended by the word 'actually.'"

My cheeks flush, and I try to backpedal. "That's not what I meant—"

"Don't worry. You don't have to like it."

"—I just don't normally drink hot coffee." I realize we are talking over each other and pause. Niko has stopped talking too and motions for me to continue. "I just surprised myself, that's all. It really is very good."

"Good. I'm glad. You can get it here anytime you want or put in a request with room service. On me."

A few sips later and we're exiting the restaurant. Niko extends an arm toward the front door of the hotel to gesture toward a waiting car.

I brush a lock of hair behind my ear. I'm suddenly extremely aware of the power dynamic in this scenario and how vulnerable it makes me. What if I change my mind or something feels off? I don't need to get into a similar situation as my last boyfriend. I hate to think that way, but it's not like I haven't been here before. Alexander knows I'm leaving with Niko and will presumably be waiting for us to return. Piper also has my location on her phone.

"Alexander. We'll be back around four, okay?" Niko calls out. Then he turns to me. "Do you want to call anyone to let them know what we're doing?"

I pause for a second. Everyone I know is asleep, so I shake my head. My gut is telling me that Niko is safe, but I wouldn't be looking out for myself if I weren't cautious.

Niko directs me to an SUV with a driver waiting by the passenger side of the car. She's dressed in a uniform and looks like she is not someone to be messed with. She smiles when Niko greets her with a kiss on the cheek. See! That's not the way a bad man would greet his driver.

"Sophia, this is Jenni. She'll be my guest for the next little while."

I reach out to shake Sophia's hand. Her grip is strong, but warm and reassuring. "It's a pleasure," she tells me, as she opens the door and ushers me in.

Niko and I both sit in the second row, water bottles and warm hand towels in a basket between us.

"Have you been parasailing before?" Niko asks as we start down the road.

"No, I haven't. I usually prefer to have my two feet on the ground, actually. It's probably safer for everyone. As you've seen, I have a knack for unfortunate events."

Hopefully, I sound more like I'm joking than panicking. A tiny glimmer sparkles in his eyes as he bites his lips together, a dimple forming on his right cheek.

"Are you laughing at me?"

"Of course not, but you do have a point." He smirks. "Your clumsiness is kind of adorable."

"For you maybe, but tell that to my leg," I retort. "Or your front desk."

At that, Niko's smile grows and he chuckles. I flush at the ease of our back and forth. Malcolm could never laugh at my mishaps; he always seemed to be embarrassed by me. Hopefully Niko's ability to laugh is a sign that it will help him fall in love with Aspen Sky Marketing.

I turn the conversation toward Niko. "I read on the hotel's press release that you went to business school in California. Was that the first time you lived in the States?"

"No, actually," he says, seeming surprised I don't know his background. "I grew up in California. My mom is American."

"You didn't grow up in Greece? I thought your family owned a series of vineyards. Was I mistaken?"

Niko inhales a deep breath, and I see his quads tighten, his feet pressing more firmly to the floor of the car.

"My dad's family," he corrects. "My parents weren't together when they had me. I grew up with my mom in California. Meanwhile, my dad was here. I'm a dual citizen."

"Oh, I didn't realize. Did you see him much?"

"He would visit when he could, and we spent my summer break in Greece most years. I never actually lived here until about six months ago, though."

I take a minute to digest this new information. I can't imagine growing up on a different continent from one of my parents. As much as they sometimes drive me crazy, I would miss them way too much. Which reminds me that I should check in with my mom when we get back.

"That must have been hard. To be separated like that."

Niko just shrugs and then unbuckles his seatbelt as the car comes to a stop. "I didn't know any different."

He tries to brush it off, but his eyes look sad. I want to say something, but I have no idea what would be appropriate.

Niko speaks instead. "Here we are! Hope you're ready!"

We climb out and make our way to a white tent near the dock where we are greeted by two guys who look like they can't be any older than sixteen, wearing matching pink muscle tanks. *This* is who I'm entrusting my life to? Panic creeps back into my gut.

After Niko and I watch a safety video and sign our lives away on a waiver, a kid named Mike asks, "Do you want to do a single harness or double harness today?"

"We'll take a double harness," Niko says and turns to me. "That way, we can both spend as much time as possible in the air."

A double harness? If that means what I think it means, I might actually puke. I feel dizzy as I picture myself hundreds of feet in the air, hyperventilating while Niko hangs next to me.

"Sounds great!" I smile back feebly. Deep breaths. It's going to be fine.

We collect life vests and walk to the end of the dock where a speedboat and two more teenage-looking boys wait for us.

Mike puts one foot on the boat and reaches out his hand to help me board. I take a deep breath to calm my shaking hands and must hesitate for a moment too long because, just as I'm taking Mike's hand to step onto the boat, Niko grabs my shoulder and I stumble.

"Wait!"

I regain my footing and turn around, expecting some sort of emergency, but Niko just scans my face diligently.

"You seem nervous. Are you sure you want to do this? You don't have to."

I'm caught off guard that he even noticed.

I glance between Niko and Mike and the brightly colored lump of polyester sitting in the back of the boat. I could walk away right now. I really don't belong here; walking away would make sense. I could go back and sit at the hotel until our next meeting and not have to deal with any of this.

"You can't do this. When have you ever been brave? He's giving you an out. Take it." Malcolm's familiar voice rings out in my head, reinforcing my fears while trying to knock me down. But wouldn't it be way worse to bow out now? I would be nailing my own coffin shut, wouldn't I? As much as Niko seems genuine that he only wants me to do this if I feel comfortable, it still wouldn't make me look good.

I can't risk that because I can't lose this deal.

"Of course! I totally want to do this," I say. "Couldn't be more excited."

Lying straight through my teeth.

At least that's a skill I got good at in during my time in Chicago. Always covering up any pain, worry, or disappointment. Being and feeling exactly the way Malcolm wanted me to.

"Thank you for checking, though," I add. I mean it, even if it didn't free me from the need to keep going.

Chapter 13

Once we're out on the water, anticipation buzzes at my fingertips, and I can't tell if it's that or the motor that is making me feel like my entire body is vibrating. I'm still terrified that something is going to go wrong, but now that I'm committed, I can't help but wonder what it's going to feel like. It must be the adrenaline. Simple biology.

Once we are a fair distance away from shore, Mike and one of the other boys ready the parachute. They work quickly and seamlessly as if they've done this a thousand times. Before I can even process what's happening, the parachute has opened, and it's filling with air, floating above the back of the boat, rippling in the wind.

The red, yellow, and purple fabric stands out against the blue sky. I turn toward Niko, watching the wind whip through his hair as he watches the men at work.

"Are you ready?" He gestures toward Mike, who is beckoning us to join him.

I step onto the platform at the back of the boat and turn my back to the sea. Mike brings the bottom of the harness up around my hips and clips me in, tightening straps around my waist, chest, and each of my thighs. Then he does the same for Niko. We both grab onto the front straps like the chains of a playground swing.

Butterflies tickle the walls of my stomach as Mike steps back and gives the all-clear signal. The boat speeds up, and I can feel the harness tightening around me, gently tugging my weight backward.

My stomach and heart drop simultaneously when, without warning, my bare feet lift off the back of the boat and we hover in the air for a second, then two, before Mike reels out the ropes that tether us to the boat. We ascend higher and higher until we reach our final height.

All I can hear is my own breath and the gentle whipping of the wind around us. The noises of the boats and people below don't reach us up here.

Beyond my toes, I see a tiny version of Mike, standing on the bench of the boat and pumping his fists, congratulating us. He looks like an action figure on a toy boat in the bathtub, which makes me feel slightly queasy.

I turn my attention to the skyline. To my right, there's nothing but the horizon, a turquoise sea, and the brightly shining sun.

To my left, past Niko, I can see the island. It's breathtaking. Brown-and-black hills flank the rocky cliffs and sandy shores. Miniature white structures line up like dominoes on the rocky hillsides.

"It's beautiful!" I say in awe.

"It is," Niko agrees, sounding far away despite hanging right next to me. "It's my favorite view on the island. Up here, everything gets put into perspective."

Sailboats dot the ocean, harnessing the wind, and a few Jet Skis and speedboats zip around, creating white trails of foamy sea water behind them. A flock of seagulls circles near the marina in hopes of catching their lunch.

I feel both powerless to the whim of the parachute and also like I'm on top of the world.

"What now?" I shout to Niko as a gust of wind powers by.

"Nothing! Just enjoy the moment!"

Niko grabs my hand and thrusts it up in a victory pose, hooting and hollering. Electricity shoots down my arm, straight to my heart, filling me with sunshine. I'm not really sure what it means that he's holding my hand, but that feels like a problem for solid ground. He did just tell me to enjoy the moment. A huge, joyous belly laugh erupts from somewhere deep inside of me, and I join in his celebration.

I haven't experienced such radiating joy in a long, long time.

Niko smiles at me, as if he feels it too.

The water glimmers like sequins in the sun while we sway in the air. The wind tosses my hair around my face. Niko lets our hands drop, and I grab back onto the straps of my harness.

"Look," he says, suddenly pointing at two seagulls chasing each other. "What do you think they're fighting over?"

"She's mad that he ate the late sardine. She was saving it for tomorrow and had clearly written her name on the fin."

Niko laughs. "They sound like my employees." He nudges me with his elbow. "You're a lot of fun, Jenni. I can't remember the last time I laughed this much. I've been working like crazy since we took over the hotel. I'm glad we did this."

I can feel the sun at my back and my heart flutters at his words. "I am glad too. I love being outdoors and seeing new things. So thank you."

"Oh, yeah? Is that what you like to do when you travel?"

That's a good question. Obviously, I haven't traveled much, but when I do it's usually a camping trip or national park.

"I've never really thought about it," I say. "But yeah, definitely. Especially hiking."

"In that case, I can recommend some trails to check out

while you're here. We don't offer hiking nearly as great as Colorado, but you can walk along the coast and see some cool things."

"That would be great, thanks. What about you? What do you love about traveling?"

"I love how traveling forces me to embrace spontaneity and get out of my comfort zone."

Is he crazy? That's the *worst* part!

"My friend Piper says her soul starts to wither if she stays in one place for too long."

Niko laughs. "Well, that's a bit dramatic, but I get it. It starts to feel suffocating doing the same five things day in and day out. Does she move around a lot?"

Piper should have been the one to come here. She and Niko would get along so well. "She and her girlfriend live in an RV and travel the US year-round. I don't even know where they are half the time. She is an associate at Aspen Sky so maybe you'll get to work with her someday."

"No way! That's cool," he says, shading his eyes from the sun. "I've always dreamed of renting a sprinter van and road tripping all over Europe. Can you imagine?"

I can't, not really. But I can pretend.

"Sounds like the grown-up version of hitchhiking and sleeping in hostels with a dozen strangers. Only better."

"Exactly. No one to steal your socks."

"No way! Did that happen to you?"

He laughs again. "Me? No, I never did the backpacking thing. I would bet it's happened to someone out there, though."

Niko traces invisible waves in the wind with his hands, like a kid sticking their arm out of a car window.

I try to picture someone sneaking under the covers in the dead of night and pulling socks off unsuspecting travelers. "I'm sorry, I just can't imagine anyone stealing used socks," I say with another laugh.

"You never know!"

Niko points to the water about a hundred yards out to sea. "Did you see that?"

"See what?" All I see are little white-capped waves rippling on their way to shore.

"I thought I saw a pod of dolphins. They're pretty common this time of year. But usually a bit further out."

"Really! Do you think it was? That would be amazing."

We spend the rest of our time in the air scouring the water for signs of dolphins. Sadly, we come up empty-handed by the time we are reeled back in. I am more disappointed than I should be, but it doesn't diminish the insane views and fun time I had. After a while, I can feel myself smiling without forcing it. Like really smiling. And for a while, I can forget all about the rest of my life—Malcolm, the job in Chicago, everything I'm trying so desperately to earn back. None of it matters right now.

I don't want this to end.

Eventually Mike waves a flag below us and we begin our descent toward the water. Back down to reality, where I have to worry about work and and find my way around Mykonos without embarrassing myself a hundred more times.

"Are you ready to get wet?" Niko taunts, kicking his feet as we descend. His legs are longer than mine and he makes contact first, sending water flying up at us. The cold spray tickles, sending a tingle up my spine. I squeal as we splash and bounce off the water a few times before slipping in. Mike jumps off the boat, which has come to a stop, and swims toward us as we bob in our life jackets and harnesses.

Mike unclips me first and I breaststroke my way over to the boat, climbing up the metal ladder on the side. Niko climbs into the boat behind me and I'm suddenly self-conscious in his presence again, as if a switch has been flipped now that we aren't alone up in the sky. I can't decide if that was the most incredible thing I've ever done or the dumbest. I can't believe I let this potential client hold my hand. I let him see me completely without my guard up. I screamed and laughed with abandon … which is not the type of person anyone wants to see across a conference room table. Shame creeps into my gut even while my fingers tingle at the memory of holding his. I feel like I'm walking a tightrope between trying to connect with him and maintaining the type of professional persona I should have on an assignment like this.

"So what is up next on the agenda for this afternoon? Should we meet to go over the proposal, or did you have something else planned?"

I look at Niko expectantly, trying to show him that I'm game for anything. Spontaneity, right? That's what he values and what I need to show him in order to land this deal. But I also need to show dedication to the job.

"I have meetings the rest of the afternoon, but—"

"Of course, of course. I shouldn't have assumed." I am quick to recalibrate, covering up what I'm now realizing might have been an inappropriate ask. "I am perfectly capable of entertaining myself."

I do my best to exude that fake confidence I had let drop during the last hour.

"In fact, I've just remembered that I have a spa session booked," I add. "Turns out, I have plenty on my schedule!"

I take a long sip from my water bottle and stare out at the approaching harbor, willing the boat to move faster so I can stop talking. Before this character I'm pretending to be falls apart and reveals who I really am—a mess.

"At the Omorfiá?"

Whoops. I forgot there was a spa at the hotel. Now he'll know I'm lying if I don't actually go. I can't exactly tell him I'm going somewhere else. What sort of message would that send?

"Absolutely! I'm getting a facial. Alexander recommended it."

Roping poor Alexander into my lies. I'm horrible.

"You'll love it. Our staff is incredible. If you need anything while you're there, just let them know you're here as my guest."

His eyes linger on mine and I straighten my shoulders, not letting him see me falter.

Niko clears his throat. "As I was saying, I have the entire day free on Tuesday, and there's something else I want to show you. Are you up for it?"

Is this a pity offering? I don't want to seem desperate.

"Sure, if you aren't too busy, that sounds good. Either way, really."

Niko puts his hands on my shoulders and looks me in the eye. "It's not a trick question, Jenni."

I smile sheepishly, face flushing.

"Okay, fine. I would love to."

"Good."

Chapter 14

It's nearly 3:00 p.m. by the time I get to my room. I'm exhausted, embarrassed, and starving after our excursion—a deadly combination. I order a pasta dish and a Greek salad through room service as a late lunch. I've been dreaming of another big block of feta drizzled in olive oil since that first night down by the beach.

As I slump on the bed, my head reels from this morning's outing. On the one hand, I felt so alive up there. The way we talked, and the moment Niko grabbed my hand, laughing … It felt so real. Like I was making a friend and having fun. Something I haven't done in eons. I felt like myself for the first time in years. Since I met Malcolm, probably.

But at the same time, I'm worried that it's going to interfere with my work. Niko and I have barely touched the proposal for the board meeting. Meanwhile, I've been receiving nervous texts and emails from Amber checking in, and I have nothing to report. While I wait for my food, I get up to type out an email.

Subject: Meetings with Mr. Psomas
Amber,

Wow. You weren't kidding about Niko wanting to be hands-on. I'm sorry I don't have much to report yet, but I do think things are going well. He seems excited about what Aspen Sky has to offer. He is pretty set on using standard metrics for the proposal and focusing on our measurable success rates. Should be straightforward.

Again, I'm really sorry I don't have more to report back, but I've been working nonstop, just waiting for Niko to really sit down with me to go over it.

I don't think you need to worry, though. Everything is under control! I can handle this. Get some rest and I'll report back soon.

Best,

Jenni

I rest my forehead in my hand, elbow on the desk next to my laptop. I should have so much more to report by now. I really need to get some concrete work done. I need to figure out how to prove, unequivocally, to the board that we are worth our salt.

Just as I open a spreadsheet to brainstorm some talking points, there's a quiet knock at the door. My stomach growls in response. My food. Thank goodness.

I quickly glance down at my outfit before opening the door. I'm still wearing my bathing suit and shorts from earlier. My hair is tangled and in a messy bun, and now that I think about it, my makeup is probably washed away or smeared all over my face.

"Jenni!"

When I open the door, Ana, looking absolutely perfect as always, is beaming in the hallway. I stand there, a bit like a deer in the headlights of her glow. "I wanted to come say hi and see how you're doing. Alexander said you had returned from your trip with Niko!"

She air-kisses me and then pushes her way into the room. "Oh, Niko gave you one of the best rooms. I just love this view.

It's so invigorating. By the way, I like to sleep with the window open all night to listen to the sea. You should try it!"

"Sure, I will." I still can't quite figure out why she is here, feeling the need to check on me.

"How was your day?" she asks. "Niko mentioned you were going to the marina?"

I guess she's staying for a chat. This is … unexpected. Ana crosses her legs and leans back in the chair, looking comfortable and relaxed.

Almost exactly the same way Sarah would if she and Piper were here. Piper would be sitting on the bed, shoes off, back up against the headboard. My heart aches at the thought. I miss them.

"It was incredible! The island is so beautiful. The parasailing was … interesting. I've never worked with anyone quite like Niko before."

"How so?" Ana leans forward as if we're teenagers about to dish about a boy at school. Talking to her feels so natural that I feel my shoulders and my guard drop.

"He just doesn't seem to take himself too seriously, that's all. I'm used to men who wear fancy suits and sit in glass offices while making demands. Niko seems more focused on having fun."

She taps a finger on her rosy lips. "You sound like you're describing Niko's dad. He sits in a glass office." She laughs. "Niko can be that way too, though. I don't think he's left the hotel in weeks. He's always behind his desk."

Really? Then why did he take half a day off to take me parasailing? "He doesn't normally have days like today?"

"Nope. I think he likes you." She shrugs. "But I'm glad he's having fun. He deserves it."

That can't be right. I mean, sure, I hope he likes me. Enough to hire our agency. But that's all it should be. Obviously.

I go to ask Ana what she means, but there is another knock at the door.

"That must be my lunch."

Ana pops up out of her chair. "I didn't mean to take so much of your time. I only came to ask about your plans for dinner?"

"Oh, um, I hadn't thought about it yet." I open the door to the room and a waitress carries a tray of food in. She lifts the plate covers and quietly exits once she has set everything on the table. I call out my thanks as she closes the door, wishing I hadn't been so frazzled and could have acknowledged her properly. Instead, I turn to answer Ana.

"I think I'll …"

Something on the tray catches my eye. It's a little yellow duck. I snatch it up to get a closer look, wondering if my brain is playing tricks on me. Sure enough, it's a rubber duck. And not just any rubber duck, it has a red rose tucked under one wing and is wearing a top hat.

"What is this?" I turn to Ana.

"Looks like a duck to me," Ana says with a grin.

"But what is it doing on my room service tray?"

I'm struck by the recollection of the conversation on my very first, jet-lagged afternoon. I had completely forgotten.

"Niko said something about these the first day I was here. There's a duck prank going on around the hotel. I think I'm the latest victim," I tell Ana. This sort of thing never happens to me. My life is usually so boring. A warmth bubbles to my chest.

"Seems harmless to me. Maybe someone was just trying to brighten your day," she says with a gleam in her eye.

"Maybe …" I turn the duck over in my hands a few times before setting it on the desk. I'll figure out what I think about it later.

Ana looks at me pleadingly. "So … tonight?"

"I'll probably just run downstairs and eat at the restaurant later, after I shower."

"That's no fun! You simply must come with me. I know of a great restaurant on the water, near a nightclub. We can eat and dance the night away!"

"I would hate to impose. You don't need to babysit me. I'll have a quiet night in, call some friends, and go to bed early."

"*Please*. You'd be doing me a huge favor! I need girl time. I need music!"

If her intent is to guilt-trip me, it's working. Plus, Piper and Sarah would be thrilled if I told them I went out and did something fun.

"Okay, if you say so. That sounds really fun. But just dancing, right? I don't want to meet any men."

"Yay!!" Ana squeals and bounces up and down on her toes, clapping her hands together. Her joy bubbles into the room, and I can't help but feel excited for the evening.

"And men? Who needs men? Meet me downstairs at eight and wear something sexy!" With that, she floats out of the room with as much energy as she brought into it and leaves me in the quiet once more.

I check the time. I've got a few hours until I need to start getting ready. I sigh as I sit down to my pasta. This is all becoming so much more complicated than I thought it would be. Rather than just minding my own business and getting to work, I feel like I'm being thrust into some social experiment to root out the fake. Not only do I have to impress in the business meetings, but I also have to play this part of someone remotely in their social circle? It feels like I'm set up to fail.

I take a sip of the orange juice that came with my lunch. Maybe it's the promise I made to myself earlier or maybe Ana's guilt trip brought up other feelings, but I dial Mom's number. I expect her not to have service in the mountains, but she answers on the second ring.

"Jenni? Are you okay? What's wrong?"

"I'm okay, Mom. I just wanted to hear your voice. Are you still camping?"

I hear some noise in the background as Mom whispers to tell Dad it's really me.

"We are, but we drove into Durango for an estate sale. You wouldn't believe the quilts this lady had. I'm making your father haul an embroidery machine home."

Her voice fills a hollowness in my stomach. I hadn't realized I was homesick. I didn't know that was a thing a twenty-four-year-old could feel. Especially when I have wanted nothing other than getting out of there.

"Have you had your big meetings? Is everything going well?"

"Not yet. But we're getting there. When I get home, I'm going to make you Greek coffee. I think you'll love it." My voice cracks. I want to tell her that I think I've made a mistake coming here. I want her to tell me it's okay and I should come home.

"If you say so," she responds.

I push the food around on my plate, feeling the weight of everyone's expectations: Niko, Ana, Piper, Amber. They all want me to be someone that I'm not sure I can be anymore. Today was good, but how much longer can I keep up this charade?

"Mom, what happens if I can't make this work?" I ask. My voice is practically a whisper. "If fail here and can't get my life back ..."

There's a loud rumble on her end, as if a she's at a racetrack rather than an old country antique shop.

"What was that sweetheart? I couldn't hear you; a motorcycle club just pulled up. I don't know how they expect to take anything home—"

I pinch the bridge of my nose and sit up straight. I can't

admit my fears to her. "Nothing, Mom. I was just saying I missed you and hope you're having a great time."

"Oh sure, you know us. We're in our happy place. Are you sure you're okay?"

"I am, just tired. I was in the sun all day."

"Well then you're in your happy place too, I guess! I'm sorry I was so worried about you. Dad has talked me down over the last couple days."

It's breaking my heart that I'm not being honest with her when she's obviously trying to support me. I'm glad she didn't hear me waver, though, because I can't go home. Not now.

Chapter 15

A few minutes before I'm supposed to meet Ana, I'm still trying to get ready. I barely ate my lunch, so I'm starving, and I can't figure out how to do my hair. I'm wearing a black cotton sundress with a sweetheart neckline with eyelet embroidery around the skirt. On my feet, are gold leather braided sandals.

Sarah had insisted on this dress in case I was invited out for drinks, much to my protestation. I had argued at first, saying I would just be attending meetings and doing a few solo excursions—how incredibly wrong I had been. I fired off a bathroom selfie to her a few minutes ago, thanking her for always thinking ahead and asking for makeup tips. But I haven't gotten a response.

I finally decide on a braided updo and natural face and rush down to the lobby. I'm out of breath by the time I get to the front doors and see Sophia, with a sleek silver sedan this time.

"Good evening, Miss Jenni. You are looking beautiful tonight," Sophia says.

"Thank you. Have you seen Ana?" I reach for my phone in my purse to check the time, and it starts ringing in my hand.

I'm sure it's Sarah wanting to know where, and with whom, I'm wearing the dress. Instead of an old photo of Sarah and me in ski goggles making goofy faces, my phone reads: "Amber – Aspen Sky."

Crap. She probably wants more details about the meetings with Niko. I can't answer her call now, though. Not when I'm about to head to dinner and have nothing concrete to tell her. I silence the call and zip my bag closed once it's inside.

"There she is," Sophia says. I look up just as Ana steps through the lobby doors, absolutely glowing. She wraps me in a giant hug.

"Darling, you look amazing!" she sings. I know she's just being kind, but I'm grateful she's so gracious. I much prefer it to the alternative of snooty looks some people give down their noses. Ana takes a step back with her hands on my elbows and looks me up and down. "Do you know what would make this outfit perfect?"

I don't have a second to respond before she's taking a necklace off her own neck and doing up the clasp around mine. The necklace is made up of gold pebbles hammered in a matte finish. The pieces are around the size of a nickel and uniquely shaped, as if done by hand, which I imagine is the case. It hangs heavy on my chest, and I realize it might be real gold. I graze it with my fingertips.

"It's beautiful, but I can't wear this." What if I lose it? Or break it?

"You don't deserve to wear that." Malcolm's voice echoes.

"Of course you can! It looks much better on you than me. Case closed. Now let's go!"

She pulls me to the car, and the next thing I know, Sophia is dropping us off outside a restaurant and telling Ana to text her when we are ready to be picked up.

When we step through the front door, people everywhere

are dressed up, drinking champagne and looking like their only care in the world is whether to order caviar or oysters.

"You don't belong here, Jenni. Stop fooling yourself." Malcolm's voice inside my head is really starting to wear on me. But he's right. Pretending to fit in is getting exhausting, but I only have to get through one more week. The board meeting is a week from tomorrow. Once I get this deal signed, I can go home and move on. Hopefully one step closer to my old life.

At our table, I pick up my menu and panic when I realize it's entirely in Greek, with no pictures. My throat constricts. "Um … what do you recommend? Everything looks so good."

Ana gives me a sly look. "You don't know any Greek, do you?"

I sheepishly shake my head with a shrug. "No, not really. I couldn't get past basic greetings on my language app."

She laughs, placing a hand on her stomach. "I love it! Don't worry. I'll order for both of us. You're going to *love* the fish."

When the food comes out, our matching dishes are steaming and sizzling. The waiter sets the plate in front of me, and I am overwhelmed by the savory aroma. The white fish is covered in a rich, creamy tomato sauce overtop a bed of potatoes flaked with salt and seasonings. I can smell hints of onion and paprika.

Ana picks up one of the lemon wedges on her plate and motions for me to do the same. "You need to squeeze lemon juice all over it. It brings the flavors together."

I take the lemon wedge from my plate and use a fork to douse the fish with its juice. I gingerly wipe the juice off my fingers with the linen napkin in my lap. When I look up again, Ana has her lemon wedge in her mouth, sucking the last bits of juice out and making a sour face to prove it.

"Sorry," she says through pursed lips. "I'm worse than a child. I just love lemon!"

Okay, I kind of love this woman. She really has no pretense. But then again, if I looked and sounded like her, maybe I would stick a lemon wedge in my mouth without a care too.

I delicately cut a bite of fish and bring the steaming fork to my mouth. It tastes like pure magic. If this is the type of traditional fare Niko is trying to bring back to his restaurant, I can see why.

"This is amazing," I say, covering my mouth. "You were right!"

We make it through almost all our food while Ana tells me stories about growing up in Athens and how happy she and her sister were every summer when Niko would arrive.

"We were three peas in a pod—running through the gardens, playing soccer on the beach. I always looked forward to it." Ana wipes her mouth with her napkin and fiddles with her bracelet before taking a sip of white wine.

"I love your bracelet. I noticed it at the beach the other day," I say, taking a break from my own meal to sip my wine. "Does it mean something?"

She glances at her wrist and runs her fingers over the two hearts. Her eyes look sad, which sends a brick to the pit of my stomach.

"It … I wear it to remember my sister. Callie."

The brick leaves my stomach to land at my feet. I'm about to apologize and change the subject, but Ana continues, barely looking in my direction. Instead, she stares at her drink, swirling it in her hand. "We were best friends growing up. But we grew apart, or were forced apart, really, and she passed away a couple of years ago."

My throat feels swollen, like I can't swallow. How awful. "I'm so sorry, Ana. Truly. Do you want to talk about it?"

A pained expression crosses her face, but she continues. "Callie started dating an older man from Italy. At first, he spoiled her like crazy and she seemed so happy. He ended up having a controlling streak. He cut her off from family and friends. I would go weeks without hearing from her in between quick calls that always came from a different phone number."

Her words are all too familiar. Of course, I was never the trophy girlfriend, but I know what it's like to be love-bombed and then treated well only when it's convenient and self-serving. Malcolm cut me off from all my friends, too. At first, it was subtle. He would make small comments about a friend being weird or rude toward him and leave it at that. Then, when any of my friends wanted a girls' night or to travel together, he would act like I was abandoning him or that they were purposely trying to pull us apart.

Once I got away and learned more about manipulative relationships, I realized it was absolutely formulaic. I hadn't talked to Piper in months by the time we broke up. When I finally called her, I sobbed while repeatedly apologizing. She immediately welcomed me back into her life with open arms. I don't think I would have survived if she hadn't.

I reach across the table, grab Ana's hand, and give it a gentle squeeze.

"I still remember the first time I noticed a bruise when we were on video. I asked Callie about it, and she immediately made an excuse about needing to hang up, and we didn't talk for a month."

I am starting to feel sick. But I have to let Ana tell her sister's story.

"He used to take her on these vacations and then just leave her there if he got tired of her," Ana said. "She'd have to find her own way home. But she couldn't call Papa because her boyfriend had already put up such a wall between all of us. She knew if she did, it would only make things worse."

What remains of our food has gone cold, so the waiter collects our plates and refills our glasses.

"Did she leave him?"

"He took her to South America a few years ago. She called me one night after a big fight. She was ready to leave him and begged me to ask Papa to get her out. She was too afraid to leave on her own and wanted us to send someone to retrieve her. Before we could arrange it, there was an accident. They were both killed in a car crash, except there were no other cars involved.

"The police never figured out how he lost control of the vehicle, but I've always known it had to be his rage. They must have been fighting, and his anger distracted him from the road. I'll never forgive myself for not getting to her sooner."

My heart is breaking into a million pieces like a glass vase dropped onto a tile floor. Callie didn't deserve that. She didn't deserve any of it. No woman does. I want to speak, but there's a burning lump in my throat. I'm afraid if I open my mouth, I'll lose all of my composure.

"That's why I always wear this bracelet she gave me. I don't want to ever forget her. I just wish I had done more over the years. I feel like I failed her."

Her grief is palpable. My shattered heart is melting into white-hot rage. I hate men like that. Men like Malcolm. They are all the same. They all treat women like objects—replaceable and controllable. They cut us off from anything good in our lives, use us up, and then throw us away—or worse. Malcolm never got that dangerous, but the psychological control felt just as life or death, as if there was nothing I could do to get out from under his puppeteering hand.

"I'm so sorry," I finally say, wishing I could change everything for her. For Callie. "Your sister never should have been treated that way, but it's not your fault. You couldn't have done anything differently."

It's all I know to say, but I squeeze her hand again, hoping she can feel the empathy and understanding in my touch. She couldn't have done anything to get Callie out of that situation until Callie decided to do it for herself. I don't know how to explain that to Ana without telling her my story, though.

"I don't know," Ana says, her voice breaking. "If I had been a better sister, maybe she would have seen the red flags sooner and not brushed them aside because he made her feel special."

She could have been describing my situation. Malcolm made me feel so special at first, and when he changed, I kept thinking I had done something wrong and needed to earn that feeling back.

It wasn't because my family and friends weren't good enough. It was because a part of me, for some reason, didn't believe I was good enough. The same part of me that desperately craved his approval.

A dullness sets in my chest when I think about it. I have to help her understand, even if it means letting her see the parts of me I've tried to hide from everyone.

"I was in a similar situation. I started dating an older man at work while I was still in college. He spoiled me, but he also kept our relationship a secret. He said it was because I was an intern and he didn't want people to judge me, but really it was because he didn't want a real relationship. He just wanted someone he could control."

She wipes her tears with her napkin.

"We were together for three years and he messed with my head so much that I was trapped in an endless loop of thinking I was the one doing something wrong. I knew my family loved me, but I thought I had to fix this situation on my own."

Even as the words leave my mouth, part of me still believes that if I was smarter or prettier, Malcolm wouldn't have treated me the way he did. Even if my brain knows better, my heart keeps trying to figure out what I did wrong.

"He eventually decided he was done with me and publicly

fired me at work. And I fled. I let him take my whole life away from me. I drove through the night from Chicago to Colorado without telling anyone, and he never even called to see where I was.

"I didn't hear from him for months until one day, he sent me a text that he went on the trip we had been planning to a winery in Greece, of all places. He had another girl on his arm in my place."

I rub my wrists. "That was probably too much information, but the fact your sister called you for help means you were exactly the sister she needed."

I take a huge breath. I feel raw, like I just peeled back layers and layers of skin to get to that story and let it out. The vulnerability feels dangerous.

"Your sister's death is incredibly tragic, but you can't carry that guilt. If you do, he just wins again. It's all *his* fault. Not yours."

I wish I could believe the same thing about myself. As hard as I try, I can't shake knowing I could have been stronger. Or at least left earlier. I shouldn't have gotten myself into that situation to begin with.

"Thank you," she whispers, tears flowing down her cheek. "You have no idea how much it means that you shared that."

Ana waves down the waiter and pays for our meal. I offer to pay my half, but she brushes me off.

"Let's go dance," Ana says, standing, and gathering her bag and sweater. "I think we both need to get lost in the music."

And as much as I hate dancing and as out of place as I feel, I know how desperately she needs it. She wants to forget and feel free. I do too. So, I follow her across the street into a club and straight onto the dance floor.

Music floods my senses, filling my ears, and thudding in my chest. We move on the dance floor as it gets more and more crowded. My mind feels like it's being spun and pulled in a hundred different directions, mourning Ana's sister and hating what happened to her with a fiery vengeance. What would her life have become if she had gotten free? Where would she be now? Where should *I* be because I got free? What should I be doing with my life?

I do not want to consider the answer to any of those questions, so I force myself to get lost in the movement. I don't want to think about how I shouldn't still be struggling to get back on my feet.

I dance until I'm dizzy and can feel the sweat, hot and sticky on my chest under Ana's necklace.

Piper: How was dinner?

Jenni: The food was amazing. But the night also kind of sucked. Why am I still such a mess post-Malcolm? Shouldn't I be better by now?

Piper: You're not a mess! Look at you, in Greece. You've got this. Just be yourself.

Jenni: I'm not sure I know who that is.

Chapter 16

I wake the next morning with a pounding headache. Ana and I danced until our feet couldn't take it any longer. Once we were back at the Omorfiá, I laid in my bed and stared at the ceiling, wanting and waiting to feel. I was met with emptiness, left wondering what is wrong with me for falling for Malcolm's games. Will I ever be able to have a normal relationship? A normal job? Or am I just a lost cause?

I drag myself out of bed. I have a meeting with Niko this afternoon. We're supposed to get on a video call with Amber and discuss our plans, which are still largely non-existent. I've worked on the proposal but haven't been able to get his thoughts on any of it. I need a nap. Or a massage.

And then I remember telling Niko I was going to the spa. After last night, that conversation feels like it happened a million years ago. Still, I know he'll ask about it.

I scrounge around on the desk and eventually find the brochure underneath my rubber duck. I pick up the cute little duck. Maybe it's a good luck charm. I slip it into my purse before grabbing the brochure.

A few minutes later, I am being greeted by a soft-spoken, calming aesthetician inside the spa. Once we agree on a treatment, I'm escorted to a changing room with pristine white lockers. She hands me a robe and headband made from the softest, plushest fabric I have ever had the pleasure of touching.

I could totally get used to this.

I slip my clothes off and fold them neatly before placing them in a locker and pulling out the key to slip it into my robe pocket. Standing in front of a large mirror with soft lighting, I brush my hair and slip on the headband. Despite the rough night, I don't look that all that out of place in the robe, headband, and plush slippers they gave me. If I saw the girl looking back at me, I would assume she visits the spa weekly. It's a weird feeling to see my face in the mirror and yet not recognize the person as a whole at the same time.

I tighten my robe and exit the small dressing room. I'm supposed to go lay down in a room she indicated, but my nerves are making me feel like I need to pee.

I head back toward the front of the spa to ask about a restroom. I hear the two women at the front talking in hushed voices as I approach.

"What are you going to do? Can you afford the surgery?"

I stop in my tracks. This conversation sounds private. I start to back away until I hear the other woman's response.

"No, but Mr. Psomas overheard me on the phone yesterday. He offered to cover the cost. Said that he couldn't bear the thought of Pebbles having to be put down."

Pebbles? Is that a dog?

"But I don't know," the second voice continues. "Would that be weird? To owe money to my boss?"

My stomach flutters. Of course, Niko would do something like this. The more I get to know him, the more I like him.

"Did he say it was a loan? I think it sounds like a gift. And you know Mr. Psomas. He would never hold it over you. He's a good one."

I hold my breath, waiting to hear what Pebbles's owner thinks. Their voices change then, and I know someone has entered the spa.

"Good morning, Ms. Psomas! Welcome. I have you down for a hydrating facial this morning, correct?"

I'm so lost in thought, picturing Niko snuggling an injured dog, that it takes me a second too long to realize they are talking to Ana. I scramble when I hear them coming. I don't want to look like I was eavesdropping. Before I can get too far, we're all standing, facing each other, in the hallway.

"Jenni! My darling!" Ana wraps me in a hug so tight that I don't quite know what to do with my arms. I shoot an apologetic expression at the aesthetician.

"So sorry to interrupt. I was just heading to my procedure room."

Ana lets out a tiny gasp as if she just had the best idea. "Ooh, are you in for a facial? Can we share a room? I'd love to have some company." She looks between me and the spa girl. "If you want to be alone, I totally understand. But it would be so nice to be together."

Both women look at me expectantly. How do I say no when she puts it like that? Besides, I need to apologize for dumping all my baggage on her last night.

"Of course," I say. "That would be great!"

"Right this way, then."

Once we are settled on side-by-side massage beds, wrapped in warm, thick blankets, and resting our heads on gentle pillows, the aesthetician begins by laying a warm cloth over my face. I instantly feel more relaxed. Soft calming music is coming from somewhere in the room and I feel like I could literally fall back asleep if I'm not careful. Although I do still need to pee, just a little.

Ana and I both start talking at the same time. She lets out a nervous laugh—something I wouldn't expect from her.

"Go ahead," I say.

"I thought a lot about the things you said last night," Ana mutters as two women get to work on us. My aesthetician rubs some sort of serum into my cheeks. It smells citrusy, like grapefruit. "It really helped me, so I wanted to thank you. Sometimes I miss my sister so much and feel so guilty that I don't know how I'm going to get out of bed. And on the other days, I work so hard to put on a happy, over-the-top personality to pretend it never happened. I know I will always miss her, but maybe I don't have to always feel so frozen by the thought that I'm moving on without her. You know?"

I hadn't really thought about that. Ana has to do everything without her sister now. Callie won't ever get a new job, get married, or have children. But Ana might. She'll have to think about her sister any time something good happens in her life.

"That sounds like a lot to carry," I comment, while the aesthetician rubs underneath my jaw. "Your sister wouldn't want you to be frozen. I think she would want you to live the life you want. You deserve that."

"I think you're right," she finally responds, sounding as relaxed as I feel. "If our situation were reversed, I would want her to do everything she ever wanted. Wear the dress, get the haircut, take the job, kiss whomever she wanted to kiss."

I try to respond, but my upper lip and chin are being slathered in something green and foamy. I settle for humming my agreement.

"I'm so glad you aren't letting your past trap you, Jenni," Ana goes on. "I don't know you very well yet, but look at you! You have a great job; you are traveling the world. You're doing things with your life. That makes me happy."

Her words are so ridiculous I almost laugh. That's the

impression Ana has formed of me over the last few days? I almost tell her how wrong she is, but the aesthetician speaks before I do.

"Sorry, ladies, no more chatting. We're applying the masks now. It's made from sea algae and is enriched with minerals and oils. We'll let it dry and do its magic for about fifteen minutes."

"Thank you," I say and hope Ana knows it's directed at her as well.

After the masks are applied, the aestheticians announce they will start the IV hydration.

"Just a little pinch," she warns, wiping the inside of my elbow.

Um, what is happening right now? I try to open my eyes, but there's a hydrogel pack resting on top of them. IV hydration? Like an IV drip in my arm with a needle?

Ouch. Yep, definitely that type of IV. I guess I missed that in the treatment plan when I picked the hydrating facial package. A bit of IV fluids can't hurt, can it? I try to relax.

Ana is right. I shouldn't let my past with Malcolm keep me from living my life. But the mechanics of how to actually do that elude me. How do I get his voice out of my head after all this time? Ignore it? Do the opposite of what his voice tells me? Maybe I need to stop worrying so much about what I'm doing or what anyone around me might be thinking. Maybe I need to stop worrying about all the ways Malcolm messed with me and focus on having a little fun.

I'm all the way in Greece. If I can't have fun and live my life without worrying about Malcolm here—an entire ocean away from Chicago—where can I?

I can feel the cold IV fluids pumping into my body. It sends a chill through me. I wonder how much fluid they are pumping in. I try to ignore the growing sensation in my belly. I definitely need to pee now.

My thoughts go back to what Ana said. I should embrace this second chance and put myself out there a bit more. Open myself to the possibility of having fun and succeeding. If only so I don't let her down. She's been through too much for me to let her see that I'm not the successful, happy person she thinks I am.

Because she needs to believe that her sister would have been okay if she had survived the car accident.

Before I know it, the women are back to wipe away the dry, cracked mask from my face with another warm cloth. It feels cleansing, refreshing. Like a new beginning. And I'm grateful it's over because now I really have to pee.

"Don't you feel amazing?" Ana asks from the other side of the room.

"Yes!" I say, as even more serum is massaged into my skin in slow circular motions. Are we not done? Panic rises in my throat when I look at the IV bag and find that it's only half empty. I need to fit that much more fluid in my body? I am going to burst.

After what feels like another agonizing hour of fragrant moisturizers and steam treatments, I literally don't know if I'm going to be able to get off the table. All the muscles in my body are being used to make sure I don't wet the bed. The women finally remove our IVs and tell us to make our way back to the changing rooms when we're ready. I slowly rise, afraid I'll burst.

"Do you have a bathroom here?" I ask, bouncing on my toes.

The woman winces. That's not a good sign. "Normally, we do. But it's out of service right now. Sorry!"

"Oh, that's okay," I say, panic rising. "I'll just get dressed and head to my room."

I run out, telling Ana that I'll see her later. I know I'm

being rude, but trust me, the alternative would be so much worse.

I get dressed as fast as possible in my current state and rush from the spa. I speed-walk to my room. I just have to go up the grand staircase in the lobby and down two corridors. I can make it. *I can make it.*

"Hey, Jenni! Slow down," I hear a familiar gravelly voice from somewhere behind me.

No, no, no. Not now. I stop and turn. Niko catches up with me halfway up the stairs. "How's it going?"

"Good, thanks! Just heading back to my room to prepare for our meeting. We're still on for this afternoon with Amber, right?"

He smiles and adjusts the cuff of his shirt. "I think so. I looked over the pitch she sent. Do you know what she meant by 'targeted video'? Ads or social content? I don't think the board is going to go for social content. We might have to take that out."

"Sure, whatever you think is best. I am pretty sure she meant ads, but we can work on that at the meeting!"

Please let me go. We can talk all about your traditional marketing beliefs and why they are wrong later. Otherwise these stairs are going to need cleaning.

"I'm looking forward to it." He smiles. "And about tomorrow ... do you have most of the day free? I want to take you somewhere. It's a surprise, but I promise you're going to love it."

I think I feel a leak. Or maybe I'm just going numb down there from how long I've been holding it. I'm going to give myself an infection. I need to get out of here right now.

"Sounds great! I love surprises." I place a hand on my back pocket where my phone is tucked away. "Oh, shoot, my phone is ringing. It's probably Amber. I've got to take this. I'll see you later."

Without waiting for him to respond, I turn and run up the stairs to my room.

I make it, but barely—I definitely need to change my underwear. I don't think I've ever felt such relief after emptying my bladder. I am definitely hydrated and definitely never doing that again.

Chapter 17

After showering and putting on fresh underwear, I make my way to the conference room for my first real meeting with Niko. We're supposed to video call Amber, which I hope means that I won't have to do much of the talking. Still, my heart is pounding when I walk through the doors to the conference room. If I thought I was nervous to have client meetings before, it's ten times worse now that I've been through so much in the last couple of days. What if after all of the effort Niko has put in to welcome me to the Omorfiá I disappoint him? What if I look like a complete fool?

"You're looking refreshed," Niko comments, after I take a seat across from him at the table. "Ana mentioned the two of you enjoyed the spa together this morning. Two days in a row?" Niko winks at me and my face flushes. Does he know I'm lying about going yesterday?

"I—Well …" I stammer, not knowing how to work my way out of this one.

"Don't worry. I am glad you're enjoying it. I should make more time to visit myself."

He stretches his neck, as if to prove he needs the self-care.

It makes me wonder if Ana was right and he does spend all of his time at his desk. So why the change the last few days? Why the parasailing and the surprise adventure tomorrow? I don't want to think about it, because any conceivable answer to those questions includes trying to make sure I can hang with the lifestyle the hotel is promoting, which means even more pressure to perform and impress.

"Shall we?" Niko asks, gesturing to his laptop, which is connected to a screen on the wall where we'll both be able to see and talk to Amber. I nod and get out my notepad, falling into old habits as her assistant, I guess.

"Hello!" Amber leans forward toward her webcam when the call connects. We get a great view of her nose. Usually, this little habit of hers just makes me smile, but I'm feeling self-conscious on her behalf now that I'm seeing it with a client at my side. "Good morning. Wait, no, I guess good afternoon!"

She laughs and Niko gives me a sly glance, like we're sharing an inside joke, but I don't know what it is.

"It's great to see you, Amber," Niko says. "I trust you are feeling well and this meeting is still convenient?"

Huh, that's a nice way to ask if she's up for this without making a pregnant woman feel like we expect less of her. I have never quite figured out how to do that, especially the last few weeks, when she has been exhausted and cranky.

"I am. Thank you for asking. But I'll let Jenni take the lead since she's the one with boots on the ground. I'm just here for any questions she can't answer."

What? That would have been good to know beforehand. I turn to face the webcam to talk directly to Amber. "Are you sure? I'm totally fine if you want to go over everything."

Please, do not make me do this. I'm not ready. Especially not with Amber looming over my shoulder on video, like a teacher proctoring an exam.

"Of course not. Take it away."

I'm feeling lightheaded as I reach for my presentation folder with shaky fingers. This feels even worse than I expected. Now that I actually know Niko and how great he is, I want even more to impress him. It feels more personal now than it ever did with clients in Chicago. I wanted their approval, sure, but it was more about how that would reflect on me in the eyes of the managers and directors at the firm. But Niko has gotten to know me; he's given me a glimpse of who he is as a person, and his approval means much more, now, than simply getting Amber to promote me.

I open to the first page of Amber's prepared materials.

"If you'd like to take a look here, we can go over the main pillars of our marketing plan," I tell Niko, before passing him a copy of the plan overview. I know he already looked at it in the email Amber sent, but it never hurts to present high-quality materials in person.

"For a resort of this size and in this market, we recommend focusing on print advertising, signage and billboard advertising, and direct mail campaigns through luxury partnerships."

The words come out formulaic, but I'm trying my best to sound confident and stick to the script.

Niko looks over the columns on the page. "What would be involved with the print advertising?"

I take a deep breath before answering, trying to stay calm and keep my voice at a normal octave. "We would place ads in luxury travel magazines like *Travel + Leisure*, and lifestyle publications targeting higher-income individuals. We would also pursue editorial features in regional tourism guides where we could give travelers a more in-depth look at the Omorfiá Hotel."

We continue on with the rest of the pillars, going through each line item. To his credit, Niko seems very invested and open to our suggestions—relying on Amber's experience to guide the plan, rather than what makes the most sense to him.

That's usually the biggest hurdle when first working with clients. They all have grand pictures in their heads of how the campaign should look, whether it's the best strategy or not.

"I had never really thought about airport signage and billboard advertising. What sort of budget does that require?" Niko asks.

"Typically, we plan for about 5 percent of the overall budget to go toward outdoor signage. But it really depends on the final budget and which aspects of the marketing plan we choose to execute when." I bite my lip and swallow as my words linger. In my experience, every client I've ever dealt with wants to nickel-and-dime the budget, and it becomes a constant pull of proving our worth and explaining the costs of things we can't change. It can get extremely uncomfortable and I never know what to say. I look over at Amber for assurance that I said the right thing.

"We can definitely talk more about specific costs and your budget down the line," Amber chimes in, putting my rising tension at ease, for now at least. "I assure you the signage and billboards will be placed strategically in airports throughout the States with affordable and easy flights to Greece, where they will have the most impact."

Niko nods and writes something on a notepad. I do the same, scribbling a note, to cover the fact that I feel even more uncomfortable than when we started.

"Let's move on toward the direct mail campaigns. There are so many avenues we can explore there," Amber continues.

I take her hint and move on to explaining to Niko how direct mail campaigns work by sending brochures to luxury travel agencies, wedding planners, and other event organizers.

"We can also partner with luxury brands to cross-promote through mailing lists and use special package offerings," I tell Niko.

"What sort of brands?"

I take a deep breath. "Watches, wine, fashion, luggage—pretty much any brand where we have a significant crossover of our target audiences."

My nerves are quickly dissipating as I feel the need to bite my tongue. None of this fits the Omorfiá, as I've come to see it. I want to show them all the ways we could reach the perfect travelers through digital marketing and targeted SEO campaigns. I want to tell them that lifestyle magazine readers are not going to appreciate the thought and care Niko has put into his hotel.

It's not my place to say anything, though. I'm just a middle man. I'm here to represent Amber and to do what the client is asking of us. That's what I will do, because it keeps me safe. If Niko and Amber want traditional marketing, who am I to tell them differently? That has only ever gotten me in trouble in the past.

Once we've covered everything in Amber's plan, Niko thanks her for joining us.

"You're in great hands with Jenni, but please, let me know if you have any more questions," Amber tells him, before ending the video call.

I stand and gather my things. "Okay, so I will work on drawing up the specifics we talked about. I'll take a few shots around the resort and create some mock-ups we can use at the board meeting. It will take me a day or two, but maybe we can meet again to go over them in a few days?"

Niko nods. "Sure, sounds good. Can I ask you something?"

My heart skips a beat. What would he possibly need to ask me? And why now, after we've hung up with Amber. "Of course, about what?"

"It seems like you wanted to say something a few times but held yourself back. Is there something we haven't covered? Do you think we should be doing something differently?"

My chest feels tight. How could he possibly have noticed

that? I said all of the right things. I went word-for-word through Amber's plan.

"No, not at all. Amber is brilliant, and I think if the board is as traditional as you say, this will all go over perfectly."

I fidget with the papers in my hand as he looks at me, afraid he's going to keep prying. Instead, he pushes in his chair and walks with me to the hall.

"In that case, I think we're done for the day. Thank you for your work on this. I look forward to seeing the mock-ups."

"Absolutely." I smile, not knowing what else I'm supposed to do here. Do we leave together? Do I turn and walk down the hall on my own?

"But don't plan on working too much tomorrow," Niko says, grinning. "We have our surprise. Meet me in the lobby. You'll need a bathing suit. And probably a hat."

Our surprise. I almost forgot. I'm supposed to spend the day with Niko on another adventure. I hate all of this back and forth. I'm terrible at balancing all of this. I can't take a whole day off working after we finally have plan and something for me to do. What would Amber think? I have no doubt she'll be calling me tomorrow afternoon expecting a progress update.

At the same time, how do I tell Niko no when I've already said yes, and he's already made plans?

"Great. I'm looking forward to it!"

"Perfect. I'll see you at nine."

I stick out my arm for a handshake—the way I would after any other business meeting—just as Niko steps toward me and places a hand on my back, like he's going to escort me down the hallway. I end up stabbing him in the side with my manicured nails. A very solid side. Blood rushes to my cheeks.

"I—I'm so sorry," I blurt out. "I'm just going to walk away now before my clumsiness causes any more bodily harm."

Niko laughs, but I'm on the verge of losing it. Can't I just be normal for a single interaction with this man?

"No, I'm sorry. Totally my fault. But those are some sharp nails you've got." He rubs his side in mock pain, and I wish I could crawl right out of my skin. "Let's go. I'll walk you back to your room on my way downstairs."

Jenni: I had a meeting with Niko and Amber today. I wanted to pull my hair out. They both refuse to see what makes the hotel so special and insist on treating it like any other hotel and spa on the island.

Piper: Really? That's so weird that Amber would think like that. How are you going to convince them otherwise?

Jenni: I don't know. Is it even my place to convince them? Amber is my boss and Niko is the client. That hasn't gone well for me in the past.

Piper: I think you should give them a chance to hear you out.

Chapter 18

"Are you ready for your surprise?" Niko says, putting his hands over my eyes. My knees buckle ever so slightly at his breath on my ear. Does he have any clue what that does to me?

I grab his wrists and pull his hands down, twisting around to face him.

"You need to stop sneaking up behind me," I say, giving him a hard time.

"Why? Are you going to stab me with those nails again?"

"Stop! That was an accident." I take a step back, despite wishing he still had his arms wrapped around me. I can't handle this … this … thing between us. At our meeting yesterday, he had acted so focused and professional. But now, it feels like he's flirting with me, and I don't know what to do about it.

"It would help if you would tell me where we're going," I say, changing the subject. "I might need a few more things than just a bathing suit."

"Like what?"

"I don't know—walking shoes, binoculars, a grappling hook?" I make a face, so he knows I'm joking.

Niko laughs, and the sound fills my heart like a sunflower in bloom, turning toward his sun. I don't know if I could ever get used to hearing his laugh and knowing I was the one who made it happen. I'm realizing I'm crushing so hard, it's not even funny. When I'm with Niko outside of the conference room, I forget that I'm terrified of this whole deal falling apart, or that I'm even supposed to be working. He makes me feel light. He makes me want to have fun for the first time in a long time.

Even though I know I should be focusing on the board meeting.

We felt pretty confident after our meeting yesterday afternoon, but Amber sent me a text last night about not losing focus before Monday. The board is our real test. Not Niko. I *should* be using all of the extra time I have at the hotel to make this the best pitch possible, not going off for a day of who knows what with Niko.

That's what my brain says, anyway. My heart tells me this is exactly what I should be doing. For the first time in years, I have been able to laugh and have fun. And it feels so good. I just want to forget about Malcolm, and marketing, and the theoretical new job I'm dying to get. Today should be about being present.

I want to have another adventure. I'll prepare for the meeting later. I still have plenty of time.

"All I'm going to say is that there are no heights involved this time," he says, putting his hands together in front of him, pleading with me not to ask any more questions.

"Okay, fine," I say, shrugging in mock defeat. "Are you sure there isn't anything else I need?"

Niko stands back and looks me up and down, stroking his chin as if trying hard to decide. My stomach flutters under the weight of his attention. I'm wearing a dusty mauve romper over a basic white tank and my hiking sandals.

In my bag, I have a bathing suit and everything else I would need for a day in the sun.

"Nope, you've got everything you need. Don't you trust me yet?"

He seems a little too happy about not having to reveal anything else about our day. I roll my eyes. "Yes, I trust you. But can't you just give me a hint? Please!"

He thinks about it for a moment and then puts his arm on my shoulder as we make our way outside. "One word: dragons."

Dragons? What am I supposed to do with that? I can't think of what that could possibly mean for our day out in Greece. "You're no help," I say, nudging him with my shoulder.

If he's going to flirt with me, I'm going to throw it right back. It obviously doesn't mean anything, aside from two people having fun.

Niko's smile melts any last apprehension as he takes my bag from my hand and points the way to the car.

When we climb into the back of the SUV, I'm happy to see that someone replaced the water bottles from a few days ago with iced coffees. "Thanks for picking up the coffee, Sophia," Niko says as we fasten our seatbelts. "You're an angel."

"No problem, boss," she says with a wink in the rearview mirror. I can't put my finger on the full reason, but I adore this woman. She reminds me a bit of Mrs. Harper—always there, watching quietly with a twinkle in her eye, as if she is orchestrating everything from the sidelines.

Niko picks up a coffee and offers it to me.

"Vanilla latte? I remember you said you usually drink iced coffee," he says sheepishly.

"That's perfect. Thank you for remembering." I'm touched. That's something my own family doesn't seem to care to remember. And Niko has barely met me.

After a short drive, we pull up at another marina. Unlike when we went parasailing, this marina is fancy—like Monaco fancy— with yachts, sailing ships and private security at the entrance.

I'm trying to keep my eyes from bulging out of their sockets as we walk past boats that must cost double the value of my parents' house. Surely, we're not going to party on a yacht, right? There are only two of us after all. We pass an entire crew of people cleaning a sleek, black yacht. A stark reminder that this isn't my world. As much as I'm having fun, I have to keep reminding myself that that's all it is. I can't expect any of this to extend past the next week. Niko and I are from different worlds, and after this week, all I'll be is a member of his marketing team. All of this fun doesn't mean anything.

"Now that we're here, I can tell you. We're going to the island of Tragonisi," Niko tells me. "I've hired a private boat to take us there. You're going to love it."

A private boat? One of *these* private boats? It's getting harder and harder to be in the moment when I feel so out of place. Nothing in my life has prepared me for this. I feel a bit lightheaded.

"Don't look so scared," Niko says. "It's not far."

"I'm not scared." Not scared of the boat, at least. Niko has just put so much thought into this, and it feels overwhelming. What if Niko grows bored of me when it's just the two of us all day? What if I don't actually love the island, and he doesn't like the way I react?

Malcolm used to do that to me. He loved to watch me squirm while he unveiled some sort of surprise, and if I didn't react exactly the way he wanted, it would send him into a rage. One time he got last-minute concert tickets. He had never mentioned the band before, but apparently he loved them. The concert was the same date as a game night I was hosting at my apartment with some of the girls from work. I had been planning it for weeks. He told me about the tickets one night when we were eating at a restaurant. I suggested he find a friend to go with since I didn't know the band and already had plans. I thought it was perfectly reasonable.

But out of nowhere, he slammed his hands on the table. *"I got the tickets for us, Jenni. Don't you understand that?"* He threw his napkin into his pasta and stormed off. I expected him to come back after a few minutes outside. He just needed to calm down, right? He never did, though. Eventually, I paid for the meal and took a cab home. The next day, when I saw him at work, he asked if I had canceled game night yet. No greeting. No apology. No checking if I was okay. He wouldn't talk to me until I rescheduled my event and agreed to go to the concert with him.

He made me hate surprises.

Niko stops walking when we reach a small catamaran. It's just as luxurious as the rest of the boats, but smaller and more intimate. A captain emerges from the small cabin to greet us. He bows as he welcomes us to the ship.

Meanwhile, Niko offers his hand to help me step down into the boat. As soon as I get my balance, he drops my hand, and I try not to notice the way my fingers ache at the absence, as if they are missing his already.

"Take your things inside, and make yourself comfortable," Niko tells me. "I'm just going to chat with the captain for a second."

I find my way inside. My jaw drops as I climb down four or five steps into an open cabin. It feels so spacious in here despite the room not being much bigger than my parents' kitchen. I half expected to feel claustrophobic, but the ceilings are tall with clear windows around three of the walls, letting in a lot of natural light. There is a sleek modern couch, a giant flatscreen TV, and a fully stocked bar. A vase of gorgeous fuchsia-pink bougainvillea flowers sits atop an aqua-colored, frosted-glass bar top. The flowers have come to signify Greece for me, as they adorn every alleyway and building I've seen on my morning walks.

I step closer to take in the scent and notice an ice bucket with a bottle of champagne behind the flowers. Next to it, a placard rests between two glasses, saying "Welcome Aboard, Niko and Jenni" in fancy script.

My heart is in my throat. Champagne and flowers mean romance, dating, love. Not friendship and business.

This has to go. The boat company must have misunderstood the situation.

I look around for a place to hide it. Because if Niko comes down those steps and sees flowers and champagne, he might think he has to let me down easily. I might expire on the spot. I'd rather jump off the boat and swim back to Colorado.

Behind the bar stands a wall of cabinets, so I rush around to see if any of them are empty. I open cabinet after cabinet, and they are all full of glasses of every shape and size. So many glasses.

Finally, I find champagne glasses on the very top shelf. Okay, I'll just put those away and hide the champagne under the sink. That works, right?

I grab the first champagne flute and stand on my very tippy-toes to get it up to the shelf—

"Need some help?"

I'm so startled by Niko's voice that I lose my balance. The glass hits the shelf and drops out of my hand as I stumble backward into the bar. If this space wasn't so tight, I'm pretty sure I would be on my butt on the floor, surrounded by broken glass. But as it stands, I'm slumped against the bar and the errant champagne flute has landed in my lap where I catch it between my thighs.

Niko rushes to the bar and reaches over to steady me. "Are you okay? I didn't mean to surprise you."

"I'm fine," I say, pulling the champagne flute from between

my legs and setting it on the bar behind me. "I was just …" I trail off because I can't come up with a convincing enough story to explain why I was going through cabinets I had no business going through.

"Hiding the champagne flutes?"

One of Niko's eyebrows is cocked, and he looks as if he is holding back a smirk. Yeah, I'm not fooling him one bit.

"You caught me," I say, wanting to hide. "I think they misunderstood the situation, maybe, and I just didn't want it to be awkward when you came down to champagne on ice. But now it's even more awkward because … well, I wasn't tall enough to hide them before you came in."

Niko raises an eyebrow and smiles. "Champagne comes standard with these boats. I don't care if we drink it or not, but if you don't want to, let me put the glasses away."

"Thank you," I say, holding out the glass to him. He comes around the bar and squeezes past me to take the glass. As he reaches up to the cabinet and easily sets the champagne flute down, I catch a whiff of his scent—sea salt, pine and warm earth, like Colorado with a bit of the ocean mixed in.

Niko turns around and we are facing each other, about four inches apart in this small space between the bar and the cabinets.

I can feel his breath on me, his chest rising and falling gently while my breathing is spiraling out of control. "I'm sorry. I tend to overthink things."

Niko takes a second to look into my eyes, a tiny smile on his perfect lips.

"I'm starting to quite enjoy it," he says. Excuse me? Did he just say what I think he said?

"You enjoy watching me make a fool of myself?" I ask, putting my hand on my hip.

"That's not what I said," he says, tapping my nose. "You're

just cute when you get nervous. Even though you have no reason to be."

A prickle shoots up my neck. "Well, you have a strange idea of what cute means, then."

"Do I? I don't think so." He steps to the side. "Now, can I get you a *nonalcoholic* drink?"

"Sounds good," I say with a small laugh, feeling all of the nerves from the champagne disappearing. I grab two glasses from the cabinet and hand them over to Niko. He pulls a bottle of sparkling water out of the fridge and pours. He adds a lemon wedge to both and gestures toward the couch.

Out the window behind it, I can see that we're making our way out to sea.

Chapter 19

I take a sip of my sparkling water, letting the carbonation soothe my nervous system. My body is still buzzing from the moment he called me cute.

I glance over at Niko. Could this be more than I originally thought? Does he feel something too?

"Have you enjoyed living in Greece after spending so much time in the United States?"

Niko inhales a deep breath. "That's a loaded question."

Well, there goes that idea. Good job, Jenni. Picking the one question for which Niko doesn't have an immediate and charming answer. Perfect.

"Oh, sorry. You do not have to answer that," I rush to say.

He waves me off. "Moving here hasn't been everything I thought it would be." He bites the side of his cheek and turns toward me, resting an elbow on the back of the couch. "Growing up, I was never close to my dad. I always thought it was because I lived so far away. I did everything I could to try and impress him. I got the best grades, attended Greek lessons on weekends, got business degree and then an MBA. I came back to Greece thinking that if I were here everything would finally click into place. We would understand each other."

I can sense a *"but"* coming.

"I've been back six months now, and when I see him, we still have nothing to talk about. You would think we weren't even related. And … I don't know. It's hard." He looks more serious than I've ever seen him.

"I'm so sorry. That must be awful."

"I really thought that doing all of this would mean I finally earned my place in his world, but I haven't. Sometimes I don't think anything I do will make a difference. He's only impressed by himself."

My heart squeezes in my chest. That sounds terrible. No one should ever wonder whether their parents love or accept them. Niko deserves proud parents after all his accomplishments. Just the thought makes me mad.

"Are you serious? You're not even thirty and you run an amazing hotel. How is that not something to be proud of and celebrate?"

Niko seems to consider this. "I don't know. He hates the changes I've been making. He would rather I make the hotel like all the rest on the island."

I take a moment to choose my words. This feels like a really important moment, and I don't want to mess it up, because Niko needs to know he is doing the right thing.

"I know my opinion might not mean much, but your hotel feels like family, like home. It's been such a great experience. I can't think of a single property we have worked with that has more heart. Your dad is wrong."

Niko shakes his head and looks out the window to the open sea, taking a sip of his water.

"I'm serious, Niko! And I don't just mean the gallery or the garden. You treat everyone you meet with respect, and that is so rare in this industry. You paid for surgery for an employee's dog! Who does that? A good person."

He gives me a quizzical look. "How did you know about Pebbles?"

Oops. "It doesn't matter. All I'm trying to say is that you care so much about the people around you, which makes the Omorfiá an incredible place to be."

I scoot closer to him on the couch and put my hand over his. He looks up at me.

"Thank you. That really means a lot." His eyes are on mine, and in them, I can see every moment he made me laugh, every time he treated me like a person, every time he cared what I was thinking or feeling. One blink. Two blinks. His eyes are bright and hopeful and if I'm honest with myself, I can see his heart, open and free. It's then that I realize, once again, how close together we are. The urge to bolt shoots through my veins.

Because if I open my heart to him and then go back to Colorado, I may never recover. I'm just having fun. Not falling in love. I scoot back to put some distance between us.

"Are we getting close?" I ask, getting up and walking to the window.

"Yeah." Niko clears his throat. "We should be. Let's go up and have a look."

We head back out to the deck and settle in on a bench to watch the water. I allow my thoughts to get lost in the teal, blue, and aqua ribbons of color bending and rippling against the hulls of the catamaran. This doesn't feel real. It feels like a dream. And not just the scenery. If someone had told me six months ago that I'd be in Greece on a private boat with a good man, I would have said they were crazy. I thought my life was over. I thought good men didn't really exist. I thought my shot at the career I had dreamed of was done. Maybe things can change. Maybe what Malcolm did to me doesn't have to ruin the rest of my life.

"You're right. We're here. Look." Niko has transformed back into his confident self. No more raw edges. I almost regret pulling us away from that couch because I want to know that Niko too. But this is how it has to be. Just fun.

I look around. We're sailing straight toward a rocky island, not much else in sight.

"Okay … and where is here exactly? Didn't you say something about a dragon?"

Niko turns and points at the giant rock in front of us like I'm missing something obvious. I search the mound for any clues but come up empty. Niko keeps waving his hand over imaginary curves.

"It looks like a dragon, right? Sleeping in the sea. Can't you see it? That's the head, and over there is the tail. The island is nicknamed Dragonisi."

He looks so excited, pleading with me to see it. Ugh, he's cute.

"I'm sorry!" I laugh. "I really don't see it. Maybe if I saw some pictures from a different angle?"

I shrug, and Niko puts an arm around my shoulder, pulling me toward the front of the deck.

"Never mind. The dragon isn't important. That's what's important."

I look to where he's pointing and see a large archway in the rock where the water disappears into darkness. Where does that lead?

"We're going in there," Niko says, as if reading my mind. "This is one of Mykonos's best-kept secrets: the caverns of Dragonisi. We're going in there to swim."

"Are you serious?" I practically squeal.

"As long as you're up for it."

"Absolutely! Are you kidding me? That sounds like a once in a lifetime experience."

He laughs. "I told you that you would love it!"

We take turns getting dressed in the cabin while the captain maneuvers our vessel into the opening of the caves. As it crawls along, I can't help but feel like we're being transported into some magical world of mermaids and sea dragons, where ex-boyfriends and failing careers don't exist.

Once we reach the middle of the expansive cavern, the captain puts down an anchor and turns off the boat. I take in my surroundings: a cathedral of rock with huge arches overhead and little caves and waterways all around. Light pours in, creating a patchwork of shimmering blues. In this moment, it's easy to forget everything else going on. All I want to do is jump into the crystal-clear water.

"See you down there?" Niko asks before stepping up to the back of the boat and swan diving into the sea, as if he couldn't wait one second longer, either.

He surfaces and hollers for me to join him.

As I toe the edge of the platform, my joy is almost too much to take. It just might burst through me like the rays of sunshine cascading through the rock ceiling.

I inhale a deep breath and jump into the water feet first. The first sensation I feel is cold, but then freedom. The water is so clear and blue it feels like I'm swimming through the sky in a cloud of bubbles.

I emerge from the water gasping and smiling. When I catch Niko staring, I splash him.

"Oh, you want to play that game?" he taunts, splashing me back before diving under the water. When I realize he's swimming toward me, I turn to race away, kicking as fast as I can while trying to breathe around my laughter.

Niko catches my ankle in his hand and tickles the bottom of my foot. Shrieks of laughter echo off the cavern walls.

Niko emerges from the water, smirks, and says, "What's so funny?" He turns to the left and right before spinning around in the water, looking for whatever must be making me laugh. I know I should stop but seeing him play innocent just makes me giggle even harder.

"Come on," Niko finally says. "Let's explore."

We swim around the entire cavern, following the rocks. At one spot, Niko hoists himself out of the water and stands on a rocky ledge, water dripping from his muscular frame. "Rate my splash," he yells before doing a cannonball into the water.

"A solid seven," I tell him, once he surfaces. "But I've seen been bigger."

As soon as the words leave my mouth, I gasp and cover it with one hand while the other treads water. *I've seen bigger?* I lock eyes with Niko, waiting for his reaction.

"Well, it's a good thing I am comfortable with my masculinity, or we'd have a real problem on our hands. I'm rather competitive about my splash abilities, though, so I need you to get up on that rock and jump."

Oh, it's on. I can't get out of the water as easily as Niko, but I'm absolutely not going to ask for a boost. Instead, I find footholds in the rock under the water and push myself up like I'm at the rock-climbing gym.

"I could have used that grappling hook right about now," I call over my shoulder. Once I'm standing, I turn to face the water. And with all the gusto of a circus performer, I wind my arms, leap off the rock, lock my hands around my knees, and crash into the ocean with my backside.

Niko is slow-clapping when I spring back to the surface. "Not bad, not bad. You get bonus points for style, so why don't we call it even?"

"I'm pretty sure that's what a loser would say," I taunt. "Another round?"

We take turns jumping from the rocks with more and more

ridiculous flare and dramatics. Niko climbs higher and higher, but I stick with the lower rocks. He never once makes me feel bad about being more cautious.

"I don't know about you, but I'm starving," Niko says after a spectacular twisting jump where he landed on his back into the water. "Do you want to head back to the boat for some food?"

I pause, as if I need to think about it, and then take off sprinting toward the boat. "I'll race you!"

I beat Niko to the stairs on the back of the boat, but just barely. As he arrives, he grabs my waist and pulls me back toward him in the water. Instead of going for the ladder to cut in front of me onto the boat, he pulls me close.

"Got you!" he says, low and steady, making me shiver in the cool water.

I can feel his fingertips on my waist, his strong hands gentle, just above my hips. Our feet are kicking together in the water. I grab onto the ladder to steady myself, never breaking eye contact. Niko looks down and goes to lean in. A volcano of nerves erupts in my stomach.

"Is this okay?" His gaze flits from my lips to my eyes, and I can tell there's a longing there. How long has he wanted to kiss me? Since our talk on the boat? Longer? When did I first want to kiss him? I don't know when my feelings started. Sometime between him encouraging my adventurous side and taking care of my nervous side. His eyes race back and forth between mine, begging for an answer.

I know I shouldn't. I can't kiss a potential client. What are the rules? What would people say?

"I ... You're my client. We're working together."

He places a hand on the side of my face, his thumb on my cheekbone, and my knees go weak on the ladder.

"Not right now we're not."

He's right. I don't want to play by the rules. I promised

myself that today would be about fun, not work. Ana's words from the spa come back to me. *"Kiss whomever she wants to kiss."*

I want to kiss Niko.

I really want to kiss Niko.

I give a small nod. He asks again, "I want to make sure that nod was consent. It's important to me."

"Yes, please kiss me," I confirm, my voice shaking with nerves and desire and probably ten other emotions I'm incapable of processing in this exact moment.

Niko doesn't need any more time. He leans in and kisses me, our mouths meeting effortlessly. His lips are soft and warm, salty from the water.

He pulls me closer, and I can feel his heart racing in his chest. He turns me until my back is fully against the ladder, his right hand holding onto a rung over my shoulder. His left hand stays firmly on my waist, holding me. I snake my left hand under his outstretched arm and grab hold of his back, feeling the muscles tense as he keeps us above water.

I'm completely lost in this kiss. It's gentle, but passionate. Hot, but sweet. It's exactly what I need. I part my lips, needing air, feeling intoxicated by this rush of sensations. He matches my breathing and kisses me again. This time, he is more confident, open-mouthed. He catches my lower lip in his mouth and tugs just the tiniest bit, causing my breath to catch as heat courses through my body.

Niko pulls me tighter and I wrap my legs around him. He takes on my weight seamlessly, holding both of us above water as the boat gently bobs up and down. He slows, and I lean in to chase his lips. I don't want to stop. Every single part of me is on fire, despite the cold water lapping around our tangled bodies.

But we can't stay here, leaning up against the boat, forever. So I let him place one more kiss on my tingling lips before unlocking my legs and smiling up at him sheepishly.

"You are incredible," Niko breathes out. "But I think we should probably find somewhere with a bit more solid footing."

I look up into his sparkling, sea-foam gray eyes. "And whose fault is that? I don't remember being the one who pulled you off the ladder and into a kiss, but I could be wrong."

"I have zero regrets." Niko smiles and then steals one more kiss before pushing back off the ladder and letting me climb aboard the boat.

Chapter 20

"So, was the surprise worth it?"

Niko and I are lounging on the boat deck hours later, our skin salty and sun-kissed as we make our way back to the marina. Niko asked the captain to take it at a leisurely pace, so we could enjoy being sprayed by the wind while still being able to hear each other. The sun is starting to set, but I don't want the day to end.

I haven't felt this relaxed or happy in years. My muscles are exhausted, in a good way, from hours of swimming. My skin feels warm. My heart feels at peace. Niko's hand rests gently on mine on the bench between us. I can't believe the day we've had. Everything feels perfect. Like nothing else matters because I belong here. I belong with him, and nothing outside of this moment even exists.

"You can surprise me whenever you want if they all turn out like today," I say, allowing my voice to reflect my pure bliss. Niko gives my hand a squeeze and I trace circles around his knuckle with my thumb. His hand wraps around mine like a pair of well-worn gloves that fit just right, no stiffness, and no stretching required.

I catch a smile on his face as he takes the opportunity to entwine his fingers with mine, as if it's the most normal thing in the world. I rest my head on his shoulder, not wanting the moment to end.

"Are you always this excited about life?" Niko asks.

"What do you mean?"

"Since the day you got here, you've been excited and game for anything. It's been refreshing, actually. You make me want to be more adventurous and chase new opportunities."

If he only knew how completely out of my element I have felt this entire trip. "I guess I just wanted to make the most out of being here. I've had an incredible time so far."

"Hopefully it stays that way," he says, pulling me close.

After our kiss in the water, Niko and I ate lunch from a gourmet charcuterie board while the boat rocked in the gentle tide of the caverns. He stole kisses in between offering me bites of fruit, cheese, and pastries. I stared at him when he wasn't paying attention, trying to memorize every detail of his face I had forced myself to ignore until now. The way his hair has a slight curl at the back of his neck. The white crescent scar on his tan left forearm. The dimple that only shows up on his right cheek when he smiles.

We talked about Greece and Colorado and all the places we each dream of visiting someday. And I didn't think once about my past, marketing, or the future. I allowed myself to just dream. We swam a bit more after we ate, but the competitive edge that had fueled our splash competitions and races melted into wanting nothing more than being together, floating in the water, or sitting on the back of the boat, our feet dangling in the water as we talked. For once, I forgot to pretend I was anyone else. I forgot to try and fit in. And Niko wanted me anyway.

As I rest in his arms, I am so ridiculously smitten. As much as I told Piper I couldn't fall for him, I have. Hard and fast. A small part of me knows this is won't end well, but I tell that part to be quiet.

I don't want to think about what comes next. Going home. Saying goodbye. That's what I'm supposed to do. It's just a vacation fling. I know that I don't want to say goodbye yet.

I want to know his favorite color and the way he takes his eggs. I want to go to a movie together and listen to him laugh while we share a tub of popcorn. I want to hike with him and feel his arms around me as we take in a summit view. I want to drink iced coffee in a cozy lakeside café and sit in silence while we both read good books.

I want to pretend like all those things are possible, that this isn't just casual fun. I want to live in this time and space forever —the time and space where Niko kisses me and there isn't anything else in the world that matters.

Niko places a gentle kiss on my forehead. "We're almost back."

I look up and see that he's right. The marina is coming into view, and Niko gently peels himself out from under me and rises to gather our things.

The moment is over.

Once in the car, I don't know whether to resume our professional interaction or the newfound intimacy we've stumbled into. I sit firmly on my side of the car, hands folded in my lap. Sophia turns the radio to a station playing soft music. When she starts driving, Niko puts up the armrest and moves to the middle seat of the bench, pulling me into him. I relax immediately. It isn't over. He's not going to pretend like it didn't happen and go back to work. He's not hiding me.

"Are you available for dinner tomorrow night?"

"Absolutely," I say, maybe a little too enthusiastically. I don't even know what day of the week it is tomorrow. I try to rein in my eagerness. "I mean, I don't have any other plans, obviously. I would love to join you for dinner."

"Perfect," he says. "I would take you tonight, but I have some late-night meetings I can't cancel."

"Oh." I pause. I hadn't really thought about why he wasn't inviting me out tonight. But the way he says it feels off, somehow. Like he's not giving me the full story. "Of course, it's no big deal."

I try not to spiral, wondering what late-night meetings he might have. This is casual. This is fun. He shouldn't—can't—rearrange his schedule for me. There's still something about it that jars me back into reality.

"Awesome. I know this great little place I want you to try —" A ring, on full volume, interrupts Niko from the pocket of his shorts. "I'm so sorry. I didn't realize my ringer was on."

He pulls out his phone and silences it without even looking at the screen. The whole thing serves as a reminder that the two of us exist outside of this afternoon, and I have no idea what that means for us. Will we steal moments in empty hallways and share knowing looks across the crowded lobby? Will we decide the work comes first? I'm not even sure what I want to happen.

I also know I can't screw up this deal. I would never be able to get my life back on track if I lose the Omorfiá.

I need to say something. I need to be sure I didn't ruin everything. I take a deep breath, trying to ignore how the car smells of ocean and sunscreen, intoxicating my senses and lulling me back into the naive bliss of the afternoon. I pull away slightly.

"So about earlier ... all of this ..." I start and stop, not knowing what to say or even what I want. I need to draw some sort of boundary. But where?

"I had a really amazing time." Niko steps in to fill my silence. "I want to keep spending time with you, but only if you're comfortable with it. I don't want to jeopardize—"

Niko's phone rings again. This time, he looks at the caller

and a grimace passes over his face, turning his beautiful features to stone.

"It must be important," I note, not wanting to keep him from work. I don't want to be that girl. "Go ahead and answer it. I don't mind."

He looks at me apologetically, his eyes full of something akin to embarrassment. I don't know who is calling, but it's clear he doesn't want to deal with it. Or at least he doesn't want to deal with it in front of me.

"Hello?" Niko answers the phone and turns to look out his window. I do the same, trying to give him some privacy. What had he been about to say? What doesn't he want to jeopardize? What means more to him: our marketing partnership or this thing between us?

What means more to me?

The deal, of course. How could I even ask myself that? The deal is the whole reason I'm here. It's what is going to fix my life, not a fling with someone I can never be with long-term. So if it comes down to it, I will choose work. I must. It's the only path forward for me.

I take out my phone to distract myself from Niko's conversation and from the thoughts swirling in my head. I have a missed call and a message from Piper.

> Piper: Hey! Hope you not answering my call means you are having a blast! We ran into Mrs. Harper and had the longest chat ever. She asked about you. We told her you were KILLING it!

I can't believe they are still in Pineview Springs. I thought they would have rolled out by now and moved on to some new, exciting spot. I wonder what's keeping them in town.

Jenni: Awww, yay! Glad you got to see her. Today was incredible. I went swimming in an island cave with Niko. It was out of this world. I have so much to tell you.

Niko is speaking in hushed tones, but he seems upset.

"—Okay, fine. I will take the meeting. No, he doesn't need to come here ... Because I already know what I want." His voice has a sharp edge to it. This is starting to get really uncomfortable. I should have never told him to answer the phone.

"Yes, okay ... Fine. Bring him, but you're dealing with him. I'll talk to you later."

Niko sets the phone on the center console in front of us, as if he wants it as far away as possible.

"I'm sorry," I blurt out, not knowing what else to say. "For whatever that was."

"I'm the one who should be apologizing," he protests. "I would have never answered the phone if I knew my dad just wanted to talk business. Though, I don't know why I expected anything else."

His dad? No wonder he was so uncomfortable. "Is something wrong? You seemed upset."

"No, it's fine. He was just being himself—arranging meetings on my behalf because he doesn't think I can do my job."

I grab his hand, knowing how much his dad's opinion matters to him. "I'm so sorry. And about us? We don't need to discuss anything now. We'll just play it by ear, okay?"

I don't want to put any unnecessary pressure on Niko when he's in this state of mind.

"It's okay," Niko says, shaking his shoulders as if to clear the remnants of the conversation with his dad away.

We are pulling into the hotel when Niko turns to me. "I

would love to keep spending time together if you are comfortable, but I don't want to jeopardize our working relationship or make you feel taken advantage of. I think you're incredible, and I love working with you. I also really like spending time with you outside of work. Do you think we can do both?"

Niko's gaze holds steady, hopeful. He's putting the ball in my court. I know what I *should* do. I should tell him that work comes first, and we can't keep seeing each other. Except, I can't make myself say the words. I don't want to disappoint him. I don't want to give this up.

And while part of me is terrified I'll mess it up somehow, the part that can't bear the thought of not being with Niko is winning out. We can do both. He just said as much.

"We can. Definitely. I would really like that."

His resulting smile consumes me. I don't think I've ever seen someone so full of light.

We climb out of the car and head toward the automatic doors of the hotel. Before we trip the sensors and the doors open, Niko grabs hold of my elbow. "Wait, come here."

He pulls me to the side of the building. Once we're behind a pillar, Niko leans in for a kiss. Our lips touch, lightly, and he runs his hands up my arms until they are in the hair draped at the back of my neck. I feel weak in the knees. After a few seconds, he pulls away.

"Can you keep a secret?"

"Oh, um, sure," I say. I guess he doesn't want anyone to know about us. It makes sense, but it stings to call it a *secret*. "Yeah, I won't tell anyone about us."

"Wait, what?" Niko asks, tilting his head in confusion. "That's not the secret. But is that what *you* want?"

"No? I don't know. Maybe." I feel like I'm playing with fire, talking any more about *us*. He'll realize at any moment that I'm not what he actually wants. "It doesn't matter. We'll figure it out. But if that's not the secret, what is?"

"Well …"

"Oh, my gosh. Yes, I can keep a secret!" I give him a playful shove on the arm, noticing once again how defined and strong he is. I need to check out this hotel gym.

"Okay, I was hoping you would hide a few ducks on your way in. Maybe in the women's restroom in the lobby? I think Alexander is getting suspicious, so I need to throw him off the scent." There's a twinkle in his eye.

It takes me a moment to realize what he's saying.

"Wait—you? You're the mysterious duck dropper?" I'm trying to make sense of this new information. Why would Niko hide ducks around his own hotel?

"Guilty as charged," Niko says, his cheeks turning a barely visible shade of pink. "It's Alexander's birthday in a few days, and I'm throwing him a surprise party at the pool. It's going to be amazing. You should come."

I must be staring at him in confusion, because he continues. "The hidden ducks have all been part of a ploy to get him to the pool on Saturday. I want him so worked up over the possibility of more heists that he doesn't suspect it's a party, let alone a party for him."

That's adorable and so thoughtful. Niko surprises me more and more every day. I've never known a man to arrange something like that for a friend. Malcolm didn't have any friends unless they were useful to him in some way. But even Jeremy, who is a good guy, wouldn't plan a surprise party. He would just buy a twelve-pack of beer and hook up the Xbox.

"Yes! Of course I'll help," I say. "Who wouldn't want to be part of a birthday duck heist?"

Niko chuckles and picks me up and spins me. "You're the best."

My heart floods with joy. Niko is one of the good ones. Though I know I won't be able to keep him, I can at least enjoy him for a few more days before my heart inevitably shatters when I have to leave. I reach up and kiss Niko, trying to smother the fear and impending pain of the future with the joy of the present.

Chapter 21

By the time I make it back up to my room, my heart is racing. But from exhilaration, not anxiety. I haven't felt this light in years; it's a feeling I'm not used to. My cheeks are sore from smiling. Hiding the ducks had felt like a secret mission. I was so worried that Alexander would spot me going in or out of the bathroom and have suspicions later when they were eventually found. So I waited until he was talking to another guest to make my move. Once in the bathroom, I put a stopper in one of the sinks and filled it with warm, soapy water before setting the ducks in to take a bath.

I snapped a quick picture and then bolted upstairs. I can't get over the fact that Niko is the duck bandit. I giggle at the thought of it and pull out my phone to send him the picture I took downstairs. Within twenty seconds, my phone buzzes, and I practically jump with excitement. I feel like a teenager.

Niko: Very nice work. Quacktastic, even. Have a good night, Jenni.

I smile at the duck pun but can't help feeling a bit uneasy.

That's it? Have a good night? That feels like such an abrupt way to end a conversation before it even starts. Who does that? Is he already regretting today?

But then why invite me to dinner tomorrow? Why kiss me outside the hotel? My cheeks burn with humiliation. I'm powerless to stop my mind from spinning.

I try to shake off the feeling that something isn't right. I'm just hypersensitive because of all the times Malcolm lied to me. Niko isn't Malcolm. He's a good guy. He has proven that.

Maybe I'm overreacting, but somewhere in the back of my mind, I remember that I thought Malcolm was a good guy at first, too. I'm not sure I can trust my gut.

Just when I'm about ready to throw my phone out the window just so I don't agonize about his texts all night long—again with the teenage behavior—my phone buzzes and I almost don't want to look at it. He clearly must have changed his mind. He got back to his office, or room, or wherever, and realized I am not remotely in his league. After a few long seconds, I can't help but open the message.

> Niko: I am really looking forward to dinner tomorrow. Just wanted to let you know that it's casual attire.

Okay … the man could learn a thing or two about texting with an exclamation point or an emoji thrown in. Maybe he's just not a big texter? I let out a long sigh and bite my lip. Should I take a chance and respond again? I don't want to be overbearing, but we have limited time left.

> Jenni: Casual is perfect! Hey, I don't know what you're doing in the morning, but I'm going to a mosaic art workshop. I saw a flyer in the art gallery. Would you want to join me?

I pick at my lips while I wait for his response. My lips are incredibly windburned and chapped. I search through my bag and instead of lip balm, my fingers wrap around the little rubber duck. I pull it out.

It makes my heart skip a beat. Niko must have put this on my room service tray. And that was days ago. Has he been interested in me before today?

I smile and lie back on the bed. When my phone starts ringing in my hand, I smile. But it's not Niko. I cringe and wish I *had* thrown my phone out the window.

It's Amber. No doubt, calling to check up on my progress.

I have to answer it despite not having any clue what I will update her about. I can't exactly gush about my hookup with Niko and promise that we are still hard at work on the presentation for Monday. Of course, I haven't touched the presentation at all today, even though I told her I would get to work on the mockups. My stomach is in knots, but I swipe to answer before I can chicken out.

"Amber, hi!" My voice comes out as a croak, my throat dry from the day spent in the sun. "How are you doing? How are you feeling?"

I sit up and move to the desk.

"I would be feeling a lot better if I knew what was going on over there. I'm dying back here, Jenni. I need to know everything. What did Mr. Psomas say after the meeting? Why haven't you sent me an updated presentation?"

I take a deep breath. She sounds intense. This is not going to be good.

"I'm so sorry that we haven't been able to connect. I've been busy. Niko—I mean, Mr. Psomas had me on a tight schedule of activities today. It's been hard to find the opportunity to sit down. But he was excited about the work we got done and wants to see the samples in a few days. I was just about to work on them now. Do you have a minute to talk about some ideas?"

"What were the two of you up to?" she asks, her intensity waning momentarily. "Wait, no, don't tell me. It'll just make me regret the little gremlin in my uterus that has had me on bedrest the last few days."

My mind flashes to floating on my back under a picturesque vista of rocky archways and bright blue skies. Yep, definitely not going to mention that.

"Well, you have me. Ask your questions," Amber continues abruptly. She is in a mood. Amber is great almost all the time, but she can spiral with the best of us when she's having a bad day. It sounds like today is a bad day. I usually try to give her some grace when she's on a warpath because she's had to be a bit cutthroat to successfully run a business, especially as a woman. But today, I'm in the line of fire and there is nowhere to hide.

"I know we've spent most of our time focusing on pretty standard marketing strategies, which are all great. But I wish you could see the hotel. It's unlike any typical luxury hotel. I really think we should play up everything that is different. They have an art gallery for local artists, a rooftop garden, community initiatives—all of these things really set it apart.

"I know we've talked about playing it conservatively, but I think that might be a mistake. If we aren't treating the hotel like the unique destination it is, it will fade into a sea of hundreds of similar properties. I've created a three-pronged strategy profiling the community initiatives, unique guest experiences, and amenities. I'd love to show it to you."

I don't know how Amber is going to respond, especially given what Niko has already told us about the board. But I think it's worth a shot.

"That's all well and good, but we've been over this," Amber responds, sounding annoyed. "Maybe once we have them on board, we could try a few small campaigns featuring the hotel's initiatives. But until then, that information is useless to us. That's not what the board is interested in hearing. They want guaranteed return on investment. You heard Niko; these guys are entrenched in the luxury market. They care only about proven ways for you to make them money."

I can hear Malcolm's voice ringing in my head louder than Amber's on the phone. *"No one actually cares about values or creativity unless those things are bringing in cash. Get your head out of the clouds, Jenni, or you'll never make it at this firm."*

I thought Amber might be more open to alternative methods, but I guess clients are clients. Money talks. Conformity is comfortable. And she's right: there's no use in spending valuable time on the other things unless we get the deal.

"I … Well, yes," I say, not knowing how else to respond. "You're right. I'm sorry, I shouldn't have gotten carried away."

I squirm in my seat. I did do a lot of competitor analysis the other day, and the opportunity for digital, nontraditional marketing is huge. None of that guarantees a return, though. It may or may not assuage Niko's board members.

Amber sighs in resignation. "Look, Jenni, we need to get this client. I need to make sure you are focusing and not just gallivanting around looking for fun content. We're marketers, not influencers."

Ouch. That was harsh. I want to defend myself. I've only been gallivanting because that's what Niko wanted. But she doesn't know that, and I'd like to keep it that way. Because at the end of the day, I need to make Amber happy if I want a promotion.

"You're right. I'm sorry. I'll get right on that. I just …" I really don't know how to finish that thought. I don't know what I can tell her to possibly make this all okay.

"I know you see a lot of possibility, but sometimes we have to stick with what works. Don't get distracted."

She's right. I've gotten distracted. She and Niko know best.

"Of course, Amber. I hear you loud and clear."

"Good," she says. "Look, I need to go, but please remember who your audience is. Right now, it's the board, not the potential travelers."

I hang up the phone and move to collapse on the bed. So much for that idea.

> Piper: ALERT! ALERT! Amber is in Devil Wears Prada mode!

A little late. But the text still makes me smile despite it all. When Piper and I were in middle school, we watched that movie probably a hundred times. We both loved it so much. We dreamed of getting out of Colorado and making it big. Piper eventually decided she was more interested in traveling and making just enough money to enjoy life to the fullest, which is exactly how her life has turned out. My dreams, however, haven't changed.

> Jenni: Thanks for the heads-up. Just spoke with her. I need to nail this presentation next week. Amber seems pretty stressed. Going to stay in tonight and hunker down.

I set my phone on the desk, deciding against a social media doom scroll, and go to the bathroom to clean up. I turn on the shower and look at my tired face in the mirror. I can't give up yet. The shower is hot on my skin, burning off the layers of dried salt from the ocean. I must find a way to make Amber's presentation work. I have to play the game. Not playing the game is what got me in trouble in Chicago. Client knows best. Stick to the script.

When I get out of the shower, I have a text from Niko.

Niko: Sounds amazing. I've always wanted to
do that. Send me the details.

I smile and send Niko the link. Suddenly working all night doesn't seem so bad when I have that to look forward to in the morning.

Piper: You still up? Feeling better about
Amber?

Jenni: Yeah, I think so. She's got a lot riding on
this, and it must be hard not to be here.
Hopefully I won't let her down.

Piper: Good. Don't let Amber rattle you. You
know how she is sometimes. Also, you never
told me the rest of the cavern story!

Jenni: Well, it's a crazy long story, but Niko
kissed me. It was magical.

Piper: OMG. Seriously? Details. Now!

Jenni: I can barely keep my eyes open. I'll call
you sometime tomorrow. But it was good. It's
so, so good.

Piper: No wonder you aren't fazed by Amber.
Eeeeek. I'm so happy for you!

Mom: Hi honey! I just wanted to check in.
Haven't heard from you! Is everything going
okay?

Jenni: It's great. I really am having the best time. I just hope I can pull this off.

Mom: Even you don't, it will be okay. You can always come home. We aren't kicking you out.

Jenni: I know. But I should be further along by now.

Mom: Maybe. But there's nothing wrong with where you are. Life isn't a race.

Chapter 22

The mosaic artist is an eccentric older woman in her sixties and she runs classes out of the front room of her home. Niko and I met for coffee at the hotel restaurant before walking to the workshop together, holding hands and admiring the beautiful cobblestoned streets.

We are one of three couples at the workshop, making it a pretty intimate setting.

"Mosaic art has been a part of Greek history since the fifth century BCE," our teacher says. "It started out as very simple terracotta patterns in red and white before evolving into the intricate and colorful mosaics from ancient Greece that depicted gods and deities, among other things."

Niko leans in to whisper in my ear. "I wish we had time to visit Delos to see the ancient mosaic artifacts there. They are incredible."

The teacher gives him a side-eyed glance for talking and he sits back up. I hold back a laugh at Niko being scolded like a school boy.

"The earliest Greeks used naturally shaped and colored pebbles. Eventually, they used glass, stone, and ceramics in a fashion similar to today. For our mosaics, we'll use cuts of porcelain and glass."

She gestures to bins on the table between us filled with all sorts of scrap tiles, dishes, and glassware in every color of the rainbow. We each have a canvas, a little pot of adhesive, and a pair of tile cutters.

"Once you decide on an inspiration for your design, you can begin gathering and arranging the pieces onto your canvas. I recommend that you don't glue down any pieces until you have a pretty good start on your design."

The students begin to discuss their ideas and gather tiles. I immediately know what I'm going to create, but I ask Niko what he's thinking.

"I don't know," he admits. "I think I need to play with the pieces and see what forms on its own. What about you?"

I have already started reaching for yellow pieces of glass and pottery. "I'm going to create a sunburst."

My answer comes easy—from my belief about there being something so meaningful about the sun. Light after darkness. Warmth after cold. Bringing new life and energy, day after day. Plus, I've always loved the way it feels on my skin. So maybe it's as simple as that.

"I can't wait to see it." Niko leans over and kisses my temple, sending a warmth cascading through me.

When I woke up this morning, I had an anxious fear that yesterday had been a dream, and that somehow the other shoe was going to drop, and none of it would be real. But when Niko greeted me this morning, his smile was as bright as ever. It's a strange feeling to struggle to trust someone who has never once done anything to make me doubt him. He's been nothing but respectful, honest, and forthcoming. But that fear is still there, poking for me to question everything. It's not that I don't trust Niko; it's that I don't trust myself. Not enough to deserve such happiness.

"Now, when you use the tile cutters, please wear your eye protection. The way these materials break is always unpredictable, and you never know what might go flying," the instructor says to the group. "You may be trying to cut a large piece and find it shatters. Or you are trying to cut a triangle, only for it to break off in a curve. The beauty of mosaics is the unpredictability. I encourage you to use the surprise cuts. Make beauty out of chaos. It will make for a much more interesting mosaic than if every cut was precise."

My life feels a bit like that a mosaic right now—a bunch of jumbled pieces, cuts that didn't go as planned, pieces that were shattered. I'm not sure if I've got them quite where they need to be to form a mosaic. But I'm working on it. One piece at a time.

"What are you thinking about?" Niko asks, as he passes me a blue piece of sea glass I can use for the background of my sunburst.

"Oh, you know, pondering the meaning of life," I joke.

"Ah, no wonder you look so deep in thought. I was thinking about how much I miss American pizza."

I give him a concerned look. "Seriously? That's what's on your mind right now?"

"No, I just wanted to see that adorable look of surprise on your face."

I scrunch up my nose at him and knock him with my shoulder. "You're ridiculous."

I pick up the tile cutters and a piece of yellow sea glass. I take my time trying to figure out where to place the blade. I settle on a corner of the glass and give the handles a squeeze. I'm worried about shattering it or sending a piece flying somewhere, so I don't go hard. Of course, nothing happens.

"I'm scared! I don't want to mess it up."

"Didn't you hear her? There's no way to mess it up. The

unexpected pieces are all part of the process," Niko encourages. "Here."

He places his hands over mine and helps me set the tile cutter. Once it's ready, Niko squeezes my hand. I hear a sharp click. A small piece of the glass falls to the table. It's hexagonal, with two sides longer than the others. It's perfect. I place it at the center of my canvas.

"Thank you," I tell Niko. Now that I'm comfortable, I do the next one on my own.

After a few minutes, I sneak a look at Niko's canvas. I can't tell what his design is yet. He has arranged a bunch of random colors and textures in an arc in the upper left-hand corner of his canvas. He's going slow and picking out each piece methodically.

"What are you making?" I finally ask.

"You'll see," is all he responds.

Around the room, each of the couples works a bit differently. One decided to work on a large canvas together, each selecting pieces and creating pink flowers in a green vase. It's intricate and delicate at the same time, and I love watching them debate on where to place each newly cut piece.

The other couple is working on separate pieces. They have barely spoken to each other since arriving and instead are focused intently on their work.

"Do you do this sort of thing a lot?" Niko asks.

"Not really," I respond, trying to figure out how to explain my relationship with art. "I think creating is such a beautiful practice. My mom knits and sews. She's always working on something, and I think it's really good for her. Over the years I've tried different things like watercolor, candle making and cross stitch. I always love it. But then work and life get in the way and I never make time. When I was in Chicago, I worked, like, fifteen-hour days and barely had time to eat, let alone craft."

Niko reaches for the bin of blue tiles and begins sorting them into shades of light and dark blue. "I didn't know you spent time in Chicago. When was that?"

Crap. I can't believe I just dropped that so casually into conversation. I usually try to avoid the topic at all costs. "I went to school in Chicago and then worked there for a while before coming to Aspen Sky."

"I'm not surprised you didn't last long."

My face flushes. What? How did he know … is it that obvious?

"Sorry, that came out wrong," he continues. "I just meant that I'm surprised you lasted in corporate life for that long working such crazy hours. Despite getting an MBA, I have never wanted a single taste of that lifestyle."

Oh, he was surprised I *wanted* to be in Chicago for that long? At least, I think that's what he means. Now that I have the center of my sunburst filled out, I open my pot of adhesive and go to glue them down.

"Did you ever want to do something other than hospitality?"

Niko laughs. "I didn't even really set out to do this. The opportunity just sort of happened. My dad knew someone who knew someone. It's been a pretty good experience."

"Was there something else you wanted to do?"

Niko takes a deep breath. He's moved on to filling out the rest of his canvas with blue tiles. I watch his fingers work, steady and calm. Just like he is.

"Have you ever heard of social entrepreneurship? It's somewhat of a countermovement to the capitalist notion of revenue at all costs, which often puts people and communities at odds with business goals. With social entrepreneurship, the approach is that we can engineer solutions to social problems, like environmental change, homelessness, or whatever it may be while also making a profit. It doesn't have to be one or the other."

He considers a white tile before placing it. "My grad program had a social entrepreneurship tract, and I fell in love with the idea. Before I came to Mykonos, I worked at a grocery delivery company that delivered produce at cost in areas of Los Angeles considered to be food deserts. That's when fresh food is either hard to find or prohibitively expensive. The company makes a profit off clients in higher income areas willing to pay a bit more in fees in order to support the mission of the company."

"Wow, that's really cool."

"It was great. I'm here now, though. And doing what I can with the hotel. It's not a lot, but it's something."

I can't tell if he has a look of regret on his face before he turns away from me to grab a bin of deep blue tiles.

I'm almost done with the sunburst in the middle of my canvas, so I start cutting purple and blue tiles for the background. I'm moving the colors around in waves, so it looks like an ombré swirl of color.

"By the way, I wanted to thank you again for hiding those ducks yesterday. It means a lot to me that you'd be willing to jump right in and join the effort to make someone else feel special."

"Of course! I didn't do much, but I'm more than happy to help."

A little while later, we are both putting the finishing touches on our mosaics. My sunburst is full of yellow, white, and gold pieces set on a backdrop of purples, blues, and silvers. My heart swells just looking at it. Like I'll always have a piece of the sunshine from this trip.

When Niko finally lets me get a good look at his canvas, I can see the arc he worked so meticulously on is a parasail. He also created a thin black line down from the parasail to a small cluster of white tiles—the boat. He created our first "date" from a few days ago. It's beautiful.

"Niko, that's amazing," I tell him. "Is that us?"

"Yeah, I thought I would do something to commemorate our first adventure," he says, placing a gentle hand on my back. "I wasn't kidding when I said I haven't had this much fun in a long time. That first night we met and I laughed at your baseball joke, I realized I hadn't laughed in days. I have been working so hard on the hotel and so deep in my own head worrying about my dad that I haven't been enjoying life. So thank you."

I take a long breath. It's funny how differently two people can experience situations. That first night I was so nervous and felt undeserving of being here. I left my interaction with Niko thinking I made a fool of myself.

I still get a pit in my stomach any time I think about the board meeting next week but hearing how that night felt so different for him gives me hope that maybe I'm not as much of a mess as I thought I was.

A wave of warmth washes over me. I sit up to kiss Niko. But before I do, the teacher taps a putty knife to her water glass to get our attention.

"Now that all of you have created your mosaics, it's time to grout them. On a table in the back, you'll find everything you need to mix the grout and then you'll want to use one of these tools to spread it over your mosaic."

Niko stands. "I'll grab our supplies."

When he returns to the table, we mix our grout together in a bowl and get to work. I can't stop thinking about what Niko said about social entrepreneurship and how customers respond to the opportunity to do good. It's so in line with my ideas for marketing the hotel.

"You know, I have some ideas for the hotel I wanted to run by you," I tell him. "I've talked to Amber, and she wasn't sure based on what you've said during our meetings, but I'd really like to take an approach similar to what you were talking about with the company in Los Angeles." I explain to him my ideas for highlighting all of the things that make the Omorfiá Hotel different. "I just think it's worth exploring on Monday. We could use your expertise from grad school. I think it could really impress them."

Niko pauses, furrowing his brow. "I'll think about it," he finally says, wiping his mosaic with a damp towel to remove excess grout on top of the pieces. "I'm not sure this board is one for such progressive ideas."

I sigh. "Oh, okay. Yeah, I understand."

Once we're done with the artwork, we leave our creations at the studio where the instructor will apply sealant after the grout and adhesive dry. We'll have to come pick them up in a few days.

As we walk back to the hotel, Niko puts his arms around me. "I hope it didn't sound like I don't believe in your ideas. They are great. I just already know the board is tolerant, at best, of the changes I've made, and I'm not sure that hinging our proposal on them is a risk we should take."

"Of course, I totally get it. You need to do what's best for the hotel. No worries."

I can't help feeling deflated. Between Amber and Niko, I think I'll be stuck giving a proposal I don't believe in whole-heartedly. I wish one of them would consider my suggestions more seriously.

Chapter 23

When I make it to the lobby for our dinner date, Niko is speaking with Alexander at the front desk. Even though we've spent so much time together now, I still stop dead in my tracks at the sight of him. He looks more handsome every time I lay eyes on him. Tonight, he's dressed in a short-sleeved cream button-up shirt with navy embroidered details down the front and around the cuffs. He's got on gray linen plants and black loafers.

I look down at the off-the-shoulder, lightweight navy sweater I'm wearing. I've paired it with a denim skirt and gold sandals. We're accidentally matching with the navy. Maybe we should take a selfie. Would that be weird? I'd love to send one to Piper and Sarah.

The moment Niko sees me, his face lights up. That smile. My knees go a little weak every time I see that smile. It takes me back to yesterday afternoon—the salty taste of his mouth when he kissed me, his hands tracing my back, his warm light illuminating long-dormant parts of my soul as we lay in the sunshine on the back of the boat.

My face flushes with the memory as I move toward him,

watching my step over a spot that has clearly just been mopped. The last thing I need right now is another clumsy accident from which Niko can sweep in and save me. A time or two is cute, but any more than that and he might start to think I'm doing it on purpose. When I look up, he's making his way toward me with a soft smile.

"Hi," I say, not know what to do with myself.

"Hello." Niko grabs my elbow and places a light kiss on my cheek. He steps back and looks me up and down. "You look beautiful. Are you okay to walk tonight? I was hoping we could walk to the restaurant. It's not far."

"Of course. I would love to." Some fresh air would probably do me some good, clear up the love-drunk way my body is acting around him.

We bid farewell to Alexander, but he is staring at his computer monitor, muttering under his breath.

"Is everything all right, Alexander?" I ask. "You seem a little stressed."

He looks up, blinking away his distraction. "Oh, Miss Jenni. Yes, yes. We found more ducks today, and I don't know what to do. Nothing like this has never happened before."

"Well, I'm sure you'll figure it out," Niko says. "Take care, Alexander."

"You too, Mr. Psomas. Have a good night."

Niko winks at me as we turn and head toward the door.

"You're horrible!" I whisper. "The poor guy is miserable!"

"He'll survive. Stop worrying so much."

I pout and can tell that Niko is holding in a laugh. "This better work out in the end, or I am going to feel terrible for being complicit."

He nudges me. "It'll work. I promise. You trust me, remember?"

"Using my own words against me—how dare you! The

boat surprise was entirely different from pranking your poor concierge."

The night is warm and lovely as we make our way down the hill toward the beach. I'm reminded of my first night in Greece. I was so uncertain of myself, fearful and alone. So much has happened since then. Now my fears are different. If I do accomplish this assignment, what am I going to do? Will I really be brave enough to leave Pineview Springs? What happens when I go home, alone, while Niko stays here? Will that heartbreak put me in bed for weeks again, like it did when I left Chicago?

Niko turns us down an alley a few blocks short of the beach. Shops line the street. We snake through a few more alleyways, walking under fuchsia flower arches and blue-painted window shutters, before coming upon a small restaurant with one small metal table out front.

"This is a restaurant my mom used to take me to. It's kind of a hole-in-the-wall, and they only have three things on the menu, but it's amazing. The same chef has run it since I was a kid. It's totally local."

Peeling vinyl lettering on the door spells out Yia-Yia's Café. Niko holds it open for me. "You won't find this on any tourist top ten lists, but it's my favorite spot on the island."

I walk into the cozy restaurant and Niko follows. It's tiny. We have a full view of the kitchen behind an old register sitting on top of a chipped counter. Two small tables with red-checkered vinyl cloths and white plastic chairs make up the dining area. Small white candles flicker on the tables alongside piles of napkins and plastic ketchup bottles filled with tzatziki sauce. An older man sits alone at a table, contentedly reading a book while he eats.

"Welcome to Yia-Yia's!" Niko says proudly, as it if it were his own grandmother's café. And I wonder if it is. Is that why he brought me here?

"*Yia-Yia* means grandmother, right? Is this another of your family's businesses?" I smile but fully recognize the absurdity of my question as soon as it's out of my mouth. The same family that owns hundreds of Greece's most luxurious wineries does not bother with tiny hole-in-the-wall cafés.

"I wish," is Niko's only response as he approaches the counter. A young teen comes to take our order.

"Niko!" The boy greets Niko excitedly in Greek, laughing and punching in an order without Niko ever opening his mouth.

"Hey, Eli, how's it going?"

It still catches me off guard when Niko interacts with everyone like they are an old friend. It is just so out of character from all the other rich and powerful people I know. "And yes, twice in one week. You caught me. But tonight is special. I wanted to share your family's food with someone. This is my friend Jenni."

I smile at Eli and say hello. The fact he called me his friend and not his associate or business partner does not go unnoticed. "Friend" sends rays of sunshine through my body. I'm afraid he'll see my goofy grin, so I turn my attention to deciphering the menu on the wall, which is written in Greek with tiny English phrasing underneath.

"We'll take two of everything. For here, please. Thanks, Eli."

Well, that makes things easier.

"Sure thing, man! Beer?" Eli switches to English, probably for my benefit.

Niko hesitates and looks at me for the answer.

"Maybe just water," I suggest. I've already drank way more than I usually do on this trip. Some water wouldn't hurt.

He nods and turns back to Eli, pulling out a wad of cash. I fish in my bag for my wallet, but Niko puts a hand on my arm to stop me. "It's on me."

"No, really, it's fine. I should be the one paying. Aspen Sky has a budget for this sort of thing."

He looks at me, confusion in his eyes at my offer to pay. Amber did send me with a budget.

"Well." He rolls his shoulders back. "So do I. It's on the hotel. Marketing expenses."

His words sound cold, and my heart sinks a degree. Did I say the wrong thing? We move to the open table to take a seat.

"So what are we having? Why is this place your favorite when there are so many five-star restaurants on the island? It must be really special." My smile feels forced, all cheeks and eyebrows. I'm trying to fix whatever tension I just created.

Niko sort of grunts, but as he talks his face lights. "It's definitely special. Not because it's fancy or groundbreaking. Sure, there are five-star restaurants on the island that most people would choose over this any day, but Yia-Yia's has heart. The food is simple and true to itself. It's just good old-fashioned Greek street food, perfected over decades. I've been begging them to take over our restaurant, but they don't want to."

I'm no longer surprised that Niko's answer has much more to do with the personality of the place than anything else. He is so far from the "30 Under 30" businessman I read about online. Of course, he prefers the home cooking place with heart instead of the upscale restaurant Ana took me to the other night.

"This reminds me of a place back home that I've been going to since I was a kid," I say, thinking about Bobby's Café and his BLT sandwiches. "But I don't think I've ever really appreciated it in the same way you do."

Before Niko can respond, Eli is at our table with two small plates. "Dolmades for the gentleman and the lady," he says as he sets the plates down in front of us.

"Thank you," I say, appreciating his use of English on my behalf.

Niko hands me a fork from the silverware basket on a shelf behind him. "Dig in!"

I prod at the green things on my plate. They look like egg rolls, but wrapped in leaves? I swear I've seen something like this in a movie, but I have no idea what they are or how to eat them.

I hesitantly stab one with my fork. "What is it?"

"Dolmades? You've never had them? Okay, this"—he gestures to the roll on his fork—"is a dolma. It's a mixture of rice, nuts, and herbs stuffed and rolled in grapevine leaves. You'll love it!"

I watch as he dips the end in yogurt sauce before taking a bite, leaves and all. I hesitantly do the same. To my unpleasant surprise, the dolma is cold and slightly bitter. The softness and creaminess of the rice counteracts the bitterness. I can also taste hints of mint and cinnamon. I can't tell if I like it, but I chew and swallow.

"That's good," I finally say. "Not what I expected. But good!" I take another bite, trying not to gag. Something about the cold temperature and slimy texture of the leaves is just not doing it for me. I've got two more on my plate, though.

Niko is on his last dolma already, and I'm barely two bites into mine. The last thing I want to do is offend him, but the second to last thing I want to do is eat another one of these.

"You look like you've smelled a skunk," he says through laughter when he looks up. I guess I didn't hide my distaste as well as I thought I did. "You don't have to pretend with me. It's okay if you don't like them. That just means more for me!"

He takes his fork and steals the dolma I'm holding in midair.

"Was it that obvious?" I ask.

"I must know you better than you think, Jenni." His words tug at my heart. He does, doesn't he?

The rest of our meal includes chicken souvlaki, lamb gyros,

and fries with salt and oregano. Both entrées are 100 times better than the dolmades, so I don't have to pretend to like them. In fact, when Eli offers seconds of the souvlaki, I enthusiastically accept.

"What was it like spending summers here?" I ask in between bites. "Was it as magical as I imagine?"

"At the time, I kind of hated it. I didn't feel like I fit in here. None of the kids really accepted me, so I mostly hung out with my cousins: Ana and her sister. And it felt like my friends back in California had a blast without me. It took forever to fit back in when I got home each fall."

He takes a sip of water, seemingly to collect his thoughts. "So I guess there were pros and cons. It's such a beautiful place, and I'm really grateful to still be connected to my culture."

"Ana told me about Callie. I'm so sorry. That must have been so tragic for the whole family."

He gives me a sad smile. "Yeah, it's been a rough few years. That's one of the reasons I decided to come back here. In addition to trying to connect with my dad, I wanted to be here for Ana. She doesn't really have anyone else who sees or supports her. Most of her family has really been stuck in denial."

"You're a good cousin."

Before I can say anything else, Eli is back and handing Niko a brown bag. The bag is covered in grease stains and a sweet, steamy aroma wafts from the opening.

"Oh, wow. That smells amazing! What is it?"

Niko takes the bag and slips Eli some more cash with a "Thank you."

"This is our dessert. I thought we could eat it while we walk."

With an excited flip of my stomach, we gather our things and walk out the door. We head toward the beach, and I wait not-so-patiently for Niko to let me have a go at that paper bag.

"Are we going somewhere special? And can I at least get a peek at those desserts?"

"I thought we could walk through the old city and catch the sunset at the windmills."

Oh, sunset at the windmills might be the perfect spot for a cute selfie. We cross the road and head around a building where the shore pops up in front of us.

"And yes, we can eat our loukoumades while we walk." He gestures toward me with the bag.

"Lou-kou-mee-des?" I say, trying to pronounce the word correctly.

"Lou-kou-mah-des," Niko corrects with a grin. "Greek donuts. They are basically donut holes, deep fried and covered in honey, cinnamon, and sesame seeds."

They sound mouth-wateringly delicious. I reach my hand into the bag to grab one. It's warm and sticky and perfectly sized to plop the entire thing in my mouth.

Even though I would have loved to scarf it down, I take a half-bite. The honey and cinnamon soothe my taste buds, and the warm dough practically melts in my mouth. It's more than amazing. It's heaven, balled up and slathered in honey. I plop the second half in my mouth.

"That good, huh?" Niko grins, plopping his own donut in his mouth whole. "I knew you would love them. *Everyone* loves loukoumades."

I giggle at the ridiculousness of a grown man talking with his mouth full of food. It's adorable.

"What?" He stuffs another donut in his mouth and exaggerates his mumbled words as I fail to hold in my laughter. "What's so funny? You're the one with honey on your nose."

My hand involuntarily juts up to cover my face, only for me

to realize he wasn't lying about the glob of cinnamon honey on my nose. I try to wipe it off but end up just smearing it across my face. Now I have honey all over my fingers. I'm a sticky mess when I look over at Niko helplessly.

"Hold on." Niko laughs and reaches into the bag and pulls out a napkin. He wets it on his tongue before handing me the bag. Using his free hand to cup my face and pull me close, Niko wipes at my nose, my cheek, and the corner of my mouth, making sure he's gotten every last bit.

My skin melts at his gentle touch. My senses seem to go into hyper-focus, noting the sharp whites and blues of the building behind him and the way my body responds to his touch. My stance softens and goose bumps cover my arms despite the warm evening air.

When he's done, I pull my gaze back to his, unable to avoid our closeness any longer. He smiles, as if waiting for a sign that it's okay to kiss me.

"Niko, is that you?"

We both snap our attention down the street. An older man in a fancy suit is striding toward us, a woman on his arm.

Niko drops his hands from my body immediately and takes a step back. "Hi, Theo. What a surprise. How are you?"

"Good, good, and who is this?" The man gestures toward me. Meanwhile, I'm frozen with donuts in hand and a sinking feeling in my gut.

Niko glances at me, blinking twice before answering. "This is Jenni Swanson. She is a marketer from the States who we're hiring at the hotel. She's here to get acquainted with the property."

The man extends a hand toward me. "Well then, best of luck. It's a fine hotel."

The woman clears her throat, nudging the man. "Yes, yes, of course. We're late for a reservation. I'll see you soon, Niko."

The couple walks away and I stare down the street, confused. Why was I a friend at the restaurant but a business associate here?

Niko grabs my hand. "I'm sorry about that. My father's accountant. I wasn't sure how you'd want to be introduced."

I can't stop my chin from trembling. All the times Malcolm introduced me as his employee, instead of his girlfriend, race through my mind, filling me with nausea.

"What's wrong? You're shaking."

My gaze snaps back to his. His eyebrows are raised in concern.

"I think I'm just cold. Let's keep walking and I'll warm up." I turn and rub at my face where he cleaned the honey, trying to wipe away the tingling sensation he left there. "I need one more of these." I take another donut out of the bag and hand it to Niko before turning back in the direction of the old town.

I can't shake the feeling that Niko is the one who wasn't sure how he wanted to introduce me to someone who might care about his reputation.

By the time we get to the windmills, I can barely appreciate the sunset. And I'm definitely not feeling confident enough to ask for a picture.

~

Piper: Hey girlie! How was today? I need so much more info. You never called me!

Jenni: Sorry, it's been a really long day. I just got back from dinner and a sunset walk with Niko. I really need to talk to you, but I'm not sure I can right now. I need to process some things.

Piper: Okay. Sure. Get some rest and call me in
the morning. I'll stay up late. Call anytime.

Jenni: Thanks. You're the best.

Chapter 24

I wake up feeling like a ton of bricks fell on me. The way Niko dropped his hands from me the second he recognized that man haunted my dreams last night. What did I do wrong? Why did he feel like it was necessary to do that?

I need to talk to Piper. I need to get a fresh perspective. She told me to call her early, so I pack my bag and head out for a walk while I talk to her. Nothing clears my head more than movement and Piper. Maybe once I sort through all of this, I'll feel better.

I make my way toward Little Venice, a part of the island I've been dying to see. It's a little alcove where the buildings are right to the water's edge. You can sit at a café table with the ocean at your feet. I'll call Piper along the two-mile walk and then find a little coffee shop or somewhere to work for a few hours afterward to catch up on all the work I should have done yesterday.

My stomach tightens at the thought of rehashing last night. Instead of calling Piper right away, I take my time, stopping to take photos and wander down little alleyways.

A tiny voice in the back of my head tells me to stop

procrastinating but I brush it away. Each corner reveals a new row of white shops with beautiful doorways, flower baskets in the windows and decorative tiles in the walkway. I could never tire of these streets. It's endlessly tranquil this early in the morning. A bit colder than I had anticipated, but it's easy to forget about last night while getting lost exploring this little paradise.

I finally find myself on the beach and pull out my phone to call. It's later than I had planned and my first call goes to voice-mail, so I keep walking. Why did I put off this phone call when I need it so desperately? I've probably lost my chance now and won't be able to speak to Piper until tonight if I can even catch her before my planned get-together with Ana.

I wander back from the beach onto another street full of shops. Most of them are still closed, so I window-shop, peeking in on pottery shops, jewelers, and florists. I'm crisscrossing the street to check out an olive oil and honey shop when a few raindrops splatter onto my forehead.

A chill is in the air and the sky is darkening. I look up to see storm clouds swirling in the sky above me. Rain pours from them. I dash to the shop to take cover in the doorway.

Of course, that's the moment that my phone rings. When I grab it out of my bag, a familiar picture of my best friend lights up the screen. Thank goodness. I didn't miss her after all. I swipe to answer the FaceTime. Piper's face pops up in a dark room.

"Piper? Is everything okay? Where are you?"

"Hi! Yes! Everything's fine. We're … at an inn." A look I can't quite decipher passes across Piper's face. Why are they at an inn? "I'm so sorry I missed your call; I fell asleep watching TV."

"Is that Jenni? Tell her thanks for winning me twenty bucks!" I hear Sarah call out.

"What is she talking about?" I ask, confused.

"We had a bet. She bet you would hook up with Niko; I bet that it would be someone else," Piper says. "Obviously, you're the real winner, though. Am I right?!"

"Yeah, sure." I say, my voice flat.

"What's up? Am I interrupting anything now?"

I sigh. "No, of course not. I'm just huddled under a shop entrance, trying to survive a flash storm."

I quickly pan my phone around so she can see the street, now splattered with puddles. "But now that I think about it, it's probably perfect weather. I've messed everything up. I don't know how it all went so wrong."

"What do you mean you screwed things up? What happened? The last we texted, you said things were going great."

My shoes are starting to swell with water, sticking out in the rain.

"I … I don't even know where to start. But Niko and I really connected, and I thought everything was great even though I can't get him or Amber to see what I think the best way forward is for the proposal. But then last night, we were out, and he totally pretended we weren't together. Things feel like they are falling apart. He is doing the same thing Malcolm did. I can't—I can't go through that again."

The words pour out of me, leaving a taste of vinegar in my mouth. It feels like a 100-pound weight is sitting on my chest. Even just talking about it makes me feel queasy, as if at any second the house of cards I've built around me is going to collapse, and I'll be left standing in the pile of waste that is my life.

"Wait, wait, wait. Slow down. Take a deep breath," Piper coaches. I do my best, but the breath comes choppy and shallow. "Back up. What exactly happened?"

I pinch the bridge of my nose, trying to pull myself together.

"Last night, after dinner, we were walking on the beach and Niko was about to kiss me when someone called his name. He dropped me like a hot potato. He couldn't have stepped back faster. To top it all off, he introduced me by my job title."

Piper adjusts herself on the bed and brings the phone closer. "Did he say anything after that? How has he reacted toward you in other situations?"

"He apologized and said he wasn't sure how I wanted to be introduced and didn't want to assume."

"That sounds reasonable. It's not like you have had the relationship talk. He only kissed you, like, two days ago. I still need those details, by the way."

I narrow my eyes. "Earlier that night he called me a friend and held my hand. He kissed me in the lobby of the hotel. The only thing that was different was that the man worked for his father. He seemed embarrassed by me. It's just like Malcolm. He never acknowledged our relationship either."

My stomach hollows into an endless void. I can't believe I got myself into this situation again. I know I said I was just having fun, but I opened up my heart and allowed a flicker of hope to grow. Then last night doused that flame as surely as this rain would have.

"Oh, hon. Your worry is totally understandable, but I really don't think that's what's going on. Do you? Niko sounds like a really good guy."

I think back to all our other interactions—the tenderness, always making sure I was comfortable, remembering how I took my coffee. All of it leaves my mind fuzzy.

"No, you're right. He has basically been perfect otherwise."

"Perfect, huh? Am I ever going to hear about the magical cave date?"

My racing heart has slowed. Maybe I'm overreacting. Niko hasn't done anything else to make me worry. I should give him the benefit of the doubt, shouldn't I? A cautious benefit of the doubt? Because when I think about needing to end it, I can't figure out how to do that without ruining my chances at the board meeting.

Doing that puts too much at risk. This whole trip will have been in vain. I'll lose everything.

"Fine, Piper. I'll tell you about the magical cave date," I offer, my mood lifting already. So I recount the other day with plenty of details. "It was totally PG-13. I am not ready for anything more than that," I add when I finish. I sigh, thinking back to the way Niko kissed me outside the hotel and how I hadn't wanted him to stop.

"Oh yeah? Then what was that little moan about?"

"Ew, that was not a moan. It was a sigh. Because it stopped raining." I step out of the shop doorway and start to wander the streets in the general direction of Little Venice.

"Whatever you say. What do you think will happen when you come home?"

"I don't know," I answer truthfully. "Obviously nothing can happen. Our lives are thousands of miles apart. Hopefully we'll be working together. I can't actually date someone I work with."

Piper rolls her eyes. "Amber met her husband at a marketing firm while she was a manager and he was a consultant. It happens."

She did? I never knew that. "Even so, Niko lives in Greece, and I'm coming back to Colorado in less than a week. It could never be serious."

Piper laughs as if I've told a joke I don't understand.

"Who said anything about serious? Casual is exactly what you need. Why can't you just have an amazing time for the rest of your trip and keep in touch? You never know what might happen."

I walk past a bakery and the fresh aroma hits me like a soft pillow with the way it wafts through the air. I stop for a minute to look over the case of sweets in the window. Maybe Piper is right. Maybe I do need casual. I mean, the only relationship I've ever really had was with Malcolm. And that went from zero to sixty in about eight seconds flat.

"Hold on," I tell Piper, and then use a combination of English and pointing to order coffee and some sort of flaky pastry with a lavender flower on top. It looks a lot like the baklava Niko fed me on that first afternoon.

I sit at a little metal table outside the café and jump right back to talking with Piper.

"Okay, maybe you're right. I still don't know if that's what I should be focusing on, though. I need to get this deal, so I can finally get out of my parents' house—go somewhere that isn't Pineview Springs."

"Small towns are for people with no ambition. If it's not a city, you're doing it wrong."

I could fill a book with all the ways I'm a failure in Malcolm's eyes. And I shouldn't care. Not anymore. But I can't help myself. Some part of me is still broken, desperate for his approval. Like if I can prove he was wrong about me, I can prove I wasn't the problem in our dysfunctional relationship.

Thoughts of Malcolm choke me up. Piper will never understand the hold he still has on me. I can't tell her any of this. It's too hard to explain.

There's silence from the other end, and Piper fidgets with her glasses. Almost as if she's gearing up to deliver some bad news.

"Wait. What is that look for? Did Amber say something to you? Is the promotion out of the picture? What happened?"

"No, no. Amber hasn't said anything. I'm sure you will figure it out. It's just ... what you said about Pineview Springs. You really want to leave that much?"

"Of course. You know that." Not a day has gone by that I haven't lamented being stuck back home.

"Well, you know how Sarah and I have always talked about settling down somewhere and running our own business?"

I do. They always have some sort of grand idea, selling climbing gear in Estes Park, surfboards in California, opening a café somewhere along the Appalachian Trail. Had they found something somewhere? My heart sinks at the notion I won't get to see them as often if they aren't roaming the country in their RV with Colorado as a home base.

"We're reopening the inn!" She has a smile from ear to ear.

"The inn? What inn?"

"The Pineview Inn. The one we used to work at in high school. When we had lunch with Mrs. Harper the other day, she joked that she wished we would take it over because she knew it would be in good hands, and I don't know … It just felt right.

"We stayed up all night debating the pros and cons. We got a loan from Sarah's dad to help with the down payment and we signed all the paperwork today."

I'm feeling a bit dizzy, so I take a sip of coffee to stall. I don't know how to make sense of this. If anyone wanted to get out of Pineview Springs more than I did growing up, it was Piper. And now she's coming back too? How did we both end up stuck in Pineview Springs?

"What? Wow, that's … surprising! I wasn't sure she was ever going to actually sell the place. Are you excited? How does Sarah feel about being stuck in Pineview?"

The joy on Piper's face deflates, and I realize I've said the wrong thing.

"Yeah, we're very excited, actually," she says, sounding annoyed. "It's been our dream to do something like this for years. Neither of us consider it being *stuck* in Pineview. We have everything there we could want—a business, my family, the outdoors, and you."

My heart sinks. I didn't mean to hurt her feelings, but I can tell I have. Let's just add being a terrible friend to the giant pile of mistakes I'm stacking up right now.

"Of course! Oh, my gosh. Of course! I'm sorry. I'm just so wrapped up in my own head right now. This is amazing news. When do you start? Are you leaving Aspen Sky?"

I don't know what I'll do without Piper at Aspen Sky. She is my lifeline. And suddenly, even though this news means that Piper and Sarah will be closer to me geographically, I can't help but feel like they are leaving me behind. They are doing something with their lives while I'm still trying to grasp at mine as it spirals out of control. It's like I'm still being punished for dating the wrong guy when I was twenty. Am I ever going to pull myself back up from that setback?

"Eventually," Piper says. "But not immediately. We're going to paint and redecorate and do a lot of DIY to update the place a bit. We're hoping for a soft opening around Christmastime. We got the keys today, which means we're going to start cleaning it up this weekend."

"I can't wait to help when I get back! You have to put me to work, okay?"

"Oh, we will. Your free labor played a big role in our decision." Piper laughs and I smile, even though I can tell I might start crying any second.

"Hey, Piper, I need to go. My phone battery is low, and I need it to find my way back to the hotel."

"No worries. I'm so glad I caught you! It's been killing me that you didn't know! And, hey, don't stress about the meeting. Just be yourself and you'll be fine, okay? I love you so much!"

Even at 3:00 a.m. or whatever ridiculous time it is there, Piper hits the "I love you" with the same energy as always.

"I love you more." I can't muster the same enthusiasm in response, but I do my best and hang up the phone.

I finally take a bite of my pastry, which is filled with lavender sugary sweetness. Any other day and I would devour it, but my appetite is completely gone, so instead I get up and keep walking toward Little Venice. I need to at least see it.

After a few numb minutes spent paying very little attention to my surroundings, I find myself on the beach in a small cove, staring across the water at a wall of buildings. The waves lap against the cement walls and I can see now why it's called Little Venice. There are balconies of red, blue, and burnt orange with matching window shutters. The cement is stained green, marking years of waves. Weathered fishing dinghies and rowboats bob close by.

I plop myself down on a chipped blue bench and watch the water swell with the tide. Why is everyone achieving their dreams except me?

Chapter 25

It took everything in me to not completely lose myself on my walk back to the hotel. I pulled myself together enough to work most of the day. I had to catch up on a few admin things, but mostly I went over the presentation with a fine-tooth comb, again. If this is my one chance to fix myself, I need to make it work. I briefly texted with Niko, but he was off property all day for finance meetings, so I haven't seen him at all.

Instead, I'm spending the evening with Ana. She has been begging me to have an "American movie marathon" where we paint our nails, braid each other's hair, and watch rom-coms. A good old-fashioned sleepover without the actual sleeping over part. At least, I think Ana is planning on returning to her room at the end of the night. I'm starting to expect the unexpected with her. She may crawl into bed, don a sleep mask, and start snoring, and I wouldn't be surprised.

She should be here any minute, so I head to the bathroom to check my appearance. I already washed off my makeup in preparation for face masks, and I'm wearing the only pajamas I brought with me: an old concert T-shirt and a pair of form-fitting black shorts. I had contemplated going shopping for something a bit chicer to wear, but after last night, I couldn't be bothered. If Ana wants the real experience, this is what she gets. I tie my hair back in a scrunchie and add another layer of deodorant to my pits.

A minute later, Ana is at the door and wraps me in a perfumed, silky hug. She looks gorgeous in pair of silk pajama pants and a button-up pajama top.

"I'm so excited! Are you excited? I've just had a message that the courier dropped off my order of goodies. Come with me to the lobby to get them!"

"Oh, sure." I turn back to slip on my sandals. I definitely didn't plan on leaving the room, but what's the worst that could happen?

"It's not a movie night without popcorn and candy, right? That's what I've always heard, at least," Ana says, a gleeful look on her face. "I had a guy track down as much American candy and snacks as he could."

She really is going all-in on the theme here. I can't help the swell of happiness over this trip having brought Ana into my life. She is so easy to love and, despite being literally perfect, has never made me feel anything less than special. If it weren't for her, I think I would have been on the next flight back to Denver after that first disastrous day on the beach.

As we make our way down to the lobby, Ana lists off rom-com movies she wants to watch tonight, including *The Proposal* and *Crazy Rich Asians*. No disagreement here.

We're rounding the corner from the elevators to the lobby when my heart stops.

That blonde hair. That broad-shouldered frame, that obnoxious University of Chicago polo shirt.

In the half-of-a-second it takes for me to recognize Malcolm, I pull Ana back into the hallway with me and slam my back against the nearest wall, my breathing becoming fast and erratic. I need to get out of here. I need an escape. Now.

"Are you all right? What's wrong?" Ana asks. "You look like you've seen a bear or something."

Trust me, I would rather have seen a bear. I know how to handle a bear. Malcolm, on the other hand, is a far bigger problem.

When I don't speak, Ana looks over me to peek back into the lobby.

"What's going on? Do you know that guy?"

I know I should lie. I should keep quiet and pull myself together. But I just can't pretend. Not right now and not with Ana. So I nod. "It's him. It's my ex."

Her jaw drops, realization dawning on her face. "Your ex? The one we talked about? How? Why?"

I take a deep breath. Why *is* he here? Is this some sick coincidence? The universe's way of punishing me for even trying to get back on my feet? Endless possibilities flood my brain, but all I say is, "I don't know."

"Oh, no." Ana looks lost for words. "Jenni, this is not okay. We have to tell Niko. We can't have that guy here, around you. Niko will book him a room at another hotel. He'll take care of all of this."

"No."

Ana whirls to face me. Clearly, she doesn't understand the gravity of the situation. I can't tell Niko. There is absolutely no telling what he will think. I don't want him to picture me as a victim. Or worse, unprofessional. I can't put personal matters in the way of work.

"I just can't." Fear laces my words, but I can't make my mouth move, to explain to Ana what is at stake here. If I let Niko know about what happened, it could change his entire perception of me. I force myself to focus on breathing. My whole body is shaking now.

I want to cry. I want to punch a hole in the wall. I want to punch Malcolm in his smug face.

"He's coming," Ana whispers. "Act surprised."

She pulls me away from the wall, slips her arm through mine before laughing as if I said something hilarious. When Malcolm approaches, Ana attempts to ignore him with an air of superiority like only an heiress would. Unfortunately, Malcolm doesn't fall for those kinds of tricks.

"Jenni?" Malcolm sounds surprised, but his face tells a different story—the cold, calculating look in his eyes, the smirk on his lips. He's feeling something, but definitely not surprised. It gives me goose bumps.

I want to respond, but I'm completely frozen. Except for my eyes, that won't stop blinking. I'm positive he can see right through me and straight into my broken heart. He rubs his hands together smugly. I'm convinced he knows how much power he still has over me.

"Excuse me, but does my friend know you? Or are you some kind of creep?" Ana says with a "get lost" attitude. She looks him up and down with a disapproving grimace as she slips her hand into mine and gives it a reassuring squeeze.

Malcolm clears his throat and squares his shoulders, clearly thrown off by her comments. Only Ana could get away with calling someone a creep to his face. She doesn't seem remotely fazed by his demeanor or interested in backing down. If anything, she stands taller, waiting for Malcolm to make a move.

"Jenni and I used to work together," Malcolm tells Ana. Of course, that's what he would say. Still unwilling to admit to our relationship in front of anyone who might be important. Turning back to me, he asks, "How long has it been now?"

One year, six weeks, and three days. I can't tell if he is pretending not to know how long it's been or if he truly cares that little about everything that transpired the last time we saw each other.

"About six months," I finally say.

Before he can say anything else, Ana asks, "What are you doing here?"

Malcolm cocks his chin, a subtle movement that I wouldn't have even noticed if not for the years I spent watching for it. It's the move he makes any time he is about to hurt me.

"I'm here to meet with a client," he says nonchalantly. I stand, stunned while he turns to Ana. "I'm a partner at Prewitt Luxury Marketing. We're going to be taking over American marketing for this hotel. And who are you?"

She scowls. "You must be confused. My cousin is the general manager, and I know for a fact that he hasn't hired anyone. Jenni has been working with him for a week already, and it's all but official that her firm will be hired. You must only be here for a courtesy interview. I wouldn't get your hopes up."

Ana's words run right through me. She said so herself at the beach that she isn't involved in the business. I'm still stuck on what Malcolm said, though. If he's really here to pitch, with everything that his giant Chicago firm has to offer, I don't stand a chance.

"We'll see," he says, forming a condescending smile that used to make me bend to his every will. Now, it just makes me feel like I'm going to be sick. "So you're still in marketing then, Jen? I wasn't sure you'd stick with it."

I hate when he calls me Jen. And he knows that.

"I am," I say hesitantly. Ana squeezes my hand again. "I work for an agency that helps independent hotels and resorts. Most of our clients are high-end bed-and-breakfasts and spas in the US, but we're expanding into the international market."

My voice is shaky and way too high-pitched. I power through, trying to channel Ana's brazen attitude. "I didn't realize Prewitt Luxury was taking on smaller clients these days."

A look of uncertainty crosses Malcolm's face. And I revel in it. But it's gone in a flash.

"We aren't. I made a personal exception for this one."

The way he says it makes me feel like he knew I was here, and this "personal exception" has something to do with me. There is no benefit to him taking on a small client like the Omorfiá Hotel. Is he really here just to mess with me? He can't be. Malcolm would never go through all this trouble just to kick me when I'm down, would he? He already destroyed my life once. Why would he feel the need to do it again?

My stomach churns like I'm about to lose my dinner.

"How gracious of you," Ana declares, with an eye roll as big as Malcolm's ego. I need to stop this. As much as I want to hug her right now, antagonizing Malcolm won't end well. He has no tolerance for disrespect.

"It was nice seeing you, Malcolm, but we have to go."

This time, I put my arm through Ana's and pull her toward the front desk, leaving Malcolm behind us. I fight every urge to look back and gauge his reaction. I can't let him see that I care. I can't let him see how he is affecting me.

By the time we reach the desk, I'm practically catatonic. "Miss Jenni!" Alexander gasps. "Are you all right? What's wrong?"

I briefly look in his direction, acknowledging that I heard him. But I can't bring myself to answer. Ana steps in. "She's being overdramatic about the fact I'm making her watch a Ryan Gosling movie. She prefers Paul Rudd."

"I don't think I know who you are talking about. But I'm sure they are both wonderful people."

Ana laughs, and it brings me out of my daze for a minute. "Don't worry. You aren't missing much," I tell him.

"Alexander, dear, I had a courier drop off a package. Do you have it?" Ana asks.

"Yes, ma'am!"

Alexander collects a bag from under the desk and hands it to Ana. "You two have a lovely evening."

Once we're upstairs, I rush into the bathroom and deposit the contents of my stomach into the toilet, collapsing on the floor. Ana sits down next to me as another wave of nausea sends my head over the toilet again.

I feel like I'm ripping in two. I have spent so much time trying to put both my heart and career back together, and it has all been for nothing. I made one mistake and fell for the wrong guy when I was young and inexperienced. Everything since then has been one colossal punishment.

Just when I thought things were starting to get better, Malcolm shows back up. He's like a nasty parasite I can't get rid of, feeding on me until I have nothing left.

"I'm sorry," I gasp out between sobs. "You shouldn't have to see this. I'm okay."

"You have nothing to apologize for." She rubs my back. "I'm here. No matter what."

She runs warm water over a washcloth and hands it to me.

"Thank you," I say, after washing my face. "I don't know what I would have done without you down there."

She hugs me. "Of course, darling. I still think we should tell Niko. He would take care of it. I promise."

I lean into her. "I just can't. I'm sorry. I have to get through this on my own."

I have to pull myself together and fix this. I can't keep being a victim, over and over.

Though Ana sighs, I can tell she accepts my answer.

"Okay. It's your decision. I won't take away your autonomy. Just know that I am here for you, okay?"

We get up from the bathroom floor. "I know you are."

She grabs my hand. "And if he so much as looks at you wrong, I'll kick him in the ... in the *psoli*," Ana spits out the last word with such disgust that I take a step back.

"What in the world is a *psoli*?" I can't help but laugh.

"His penis. The translation is more like, ugly little pecker."

At that, I full-on snort, which makes Ana laugh, and then we both laugh until we cry.

I don't know how to navigate a world in which Malcolm is present in my life. When I left Chicago, it was supposed to be a new start. One where I could pretend he had never existed or was at least buried in the past. But now, he has crash-landed back into the present. And he has the potential to destroy everything again.

I don't know if I am strong enough to keep it all together.

Jenni: I know you're at rock climbing, but I need help. I can't sleep. Malcolm is here. Everything is falling apart. I've been shaking and ill all night. He's stealing the hotel from me. I know that sounds ridiculous, but he must have known I was here somehow. I'm feeling so paranoid. I can't do this. I need to come home. This was all such a mistake. I'm falling apart. Please call me.

Undo Send

Jenni: Sorry I haven't checked in. We've been sooo busy. Got back super late from dinner, and then I crashed (Alone. Because I know you'll ask). Just woke up to pee and thought I'd send you a text! I hope rock climbing is a blast tonight! Ok, love you! Give Sarah a hug for me!

Chapter 26

At my meeting with Niko the next day, I can barely focus on the presentation. My mind is too consumed with Malcolm.

I want to ask why there's another marketing firm here. I want to beg Niko to tell me it's all a huge misunderstanding. Except I can't do that without explaining my entire messed-up history. So instead, I pretend I know nothing and try to act as normal as possible.

I want to crawl in a hole and hide from the world. Only, I am supposed to be able to handle this, so I sit still.

I need this deal to work out, now more than ever. I can't lose to Malcolm, again.

As we go through each slide, I can't quell the small part of me that fears Niko might have brought Malcolm in because he has lost confidence in Aspen Sky. Has he lost confidence in me? It had to be Niko who called Malcolm, right? The general manager is the one in charge of hiring and planning.

I hate to think he did, but I'm struggling to come up with any other explanation.

"—magazines?"

What? My eyes dart to Niko across the wide conference

table from me. Amber was supposed to be on a video call with us, but she canceled last-minute.

I clearly haven't been paying attention. What did Niko ask me? Magazines? "Yes, magazines! We should definitely run advertisements in magazines."

"I meant to ask whether you have any editorial contacts? Isn't that the best way to get on those top ten lists and recommendations? You have to have connections—know someone who knows someone."

His smile wavers.

Connections.

"We're going to be taking over American marketing for this hotel." Malcolm has connections everywhere. His firm—my old firm —has a foot in the door at every publication and major website in the industry. We have a grand total of two. Aspen Sky can't compete with Prewitt Luxury. I can't compete with Malcolm.

"Sure. Amber used to work with the editor at *Passport Monthly* and has a friend at the website *European Vacations Now*. But we're developing more relationships every day. We will definitely work to get you at the top of any appropriate lists."

Not that any of that will do much good. Top ten lists and magazine awards are such an outdated form of marketing. No one pays attention to them outside of the industry. Real travelers aren't looking at those things. They want to see a hotel through video, hear its story, and most importantly, connect with its message. A multimedia piece by a travel writer featuring everything that makes the Omorfiá Hotel special would go so much farther than a line of text on page thirty-eight of a random magazine in a waiting room somewhere.

But that's not what Niko and his board seem to think. I have learned my lesson. My place is to listen and do what the higher-ups want. Malcolm made sure of that.

"Cool," Niko finally says.

I think I need to end things with Niko. Now that Malcolm

is here, I can't let this thing go any further. And I absolutely can't let Malcolm figure it out. There's no telling what he would do with that sort of information.

"Is there anything else you think I should prepare for the pitch on Monday?"

Niko ruffles through the pile of papers in front of him. "No, I think that's it. Good work."

I stand and start to gather my things.

"Okay, work time's over. Now, it's play time." Niko is around the conference table within a moment. He pulls me in for a kiss. I comply stiffly, and he notices immediately, letting me go. "I'm sorry. Was that incredibly cheesy? It was, wasn't it? I wouldn't want to kiss me after that line either."

I smile so I don't cry. He's so perfect. Why did it all have to turn out this way? Why is Malcolm ruining everything?

"You're fine, it's not that. I just can't switch my brain over that quickly. That's all."

"Understood. Can I take you out to dinner, then? Ease into it?"

This man knows how to woo me—with food. The only problem is I know that if I go to dinner, I won't be able to stop falling. I won't be able to put an end to our fling. But if I stay here at the hotel by myself, I'm afraid I'll spiral. I wish Ana were here.

"We should invite Ana," I say. If she's there as a buffer, dinner will be a lot more manageable.

Niko considers my suggestion. "Sure, that would be great. I'll send her a text."

I continue to pack up my things. I have no idea how to end this, but if Ana is there, at least things won't get out of control.

"In the meantime, would you want to go check out the party supplies I have stored downstairs? Alexander has gone home for the day, so we're in the clear."

"The ducks? Yeah. Of course I do."

My voice comes out a little too high-pitched, a little too desperate for something to focus on that isn't this thing between us. If Niko notices, he doesn't say anything. I will break things off after dinner. I'll tell him I don't want anything impacting the meeting and hope that he understands.

Once downstairs, we find ourselves knee-deep in party supplies. There are three giant inflatable rubber ducks for the pool, banners, strings of lights, and a plastic mini pool for a carnival-style game station. And my favorite: a huge wooden board with cutout circles for guests to put their faces through for pictures.

"You did all of this?" I ask, my eyes wide as I take it all in.

Niko turns over a to-be-inflated helium balloon. "I had a lot of help from Ana. I have actually been considering asking her to come work for me. I think she'd be fantastic as the hotel's event coordinator."

"Really? That's amazing. She'd be fantastic, and I know she'll be thrilled that you thought of her."

"I hope so." Niko grabs the photo board. "I think we need to test this out, though. I want to make sure I look good as a duck. Can you grab that tripod and bring it out into the hallway with me?"

He is so utterly unserious. It's my favorite thing about him.

Niko places the board on its stand in the hallway and then attaches his phone to the tripod. "Okay, I'm going to put my phone on self-timer mode. We'll have ten seconds to get into position ... Now!"

I scramble over, putting my face through the hole of the duck wearing a purple polka-dot bikini top over rounded breasts. She even has a book tucked under one wing. Niko fills the other cutout with a duck with a mohawk and an inner tube about its middle. I smile when the flashing light counts down.

Niko checks the photo. "Okay, it worked. But I think you

should give the camera a little more spunk. Your duck looks like she knows how to have fun."

He winks at me before .putting his phone back on the tripod. That wink, those golden wrinkles around his eyes—they make me melt. "I'll put it on continuous shutter every three seconds. Let's take a few more."

He bounds back to me, racing the camera. I make a duck face, straight out of the 2010s, and a laugh erupts from Niko as he climbs behind the board. *Click.* I try to look over at him and am still craning my neck when the next shutter goes off. I start laughing too.

We both make goofier and goofier faces until we are stopped dead in our tracks at the sight of two people coming around the corner from the front desk area. No one should be coming back here at this time.

My stomach drops when I realize it's Malcolm talking with an older Greek man. I scramble to get my face out of the duck. I go to turn around before he sees me. Niko, on the other hand, surprises me. He jumps up from where he is crouched in the photo board and clears his throat. "Dad?"

No. No, no, no. I spin around, desperate to get a bearing on what is happening. This guy is Niko's dad? The man with Malcolm?

"Niko," he responds. "I was hoping to catch you in your office. I'd like to introduce you to someone." He gives me a look of disdain as I step out from behind the photo board. "But perhaps you're busy."

"Dad, this is Jenni. She is from the marketing firm I told you about. The one I'm bringing in to run our marketing in the States."

This is quite possibly the most embarrassing thing that could be happening right now. Niko's dad just saw me sticking my tongue out with my head in the body of a bikini-clad duck.

How much worse could it get? I shrink back, as much as I can without completely disappearing behind Niko.

"Ah yes, you seem like you're … having fun." He spits out the word "fun" like he's disgusted by it. "Her proposal still needs board approval on Monday though, doesn't it? Or did I miss my own board meeting?"

His board meeting? Are you kidding me? Niko's dad is on the board? The same dad Niko has repeatedly told me understands nothing about the hotel or what he is trying to accomplish? He certainly never told me his dad was part of the board. I would have remembered something like that. Niko only ever referred to it as "the board" or the "board members." He never mentioned his dad.

And now that he is here with Malcolm? We're even more screwed than I thought. From what I know about Niko's dad, he is completely Malcolm's type.

"That should only be a formality," Niko says, none of the usual spark on his face.

Niko's dad adjusts his suit, as if he's in negotiations and not having a conversation with his son. "I know I told you you'd have free rein, but trust me, son, this is who you will want to work with in the end."

Malcolm steps forward as if being presented as some sort of hero. "Malcolm Prewitt of Prewitt Luxury Marketing." He puts his hand out toward Niko, who ignores it. Every inch of me warms at that. I might love this man. Even if I can't actually love him.

"I told you I didn't want him coming here. I told you to meet with him if you wanted, but that I didn't need to," Niko defends, crossing his arms over his chest. The phone call on the way home from the caves. He had been so upset on the phone with his dad that day.

"Look, it's not a big deal. Malcolm's father, Carlisle, has done the US marketing for our wineries for twenty years. I asked if he could take a look at the Omorfiá as a personal favor. Next thing I knew, Malcolm was volunteering for the job."

By now, I'm feeling like I really shouldn't be anywhere near this conversation. Both Psomas men have stiffened and reddened, seemingly in a standoff. I stare at my feet, wishing I could disappear.

"I have years of experience in luxury hotel marketing with properties much larger than this," Malcolm chimes in. "I'm sure you'll find that we have every resource you could possibly want and a team of associates willing to work around the clock to meet your needs."

Niko rubs his forehead, pushing his hair back. "I'm sure you do."

Niko barely takes his eyes off his father. I want to grab his hand and tell him it's okay. He doesn't need to defend me. All three men are staring at each other, digging in their feet.

"How about this?" Niko's dad finally breaks the silence. "On Monday, both of them can make their proposals and we'll vote—you, me, and the four other members of the board. Then we'll decide. But if you are ready to stop playing dress-up, or whatever this is, and take your hotel seriously, you should strongly consider my recommendation."

He turns away from us and our duck board.

"Malcolm, let's continue our tour."

"It was great to meet you," Malcolm says to Niko. "And, Jenni, it was nice to see you, too, as always."

The two of them walk back out toward the lobby, leaving Niko and me behind in silence. He turns around, making fists with both hands.

"Niko? Are you all right?"

"Yes," he says, without turning around. "I'm fine. He just always does this."

He takes a minute before turning around, and when he

does, his faces softens immediately. "You look like a ghost. Are you okay? It was wildly inappropriate for him to talk down about you like that. I'm so sorry."

His dad clearly has zero respect for me. I don't stand a chance on Monday. Niko starts pacing back and forth across the hallway. If he notices I haven't responded, he doesn't let on. I grab the tripod and then the photo board, putting them back in the closet to keep my hands busy.

"I mean, the nerve. To show up here, when I explicitly told him I didn't want to use one of his big flashy firms? And that guy? Are you kidding me? He looked like he was straight out of *Mad Men*."

I need to say something. It's starting to get weird that I haven't opened my mouth since we were laughing and taking pictures. "He does pride himself on first impressions …"

Niko stops and faces me. "Wait. He said it was nice to see you, 'as always.' Do you know him?"

Crap. Why did I remind him of that? There is no way this ends well.

"We've met. I was an intern at his firm a few years ago. We crossed paths a bit."

My head is spinning. I absolutely, resolutely cannot give him any more information about my past with Malcolm.

"That's so weird. What are the chances?" Niko's phone rings. "It's Ana. She must be ready. Should we go wait for her in the lobby?"

I realize this is my chance. The only one I'm going to have before things get any worse. Because now that I know Malcolm is here with Niko's dad—on special favor to the board—there is absolutely no way that I can be with Niko. It will only end badly, with Malcolm humiliating both of us.

"Actually Niko, we need to talk."

"What's up?"

I swallow, hard. This is going to be absolutely miserable. "I think I made a mistake the other day."

My words hang between us. Niko's face drops, but his eyes never leave mine, as if he is waiting for what he knows is coming. "I lost track of why I'm here. You are great, and I think what you are doing here is amazing. But I … I've made this mistake of getting involved at work before, and it didn't turn out so well. I need to remain professional—keep focused on the job at hand—so that we both get what we want."

Niko's eyebrows are pinched together, and for a second, I think his eyes are clouded with pain. Remorse, maybe? But just as quickly, he straightens, wiping all emotion from his face.

"Is this about last night? The second I introduced you to my dad's accountant, I regretted how I did it. I just kind of freaked out. My dad really rattles me. I didn't mean to make you feel like I was hiding this thing between us. I just didn't think he was a safe person to tell."

His words are rushed, like he is desperate for me to hear them all. Tears prick at the corners of my eyes. If only that was the problem.

"No, you didn't do anything wrong," I tell him. "I just need to focus. And I think it would be better for everyone involved if we don't go into that meeting on Monday as anything more than business associates. I don't want anyone to get the wrong impression and doubt our ability to work together."

Niko runs his hands through his hair, a look of sorrow crossing his face. My heart tightens as guilt washes over me. I don't want to hurt him. But when he straightens, the look is gone, replaced by one of surety.

"Of course. I understand. I don't know what I was think-ing. I'm so sorry if I made you feel taken advantage of. That was never my intention."

Ugh, even when I'm breaking things off with him he wants to make sure I'm okay. It's such a cruel joke that when I finally find a good man, circumstances completely beyond my control are keeping us apart.

"You didn't. I promise," I say. "I have no hard feelings. But … I should probably go. I hope you have a good dinner with Ana, and please talk to her about the job. She'll be happy."

Niko reaches out, as if not ready to let me go. "Wait, will I still see you at the party?"

Alexander's party. A kernel of sunshine in this complete disaster. The reminder that most people are good, even though I can't seem to shake the worst one.

"Yes. Wouldn't miss it for the world. I'll be there."

Piper: Hey hot shot! No updates tonight?
Miss you!

Chapter 27

I spent Saturday hiding from everyone. I never left my room. To his credit, Niko left me alone. Ana, on the other hand, stopped by my room a few times to check on me. I told her I was fine but had a lot of work to catch up on, which was true. It just wasn't the reason I couldn't get out of bed.

In similar fashion, I spent most of this morning debating whether I should attend Alexander's birthday party. I don't want any more accidental run-ins or problems. But I promised Niko I would be there, so I put on the only clean outfit I have left other than my suit for the board meeting tomorrow. I head to the pool in a white-and-lavender seersucker sundress and pray I'll be able to avoid Malcolm. There's no way he would want anything to do with the party. At least I have that on my side.

When I arrive, I'm awestruck. The party looks incredible, even better than I imagined. Ana and Niko are directing last-minute preparations when I sneak in with a group of arriving guests. Alexander is supposed to start his shift in ten minutes, after which someone will go to the front desk to report a duck prank at the pool. When Alexander arrives to investigate, we'll all yell "surprise" and send a replacement concierge to the front desk.

Excited energy crackles in the air as everyone waits for the big moment. But I feel more like I'm walking through water—trying to find excitement when the prevailing emotion I've felt for the last forty-eight hours is dread.

I walk around the pool deck, surveying the party. A giant banner reads "Happy Birthday, Alexander," and the pool is full of inflatable ducks and pool toys. To one side of the pool is a photo station, complete with the photo board Niko and I had played with in the hallway and a more glamorous photo back-drop with lighting and a photographer. On the far side of the pool, a giant balloon arch stretches over a handful of carnival games and prize boards.

I want to love it, to feel *something* other than the uneasiness in my gut, but I can't find the emotions I need. The party is so quirky and silly, even with all the glamour. However, the only the thing I can think about is how disturbed Niko's dad was by our photoshoot in the hotel hallway. That's going to be the only thing he sees when I stand up in the board meeting on Monday: a rubber duck with a purple polka-dot bikini. He's never going to take me seriously.

I turn away from the games and wander over to a tent filled with mountains of food: salads, fruit, pastries, and a gyro station where a chef waits to cut fresh slices of lamb from a rotating spit. It all looks amazing, and yet I have no appetite.

As if on cue, I hear Ana call my name. I turn to see her walking toward me in the most gorgeous bohemian-style yellow dress, her hair in a loose braid over her shoulder. "Jenni, I'm so glad to see you. Are you okay?"

When Ana wraps me in a hug, guilt sinks into my stomach, cold and heavy. If I tell her how badly I'm hurting right now, she'll try to convince me, again, to tell Niko what is going on. After the way he had reacted to Malcolm last night, the thought of telling him about my past feels excruciating. He would never understand. I have had too many people ask me how I ended up in a relationship with someone so awful. I have had too many people ask me why I didn't leave earlier or tell anyone what had been happening. I don't think I could handle that kind of judgment from Niko too.

"Oh, yeah," I say when she lets me go. "I'm feeling much better."

I'm no longer puking into my toilet, so I guess it's not a lie.

"Did Niko tell you? That sneaky, sneaky man!" She looks around as if wanting to slap him on the wrist. "He offered me a job! Doing events and community outreach!"

Ana squeals in excitement and gives me another hug, just in time for a hush to go over the crowd. Alexander must be on his way. Ana and I join the back of the crowd congregating on the pool deck. Within a minute, Alexander bursts through the doors of the hotel, a look of determination on his face. The crowd erupts in cheers, and he appears to melt, his hands rising to his mouth in shock. Niko shouts, "Happy birthday!" and claps Alexander on the back.

"What—what is all of this?"

"There was a little rumor going around the hotel that you have never had a birthday party," Niko replies. "We couldn't let that continue."

"All of this for me? For me?" Alexander takes in the party, looking like he might cry. Then he bursts into laughter and turns on Niko. "The ducks! You! You are the one with the ducks!"

Niko puts his hands up in the air. "Guilty as charged. Now let's party!"

With the crowd cheering again, Niko and Alexander get swept up in people wanting to wish happy birthday to the man of the hour. It's so full of joy.

Ana squeezes my hand. "Should we go say hi?"

Niko and Alexander are moving in our general direction, both looking like the sun is shining just for them. Niko's hair is relaxed, and he has a five-o'clock shadow I haven't seen on him before. All I want is for that smile to land in my direction. I crave it. Except I'm not ready to face him. I feel dizzy just thinking about it.

"Actually, I need to run to the bathroom," I tell Ana. "I'll be right back."

I sneak past the crowd and into the hotel, looking for the nearest restroom. I just need a minute to collect myself, to throw some cold water on my face.

I cross the hallway from the pool door and head toward the exercise suite. There's a changing room in there, and I'm willing to bet it has a bathroom.

"Hey, Jen! Slow down."

The voice sounds like nails on a chalkboard, just like it does when it's in my head. I turn. Malcom has caught up to me in the hallway. I'm too drained to panic the way I did the last two times I saw him. Now all I feel is akin to defeat.

"Can you please just leave me alone? No one here knows about us, and I'd like to keep it that way."

"Whoa, whoa, I'm not looking to fight," he says. "I just wanted to thank you."

What does that mean? Thank me for what?

"If you hadn't posted on Instagram about your trip, I wouldn't have recognized this hotel when it came up in a planning meeting. Dad was planning to pass it off to an associate. I told him I would take it as a favor to Dimitri. Like he said, he's been a client for years. My family vacations at his vineyards every year. Don't you remember?"

I can hear my pulse pounding in my ears. I remember my second summer internship at Prewitt Luxury. Malcolm and I had been on-and-off for a year, and I was ready to break things off. But then he said he would tell his family about us and make it official. He said he would bring me on the family trip to Greece. But at the last minute, he told me it wasn't going to work out. He hadn't told his family and it wasn't a good timing. I had my bags packed and everything. He left without me.

That was a Psomas winery? And the one he went to last fall with his now-fiancée? How had I missed this so completely? How had I missed the connection?

But Malcolm didn't. Because that's the way his mind works —always finding some opportunity to manipulate and control. I should have seen this coming.

"You knew I was here, and you came anyway?"

"Dimitri was thrilled at the prospect. He thinks this hotel is just the start of a catalog of properties across Greece, maybe even into Italy. He just wants his son to be successful. You understand."

I feel weak, as if blood is draining out of my body. Malcolm did *all* of this. On purpose. He knew I was here, and he sought Niko out as a client because of it.

"Why?" I whisper, unsure if I really want the answer. "Why did you do all of this? Just to hurt me?"

"No. Absolutely not. I'm devastated you would think that."

Give me a break. Malcolm is the king of turning everything back around to favor himself—make it look like he's the victim. I shake my head, fighting off tears, fighting for words.

"I'm a director now, and I need to start building my own portfolio of clients. I saw an incredible opportunity, and I had to take it. That's just business. It's nothing personal."

I want to scream. *Just because you want a client, you think it's okay to steal them from me? After everything else you have done to ruin my career? That's not personal?*

I don't have it in me to start that fight. I never won an argument when we were together, and I'm not going to win this one.

"Fine. Whatever. What do you want from me?"

"Jen, come on." Malcolm's words drip with condescension, as if I'm crazy to think he would be anything less than cordial. "Can't we be friends? Just because we broke up doesn't mean there has to be any animosity."

I roll my eyes. Malcolm has always been a bit delusional, but this is just too much. "Do you really think I want to be friends with you? Please, just leave me alone."

I try to turn toward the bathroom, but Malcolm puts a hand on my arm, turning me back toward him. I brace myself, ready to push him away, but he throws his hands in the air, feigning innocence.

"I'll admit that mistakes were made, by both of us," he says, with emphasis on the word "both." Heat blooms across my cheeks. I am not proud of the way I acted toward the end of that relationship. We had some pretty big fights, and I was so desperate to defend myself and prove that the manipulation wasn't just in my head that I said and did some pretty ugly things.

"And I'm really sorry about that," Malcolm continues, motioning for me to take a seat on a nearby bench. I sit, but only because if I do what he says, this will be over faster.

"I think you should come back to Chicago, back to your old job. It was a mistake to fire you like that."

I laugh out loud. It's an angry shell of a laugh. That is honestly the last thing I expected him to say. In fact, I would have been less surprised if he had told me he was buying me a house.

"At Prewitt Luxury? Working with you? Are you kidding?"

"No, I'm not." Malcolm acts hurt I would even suggest it. "I tried to fix things as soon as I got back to the office. I was going to tell everyone it was a misunderstanding. I had just been trying to save face in front of the client. But you were already gone. You ran away before the dust could settle."

He's right. It has been my biggest regret. For months afterward, I had lain awake at night thinking of other ways I could have handled the situation. I knew he couldn't just fire me like that. I could have gone to HR and asked for a performance improvement plan or to be moved to a different management team. I didn't, though. I just ran away. I should have stuck it out in Chicago until I found another job. I should have told someone about our relationship and how Malcolm mistreated me. Desperation and fear kept me silent. It felt like people would have taken Malcolm's side anywhere I turned.

I stare at the wall, not daring to consider what he's offering.

"You're far too talented and smart to be an assistant at some tiny, play-pretend agency." Malcolm inches closer to me. "You deserve better than that."

So he knows I'm just an assistant? What did he do, call Amber and snoop around? I wouldn't put it past him. I hate myself for feeling some tiny validation in his words, even though I know it's all part of some game he's playing.

"It's a terrible idea for us to work together again."

"I know what you're afraid of. I really do," Malcolm says, grimacing. He puts his head in his hands and groans in regret. "I threw you under the bus a few times, but I was under so much pressure to make director that I was desperate. It would be different now. We can start over. You don't even have to work directly under me. I can get you a spot anywhere in the firm."

I laugh. Does he really think I'm going to fall for this? I want my old life back, but not this way—not by his hand.

"Jen, you and I both know the board is never going to choose your agency over my firm. It's simply a matter of experience and resources."

He puts his hand on mine, and I flinch, but Malcolm pulls away immediately, acting like he doesn't understand my aversion to his touch.

I don't respond. I'm not considering the job. If I had to

bet, there is no job. He'll have some excuse when push comes to shove. But what he said about the board meeting cuts like a knife, because he's right. Who, in their right mind, would choose me over Malcolm?

"All I have to do is make one call, and we could get you signed on as a senior associate."

I stare at the floor, not speaking.

"I know it's a lot to consider," Malcolm says. "Just let me know, okay? Preferably before the meeting, so we don't waste anyone's time tomorrow."

Malcolm walks away, knowing he has sufficiently shredded any confidence I had left. I don't know what I was thinking, hoping I still had any sort of shot of making this work. The only way this ends is in humiliation.

Chapter 28

I need to get out of here. I need space to breathe. I make my way through the lobby in a blur. I don't know where I'm going. I just know I need to be anywhere but here.

Once outside, I remember the complimentary bikes Niko mentioned on our tour. I need a bike ride. Riding will help me think. I find the rack and tap my room key to unlock a bike. I don't want Ana or Niko to come looking for me, so I text them I'm not feeling well, and I went back to my room. Hopefully, they are too busy with the party to check their phones.

I take off cycling up the hill. I need to feel the burn in my calves and quads. I need physical sensations that match the emotional turmoil inside my body. Like that will somehow help get rid of it. Or at the very least, satisfy the part of me that hates myself for getting into this mess.

I know Malcolm's offer isn't real. I know I could never go back there even if it was. But the conversation reminded me of how far away my dreams really are. They feel so incredibly impossible. I'll never convince the board to choose me over Malcolm. I'll let Amber down. I'll never get the promotion or find a new job. It all just feels so incredibly impossible and out of reach.

I should just give up now.

Once I pass resorts and restaurants, I find myself on a long stretch of road without much in sight other than industrial warehouses. My breath is coming sharp and painful. I'm getting a side stitch right between my ribs, but I don't want to stop. Not here, where I don't recognize anything, and it's clearly not a touristy part of town. I force myself to keep going.

Finally, I see an air traffic control tower. I'm by the airport. I pull over and lean my bike against a chain-link fence separating the road from the runway and try to orient myself. If I can get to the front of the airport, I should be able to cycle back down toward the coast and end up somewhere in the old town, near the windmills. I think.

As I fully take in my surroundings, I realize I'm completely turned around. If I make the wrong choice, I could end up on the wrong side of the island with no idea where I am or how to get back.

I could turn my phone on and use the map app, but at this point, I'm sure Ana and Niko have noticed I never came back to the party, and I don't want to see any messages or phone calls from them. Or Piper and Amber, for that matter. I cannot talk to either of them right now. Not when I'm on the brink of completely losing the deal. Amber will never forgive me.

Sweat drips down my forehead. The afternoon heat is making me wish I had some water or had thought to put sunscreen on for the party because my skin is feeling toasty. The old part of town is west of the airport, which I'm pretty sure is to the left from this vantage point. I'll just have to keep heading that direction.

I can't shake the feeling that if I continue to pursue this deal, only bad things are going to happen. I thought I was finally getting myself back on the right path. I really thought I was going to be able to do it. That's all gone now. It's all been taken away. I'll never win this contract. I don't have what it takes.

What hurts the most is that, despite all of the ups and downs I've experienced this week, it's been amazing to be doing "the thing" again. After all this time, I wasn't sure I could do it anymore, like maybe I hadn't been very good at marketing and Malcolm had been right to fire me. But being here, working with Niko, lit that spark again. And it was all for nothing. No matter what I do, I'll end up back in Colorado in my same job, in my same bedroom, seeking out the same job interviews that won't go anywhere. Even if Amber doesn't hate me for losing the client, she won't have the budget to promote me without this revenue.

I might as well leave and save myself the humiliation of even trying.

After about twenty minutes have gone by since leaving the airport, I realize I haven't seen anything resembling the old town yet. Have I ventured too far north? Too far south? I'm turned around thanks to the winding roads. I stop my bike at what looks like some sort of school. It's a Sunday afternoon, so not many people are around, but I spot a few teenage boys hanging around out front.

"Excuse me, do you speak English?"

They look at each other before responding. *"Ti? Ti eípate? Óchi angliká."*

I guess not. How am I going to get through to them? "Sorry. Windmills? How can I get to the windmills?"

I wave my hands in a big circle in the air, trying to imitate a windmill. The boys point and laugh. Lovely. I start to walk my bike back to the road. This was no help. No help at all.

"Stási!" I turn to find one of the boys chasing me down. *"Eísai tourístas? Oi várkes eínai ekeí káto."*

He points at the main road and gestures to the right. Did

he say tourist? He understood me! I repeat his gestures. "Down the road and to the right?"

"*Naí!* Yes!" He nods enthusiastically.

"Thank you, thank you!"

He's already turning back to his friends, who are still pointing and laughing. Apparently, a lost hot mess of a tourist is comedic gold.

I follow his directions, but when I reach the coast, there are no windmills or Little Venice in sight. I'm at a commercial port. Two ferries sit at the closest dock, waiting to carry cars and people to other islands or the mainland. And in the distance, a giant cruise ship looms over the port. *Tourists.* The boys must have thought I was from a cruise ship.

I have no idea where the port is in relation to the Omorfiá Hotel.

Everywhere I look there are security gates, busy roads, and dusty parking lots. I pull over in the parking lot of a rental car company and sit on the wheel stop in an empty space. I peel off my sandals, bloody blisters covering the back of my heels.

I'm lost, bleeding, exhausted, sunburnt, and filthy. And I'm no closer to figuring out what I'm going to do.

I give up and turn on my phone, hoping I have enough service to pull up the map and find my way back. My phone pings the second it lights up, filling the screen with messages and missed calls. Piper. Ana. Niko. An unknown number. I swipe away all the notifications just as a car pulls up.

I jump up and drag the bike out of the way, but the basket gets caught on the wheel stop. I yank the bike again, but it screeches. I look up, flustered, to wave an apology that I'm taking so long. But's not a random car. Sophia smiles back at me from the driver's seat, her eyes sympathetic. What is she doing here? I drop the bike and stand, confused.

The car door opens and Niko steps out. I don't know

whether I'm relieved he's here to save me, yet again, or terrified he'll figure out why I was running.

"Jenni," he cries, rushing over to me. "Are you okay?"

He grabs my elbows and looks me up and down. Worry lines on his forehead quickly morph into a look of relief when he sees I'm not physically harmed.

"What are you doing here? How did you find me?" I literally just turned my phone on. I hadn't even called anyone for help yet.

"Ana told me you weren't feeling well, so I came to check on you. When you weren't in your room, we got worried. We tried calling you and searched the hotel, but we couldn't find you anywhere. Then I noticed a bike was gone and the key log showed you had checked it out. The bikes all have GPS devices on them in case guests leave them somewhere around the island."

"Oh … that makes sense." I shake my head. I should have suspected something like that. Guilt tears at me. My leaving disrupted the party. Niko should be there, enjoying himself. I really screwed up. "I'm fine. Are you okay?"

He looks so worried—scared, even. His hair is a mess, and his clothes are askew in a haphazard way I've never seen on him before.

"Ana saw that guy Malcolm lurking around the lobby, and I don't know, I just got this really terrible feeling that he had said or done something. I just can't stand that guy."

Niko squeezes his hand into a fist, probably without even realizing it. How did he know? How did this amazing man know who he needed to protect me from? I want to cry. I want to lean into him and let him make everything better.

But letting Niko take care of me won't fix anything. It won't fix the fact that I'm losing this client. It won't fix that my life is still in pieces.

"We talked … He wanted to catch up, but—"

"Wait." Niko reaches a hand out, stopping before I can say anything else about what happened. "If you're not sick, then why did you leave the party? What happened?"

He swallows, his eyes pleading with me to open up to him.

I don't have an answer for him. What can I say? "I ... I don't know. I just needed a ride."

He looks confused and hurt, as if he knows I'm not telling him everything.

I really didn't think leaving would be a big deal. I thought they would just forget about me and have fun. But the look in his eyes stings like a thousand paper cuts to my heart.

"I didn't think it would matter to you," I admit, before dropping my gaze to my bare feet.

"Of course you matter to me, Jenni! How can you say that? What have I done since the moment we met that gave you the impression I don't care? Since the day you arrived and swept me off my feet, I have wanted nothing but to make you smile. You have no idea what your smile does to me. And when you asked for space, I gave it to you—even if it killed me to let you go. That's how much I care."

None of the things coming out of his mouth make sense. In what world did he think anything would ever work between us? He's ripping me apart with false hope, throwing reality out to sea.

"What did you think was going to happen, Niko? That I was going to pick up and move and we would live happily ever after in Greece? That could never happen for a hundred different reasons. I don't understand what you want from me."

His shoulders crumple with the weight of my words. Hurting him is the last thing I want to do, but maybe it's better this way. Maybe he shouldn't want me. He could move on and forget this week ever happened. He'll be better off for it.

"I don't *want* anything, Jenni. I understand all of that. I don't expect you to drop your life for me. I don't know how any of it would work. We can't date like normal people, and I know working together might be weird, but I just … I feel something different with you, and when I think about not having you in my life, it feels cold and empty." He grabs my hands. "I want to do whatever I can to have you in my life, no matter how that looks."

He sucks in a breath, waiting for me to say something.

"Well, maybe you shouldn't." I don't deserve it. If he even knew half of the truth about me—if he knew this person he finds to be so confident and excited about life is really a fake—he would never have said what he did.

"What is that supposed to mean?" Niko looks sick, like I've punched him straight in the gut.

"We barely just met. You don't know anything about me. You shouldn't be risking your business, your relationship with your father, your heart, or anything else on me. What if I have no idea what I'm doing? What if Prewitt Luxury could triple your revenue and expand the hotel—give you everything you've ever wanted? They are great at what they do, but you don't even want to hear them out because of me? You shouldn't do that, Niko. This was just a fling. Nothing more."

The words feel like acid coming out of my mouth. But I've said them, and I can't take them back. It would be foolish not to consider what Malcolm has to offer him. I'm not worth it.

"Everything I've ever wanted? According to who? I told you I don't want any of that. I don't want my father's life, where business is more important than the people around me. I thought you understood that." He takes a step back. "It's starting to sound like you don't want anything to do with me or the hotel."

I stand still, waiting for tears to run down my face because nothing rips my heart out more than him thinking that. Nothing feels worse than him thinking I don't care.

My body betrays my heart, and the tears don't come. The

moment for fixing all this passes, and I'm too frozen to reach out and seize it.

"Well?" Niko asks. "Do you?"

"I …" This is all moving too quickly. Why can't I just tell Niko that I feel the same way and we'll figure it out? Something broke in me last year and, as much as I want to let him fix me, I can't. I can't make the words come out of my mouth even as my heart shatters.

"Well, I think that's my answer." Niko turns and looks up at the sky, his face buried in his hands. His heart is breaking too. Another casualty of my messed-up life.

"That's not what I meant," I say, desperate for a pause button to make time stop moving so damn quickly. "There's just …"

My voice catches in my throat. I still can't tell him about Malcolm. I can't bear to open that trauma to him, to expose myself and lay everything out there.

"No, it's fine," Niko protests, turning back to me but refusing to make eye contact. "I understand. Look, Sophia can take you back to the hotel. Your feet look like they hurt. I'll take the bike. The hotel room is yours as long as you need it. If you want to bow out of the meeting tomorrow, I won't stop you."

I can't think of anything to say to undo this. I'm not even sure I should. So I walk past Niko toward the car, dangerously close to breaking into tears.

When I've opened the door, he calls to me, his voice damp with emotion. "Jenni? I just want to say I'm sorry. I don't regret anything, but I'm sorry for the mess I caused."

"I'm sorry, too." My voice is weak and pathetic. I know if I say anything else, it will only hurt him more. I climb into the backseat of Sophia's car. Niko sits on the ground next to the bike, his face in his hands.

Sophia pulls away. "I won't pretend to know what any of

that was about, but I'm sorry," Sophia says when I pull my gaze from the window. "He'll be okay. You both will. Life is very long, and everything works out in the end."

She gives me a gentle smile, and I wish I could respond. But I'm empty and my eyes are still dry, though I ache for a release of the grief coursing through me.

"Sophia, would you be able to take me to the airport after I grab my bags?"

"Of course, dear."

Chapter 29

I book a ticket on the next flight to Athens, wanting nothing more than to get off this island. It cost more than I make in a week, but I don't even care. Breaking Niko's heart like that made my decision final. I can't go through with the meeting. Not after that. I don't know what I'll tell Amber, but I guess it won't matter either way. If she fires me, it's not like I haven't been at rock bottom before.

I'm sitting at the airport waiting for my flight and all I can think about is the look on Malcolm's face when he first arrived. That self-satisfied look that everything was going to go his way. I still wasn't strong enough to prove him wrong in the end.

I grab my phone to email Amber, just to get it over with. I tell her I've had a personal emergency and won't be able to attend the board meeting on Monday. I don't want to drag this out any further than I need to. I'm sure she's going to flip out when she reads it, but I don't know how else to break it to her.

Honestly, nothing she can say will make me feel worse than I already do. I keep replaying the moment Niko realized I was trying to back out. He looked so betrayed, so devastated. I know the feeling of betrayal so well that I'm furious with myself for having put that look on someone else's face. Every time Malcolm betrayed me, every time he pretended we weren't together, every time he acted like I was no one of importance, all the way up until he told me to leave that final meeting in Chicago without an ounce of sorrow on his face.

And now I've done that to Niko. I walked away, leaving him to feel confused and alone. His gray eyes, streaked red with pain—begging me to explain, to give some sort of reason that would make sense. But I couldn't. Not in any way that would help him feel better.

It's haunting me, pulling at the very fabric of my heart, unraveling all my resolve not to fall in love. Not to care too much. Not to let my feelings for Niko get in the way of fixing my career.

THE FLIGHT GOES by in a blur. Shortly after landing in Athens, I turn my phone on, but there aren't any new messages. Amber doesn't usually check her emails on Sundays. Or at least, not every five minutes.

I also notice, not surprisingly, that there aren't any messages from Niko. I don't know why there would be after the way I treated him, but I still yearn for contact.

I could take it all back and start over. But I think I've hurt Niko enough that he won't think twice about moving on without me.

My mind is in a distant haze as I walk to baggage claim. Once I've got my bag, I need to head to the ticket counter for a flight back to Denver. When I left Mykonos, I only thought one step ahead. I don't have a flight to the US, a hotel or anything else figured out. I am completely winging it.

I find the ticket counter, but there isn't a single person in sight. I sag when I see it's almost 10:00 p.m. I didn't even think about the ticket counter being closed since all of the flights are done for the day.

I find a bench to drop my suitcases and collapse. This whole day has felt like a lifetime. Everything has changed.

I pull out my phone and open the airline app to search for a morning flight. Monday must be a hot travel day because nothing is coming up except $10,000-plus business class tickets. Even if I was that desperate to get out of here, my credit card would decline.

I need to talk to a living human who can help me. A glance back at the ticket counter, which is now totally dark. Something tells me that won't happen any time soon.

My phone rings, and the caller ID announces that it's Amber. I can't answer right now. Not yet. I send her to voice-mail for only the second time ever. I need to figure out how I'm getting out of here before I have that conversation.

I wander the airport, my feet as aimless as my thoughts. Should I get a hotel? I don't want to worry about a taxi or waste any time before figuring out how I'm going to get home. My phone pings with a text from Amber, but I'm too scared to look at it. Eventually, I wander back to my bench. I'm sure I won't be able to sleep tonight, no matter how exhausted I am, so I decide to make the bench home until morning. I pull out a sweatshirt and my neck pillow to try to get comfortable. And finally, the tears flow—mourning everything that has gone wrong.

Hours pass and I drift in and out of semi-sleep, never able to fully shut down. During one of those waking periods, I hear a loud buzzing that has me jumping up, hoping someone is here to open the ticket counter. When I don't see anyone, I realize it's my phone vibrating against the metal bench. Piper is calling. I debate not answering, but I need my best friend.

"Jenni, are you okay?" Piper asks in a rush. "Amber called me worried about you and when I checked your location, I saw that you're in Athens? Why aren't you in Mykonos? What happened?"

"No, I'm not okay," I finally sob into the phone. "I think I really messed up. I don't know what to do."

"Okay, slow down. Tell me what happened. But first, are you physically okay? Are you safe?"

"Yes, yes, I'm okay," I say through tears.

I tell Piper everything. From that first night I saw Malcolm in the lobby up until getting stranded at the airport earlier tonight. The entire time, I'm barely holding on, afraid she is going to judge me for all my obvious mistakes. I should have done everything so differently.

"Oh, girl, that just plain sucks."

I laugh through my tears. "Yeah, my thoughts exactly."

"I only have one question. Why do you care at all that Malcolm is there? I know he represents a lot of trauma, and you should never have to be in a room with him if you don't want to, but I also know that you are just as worthy of being there as he is. You shouldn't have to back down."

"I … He just represents so much—everything I've lost, everything I want to get back but can't. He has all the power. When he showed up just as I was succeeding, it felt like a giant slap in the face. I can never get my life back because he is always standing in the way."

"I know you have *said* you want that life back. But honestly, Jenni, you weren't very happy in Chicago. Think about it. Is that really what you still want?"

I'm taken aback by her words. What does she mean I wasn't happy? Of course I was. I was living out my dreams. I was working so hard. I didn't have time for anything else, but that's normal. No one has time for life when they work in the corporate world. In Chicago, it was only ever work. That was what was expected of me, and I was proud to do it. But Piper's right. I never laughed.

Not like I have this past week, anyway.

"I thought I was."

"Do you want to know what I think?" Piper asks. "I think you were so focused on your dream that you never stopped to figure out if it turned out the way you expected, if you actually loved it. And I think your grief over losing it has taken up so much of your mental energy that you still haven't stopped and thought about whether you still want that life. Does it really make you happy?"

I have wanted a big corporate job since I knew that sort of thing existed. It always seemed so glamorous, so powerful. Except, once I found myself there, I had no time for real relationships, friends, hiking, or doing anything that wasn't bending over backward for bosses and clients. Honestly, I have felt more alive since moving home to Colorado than I ever did in Chicago. Even with all the regret, grief, and resentment, I was doing things I loved again.

What if I was pretending to be happy because I didn't want to admit that the dream I had chased my whole life wasn't what I pictured? I think I fooled even myself.

"I don't think I was happy," I say in defeat. What was the whole point? What do I do now?

"Ding, ding, ding!" Piper sings on the other end of the phone. "You were chasing that dream so long that you lost yourself somewhere along the way."

"What do you mean?"

"You started following Malcolm and only Malcolm. Every client, every director you worked for—everyone you associated with had to be approved by Malcolm. You didn't do *anything* without worrying what he thought. I think you're still doing it."

No, that can't be true. Yes, I was always a bit afraid of his reactions to things, but I didn't live my entire life around that. Did I?

"But I left. Malcolm hasn't been my boss for a long time."

"And yet, you still hear his voice in your head any time you have a decision to make. Don't you?"

I don't answer. It feels unfair of her to weaponize that information. I told her that in one of my darkest hours, when I needed someone to understand, not so that she could use it against me.

"I'm sorry. I know that's really harsh, but Jenni, Malcolm is *not* the guidepost of your life. He is not leading you up the mountain. Malcolm leads you straight off the cliff. Or better yet, he is nothing but a blip on the trail map, a fallen tree you have to climb over. But you? You are the waterfall. You are the summit. *You* are the person who can get through every obstacle thrown at you. You just have to stop living your life for someone else."

My throat feels drier the more she talks. Is this all true?

"Tell me you've been desperate to get your old life back because it's actually what you want. Or tell me it's because you want to prove yourself to Malcolm. Tell me which is true."

"I do *not* care about proving myself to Malcolm. I hate him. I have spent the last six months running from him—trying to forget that part of my life."

"And yet, what was one of the first things you said when you got this assignment?"

I rack my brain. "That I didn't want to get mugged?"

"No, you said, and I quote, 'I could prove him wrong.'"

"I did not."

"You did! You said it under your breath, and you thought you tricked me into believing it was about someone else, but I knew."

"Okay, and so what? If you had been through what I've been through … you have no idea what it feels like to have your whole world taken from you."

"You're right. I don't. And I definitely don't know what it's like to live in the type of relationship you were in with

Malcolm for years. What I do know is I've watched you wither away, and then come back to life over the last few months, especially the last two weeks. And I really, really don't want to see you fade to black-and-white again. It will break my heart."

"What is there left for me? I've ruined everything."

My job at Aspen Sky. Niko. I've lost it all.

"You haven't lost anything, hon. Amber is worried sick about you. She's not firing you. And you have us. Starting over is not the end of the world. There are a million futures for you out there. This could be your chance to find a new dream you actually love, rather than continuing to chase one just to prove you can do it."

Wait, Amber is worried about me? She wasn't calling to yell and scream? I quickly check my text messages and, sure enough, she told me not to worry about the meeting and that we'll figure it out. She wants me to let her know what I need and to know if I'm okay.

The contrast between her response and what happened to me in Chicago practically brings me to my knees.

Is Piper right? Could I let go of my corporate dream and find another, better life?

I have a job with people I like and a boss who is not only excited to give me opportunities, but who is worried about me when something goes wrong. I have friends who have never deserted me despite pushing them away for years.

I met a man who is kind and wants me for who I am, not because he can control me.

I live in my parents' house, and my job looks different from what I thought it would. Who cares? Am I still so desperate for Malcolm's approval that I've never seen all the positives of my life? Have I thrown all that away because of it?

"It's too late." My voice cracks as I softly admit defeat. "I ran away. I can't believe I did this again."

I'm completely numb. Unable to even process what to do next.

"No, you haven't. There's always time—always another chance. We're going to get this figured out. You just have to decide what you want. Do you want to come home and move forward, or do you want to fix things with Niko and go from there?"

How? How do I fix this? It seems impossible without ripping open every wound and begging forgiveness from people who owe me nothing: Niko, Ana, even Alexander.

"I don't know if I can."

"You can. But you have to choose to do it. I know it feels like there are too many obstacles, but the biggest one is not believing yourself. You can change that."

Tears stream down my cheeks. I inhale a deep breath. "I'll think about it."

"Let me know when you figure it out. Either way, I'm here for you."

I try to lie back down, only to toss and turn for the rest of the early morning hours. By the time the lights turn on at the ticket counter, I know what I'm going to do.

Chapter 30

I gather my things and make my way over to the ticket counter now that a lone woman is starting up the computers and setting up the desks.

Since I can't find anything to book online, I'm hoping she can help me find an open seat on a flight that leaves as soon as possible. I'd take anything right now. I stand at the counter for a few moments before she bothers to acknowledge me.

"We're not open yet. You can't check in until two hours before your flight."

No. I need her to help me. Right now.

"I'm not actually booked on a flight. I need to buy a ticket. I've been trying to do it online, but nothing is coming up in the app. Can you check the flights for me? Please? I really need to get somewhere. It's an emergency."

She looks at her computer for a moment and I can tell she's not looking at flights because I didn't even tell her which airport. My hands shake as I wait for her to respond.

"Can you help?" I press, not bothering to hide the desperation in my voice.

"Nothing on my computer will be any different from your phone. If no seats are coming up, there are no seats."

That's what I was afraid of. "Okay, thanks anyway."

I take a few steps back from the counter and go to pull up a search engine on my phone. There has to be a boat or an airline that doesn't show up on my flight app. There has to be a way to get back to Mykonos and fix this.

After a few airline ads, the very first search result is a ferry. It's a car ferry and as I read more on the website I realize it's a slow, almost day-long trip. That will never work. I have to be back on the island by noon.

The next search result looks like a high-speed boat from what I can tell. I tap on the link and wait for the website to crawl to life. Of course, once it loads, I realize the website is in Greek.

I look around the airport, which is starting to fill up with the day's travelers. Everyone seems in a rush. I need someone to help me, and fast. Searching the large hall, my eyes land on a woman who is sitting, feeding grapes to a young child in her lap.

"Excuse me? Do you speak English?"

She nods and sets her toddler on the bench next to her.

"Can you help me? I'm trying to book a ferry to Mykonos and the website is in Greek. It would take me forever to try to and translate. I was hoping you could help me book a ticket?"

She gives me a quizzical look. "You're not flying?"

"Well, no. There aren't any flights."

Something about the way she looks at me with kindness, makes me spill everything. "I just ran away from the most perfect man in Mykonos out of fear—and I need to go back to him. Fast. I've already checked flights, and nothing can get me there before tomorrow, so I think that leaves me with the ferry as my only option."

The woman nods, a knowing glint in her eye as if she, too,

has gone to desperate measures to get to a person she loves. She grabs my phone.

After a series of tapping and typing, she smiles. "There's a high-speed ferry in two hours. It can get you to the island around eleven in the morning. There's also a slow boat in three hours that won't get there until evening."

Two hours? Can I make that?

"How far is the port from here?"

"Maybe one hour or so? You can make it if you leave straight away. Good luck!"

I thank her profusely and start running toward the exit that reads TAXI.

When I find a cab, I open the door and start to climb in. "Piraeus Port, please! I'm in a hurry!"

"Too far, sorry," responds the driver, stopping me in my tracks.

"Too far?" Seriously? Why do the transportation gods have it out for me today?

"My shift is over soon. I just want to get home to my family," he says with a shrug. "Look, there is a bus right there. It will go straight to the port and save you seventy euros."

The bus is at the other end of a long curbside, and I have no idea how long it will wait. I sling my backpack over my shoulder, grab my suitcase, and start running again, my sandals slapping against the pavement. I'm sure I look ridiculous. But for once, I don't care. I know what I want and going for it feels intoxicating.

I reach the bus just as the doors are closing. No, no, no. I bang on the doors.

"Please! Wait!"

The hydraulics sound on the bus, and my heart drops. You have to be kidding me. Then doors open.

"Thank you! Thank you! I thought you were going to leave

me." I hoist my suitcase up the stairs to the driver. "You have no idea how much I needed this."

"Calm down, lady. We aren't leaving for five minutes." He gestures to an overhead ticker board that has our departure time listed. "Oh, sorry." I pay for my ticket. "Do you think we'll reach the port by eight-thirty? I'm trying to catch a ferry."

"Everyone's trying to catch a ferry," he grumbles back.

Sufficiently humbled, I find an empty row halfway back. I take the window seat and pull my suitcase in from the aisle. I'm sweating and panting, but I made it.

I text Piper.

> Jenni: On a bus. Headed toward the port to take a ferry to Mykonos. Can you text Amber and let her know I'm taking care of everything?

> Piper: I will take care of Amber. And cool re: the ferry. You little world traveler.

> Jenni: Well, let's hope it actually gets me there on time. Wish me luck because I'm going to need it. I have to convince everyone that I deserve a second chance.

> Piper: All my fingers are crossed. I'm so proud of you.

I settle in as the bus starts its journey. What do I do now? They never show this part in movies—the waiting part. They just show someone bolting off and then two minutes later, tracking down their loved one, panting and sweaty as if they've crossed all of Manhattan by foot during one Coldplay song. But that's not really how it happens, is it? I have to sit here, second-guess myself, and imagine the conversation I am about to have with Niko over and over again until I drive myself crazy.

There's a USB port in the seat back in front of me. With

my phone hovering at 8 percent battery life, I pull out my phone charger. It's kind of my like the rest of me. Now that I'm still, it's all catching up to me and the hot air on the bus is making me feel sleepy. I'm just going to close my eyes for a few minutes and try to calm myself down. It's all going to be okay. I'm going to make it with plenty of time to spare and everyone is going to listen to me.

A girl can dream, right?

I JOLT awake after what feels like a minute. The bus has just screeched to a stop at the port. I yank my phone charger out of the seat back and shove everything into my backpack. Lugging my suitcase off the bus, I nearly fall into a puddle and bump right into a man in front of me. He turns, ready to lay into me, but I push past him. I do not have time.

"Sorry!" I call over my shoulder as I frantically search for my ferry. I find it all the way at the end of the dock, so I race to catch it.

Once onboard, I put my luggage in a rack and find my seat. I have a middle seat between two people who are already fast asleep. Instead of climbing over them, I make my way to the café. My stomach is cranky, considering I haven't eaten since the bag of chips on the airplane last night.

I pick up a breakfast sandwich and a coffee before sitting at a small table near the window. I slowly eat the sandwich as I wait for the coffee to cool. They didn't have any iced coffee, but I need the caffeine boost if I'm going to survive this day. I watch the water ripple and flow in the morning sun. It takes me back to the cave, behind the boat. The moment when Niko kissed me. He saw me then. He wanted me. I hope that is enough for him to forgive me—once I tell him everything. I *am* going to tell him everything, from the way Malcolm tried to sabotage the deal to the way he used to treat me and why I was trying so desperately to run away. I can only hope he'll understand.

When I finish my breakfast, I go back to my suitcase and scrounge up the outfit I had been planning to wear to the meeting—the beautiful suit Sarah helped me find. It's wrinkled and smells a bit like dirty laundry, but I take it to the restroom to change in a small stall. At least I'm not on an airplane in a tiny bathroom where I can't even turn around.

I emerge from the restroom looking a bit worse for the wear with frizzy hair and puffy bags under my eyes. I'm determined to make this work. I let my hair down and head out onto the deck. Maybe this will make my hair look intentionally windswept. Either way, the fresh air will help clear my head, so I embrace the chill.

"You look like you are about to do something important," a calm, gravelly British accent says from over my left shoulder. When I turn, I find an older man sitting with a cigarette and a coffee. He motions to the other chair at his table. "Care to join me? I can spare a light."

I look over his shoulder and realize I've walked out into the smoking area.

I take a seat, grateful for the distraction. He hands me his pack of cigarettes. "No thanks, but I'll take the company."

"What's on your mind, love?"

"Oh, you might not want to open that can of worms." I laugh, gazing out at the water.

"Try me. I've seen a lot."

"Well, I have an important meeting in a couple of hours, and I am worried we're going to be late. It's … they aren't really expecting me, but I really want to get there. I screwed up and I need to fix it."

"Screwed up how?"

I briefly explain the situation to him.

"Well, I don't know what sort of business you're in, but if it were me and someone took a last-minute ferry to rush back to a meeting they were forced out of, I would think that showed quite a bit of dedication."

I hope so. It could also further Dimitri's impression that I'm a wreck, though.

"I'm not sure the man in charge is going to see it that way, but I appreciate it."

"Tell me about him. Maybe I can help."

I give this stranger the basic information about Dimitri Psomas and the history of the hotel. I leave out the part about falling in love with Niko and the fact that the competition is my vindictive ex-boyfriend.

"That's an interesting scenario," he comments, tapping his cigarette on the ashtray. "As a businessman, this Dimitri is going to want to see competence and ability. If your way of doing things is different from his, you just have to show him you know what you're doing. Hold your ground. It's the only way."

And how would I prove that? How can I show that, even with fewer resources and backing, Aspen Sky can deliver better service?

"Well, love, I have to get back to the missus, but good luck."

He gets up and heads back inside. I sit for a few more minutes before deciding what I need to do. I head back in to find my row. My aisle neighbor has woken up, so it's easier to squeeze into the middle seat and pull out my laptop. For the next hour, I pour over the presentation, making changes, and memorizing everything I'm going to need to convey.

When we finally pull into Mykonos Port, I check my watch. We're twenty minutes later than we were supposed to arrive. I race to get to my suitcase and see there is already a large line at the gangway to exit the ferry. My hands are shaking with anticipation by the time I finally disembark. Once on ground, I find an even longer line to grab a taxi.

That's when I hear someone call out.

The old man from the ferry—he's in what looks like a private car. "You'll be late if you wait for a cab. Come with me! We'll drive you."

I can't believe my luck. This has to be some sort of sign. The universe is helping me. Things are finally going my way for once. I pick up my bags and jump in the car.

"Thank you! I can't even tell you how much I appreciate this."

"Where to, ma'am?" the drivers asks from the front.

"The Omorfiá Hotel." I give him the address and then turn to the British couple. "I'm Jenni, by the way."

"Emma and Barnaby. Pleased to meet you, love," Barnaby's wife says. "Thanks for keeping him company on the smoke deck. He keeps promising me he'll quit, but the water makes him nervous."

"Emma's just glad she didn't have to sit out there with me." He laughs, which turns into a raspy cough. "Feeling any better about your presentation?"

I take a deep breath and check my phone. "I don't think I have a choice. The meeting starts in 20 minutes. I'll be walking in late as it is. So I'm as ready as I'm ever going to be, I think."

We pass the rental car parking lot where Niko found me yesterday, and my heart feels like it might take flight. How could that have been less than twenty-four hours ago and yet feel like a completely different universe? All I can do now is try to make things right. Because even if they decide not to go with Aspen Sky, Niko doesn't deserve to be saddled with Malcolm, who will never understand his vision for the hotel or what makes it unique.

"If you ask me, your face looks like you're chasing love rather than business," Emma says.

"How did you know?"

"A nan's intuition. I've seen my fair share of lovestruck young people. Tell us about him."

"Where do I even start? He's kind and handsome and just a good man."

"So what happened?" Barnaby asks.

Emma slaps him on the thigh. "Barnes! That's none of our business."

Before I can figure out how to respond, we're pulling into the hotel. I turn to Emma and Barnaby. "I can't thank you enough—"

"Go" Emma urges. "No time for this! Go!"

I smile, jump out of the car, and run into the lobby.

Chapter 31

Alexander jumps up from behind the desk when he sees me. "Jenni! What happened? We all thought you left. Are you okay?"

He runs over to me and takes my bags. I straighten my suit and run my fingers under my eyes to get any remaining smudged mascara.

"You have no idea how okay I am, Alexander," I say, wrapping him in a huge hug that, of course, makes him blush. I love him even more for it. "I need to get to the board meeting. Is it still in the conference room? Is Niko in there?"

"Yes, but I must warn you. He has been terribly upset since yesterday."

"That's probably my fault."

Ana's voice rings out from the stairs. "You're back!"

"Ana, thank goodness. I need your help."

She rushes to my side. "What can we do? Are you here to see Niko? He just went into the meeting, but one of the board members still isn't here so they haven't started yet. Should I get him for you?"

I need to talk to him. Preferably alone before I talk to the entire board. I would also like to not look or smell like I've been traveling for the last fifteen hours. "Yes, but let me find my makeup. I look like a mess."

I unzip my suitcase and start throwing clothes out, searching for my toiletry bag. Half of my things are on the floor before I find it.

"Come to my room. We'll clean you up. Alexander, pick up Jenni's things and then go stall the meeting. Tell the kitchen to send in coffee and pastries—do whatever you can. And tell Niko that I need him in my room in ten minutes."

"Yes, Miss Ana. I'm on it."

He quickly dumps everything into my bag, kicks it behind the desk and runs to the kitchen with the determination of a royal messenger.

"You know he worships you, right?" I ask Ana as we walk briskly to her room. "He would go in there in a clown suit if you asked him to."

"And that's why I didn't ask him to go in there in a clown suit. Alexander is such a sweetheart and also way too young for me. He will have to settle for us being friends."

When we arrive at the room, Ana ushers me into the bathroom.

"You do your makeup. I will do your hair." She grabs a barrel brush and her blow dryer. While I apply foundation, she brushes through my hair. Expertly, she curls the layers to frame my face, and my hair miraculously smooths out.

While I finish up my lips, Ana plugs in a steamer and runs it along my slacks and suit coat. I didn't think you could steam clothes while wearing them. Then, she lingers a little too long in one spot and I can feel the hot steam burn through the fabric. "Ow!"

"I'm sorry! Almost done."

Ana hits one more sleeve with the steamer and then sets it on the counter. I appraise myself in the mirror. I look ten times better. I could have never done any of this alone. Ana picks out a perfume from an acrylic case on the counter and spritzes me. "Perfection."

I raise my eyebrows at her. I'm far from perfection, but I can at least show my face without worrying that I look like I've been spit out by a whale.

"Thank you, Ana. I can't tell you how much this means to me. And I'm so sorry about yesterday. I don't know how to explain it right now without ruining all this makeup, but I know I messed up, and I'm so sorry."

Before she can respond, there's a knock on the door. "Ana?" It's Niko. Ana opens the door.

"Are you okay? Alexander said it was urgent." He looks her up and down, his face strained.

Without saying a word, Ana steps back, letting Niko into the room, where he finally sees me. He stops a few feet away. His face is still full of hurt.

"Jenni? What are you doing here?" He sounds eager, but tired.

"Can we talk?" My stomach flutters with nervous excitement.

"Of course. Can it wait? Alexander just pulled me from the board meeting, and I am afraid of what my dad might try to do in my absence."

This is going to be hard. But I have to do it. I hurt him.

"I know, but I need to explain everything. If you can give me a couple minutes, I can tell you everything. Then hopefully, if you'll have me, I can join you at the board meeting."

His eyes dart to mine and I can tell he's confused.

"I'll give you two a moment alone." Ana says and steps out into the hallway, closing the door behind her.

Where to start? I practiced this speech over and over again on the boat, but now, with Niko in the flesh, all I want to do is bury myself in his arms and beg for forgiveness. He deserves more than that, though. I have to be honest with him and tell him the whole truth.

"I'm sorry about yesterday," I start. "I was scared, and I didn't know how to make things right. So I ran. It's kind of what I do. This is a first for me, though, because I came back."

I swallow against the lump in my throat before I continue.

"For the last six months, my life has been a wreck. I'm not technically a marketer despite what Amber and I led you to believe. I'm her assistant. She sent me here only when no one else would do it. This trip—this job—was supposed to be my ticket to put my life back together. I thought that if I came here and convinced you to work with us, I would prove everyone wrong about me. I could get a promotion and get my life back on track.

"At first, everything was going so well. But then I started to fall for you. And I hadn't felt that way about anyone in years. You made me feel like the sun was shining on me again after years of storms. My last boyfriend was horrible. He was manipulative and controlling, and ... we worked together. Getting involved with him is what eventually led to me losing my job in Chicago. So I freaked out. I thought that might happen again if I got too involved with you. So I put walls up."

"And I respected them," Niko interrupts, finally speaking. He looks so desperate, and I feel the weight of his heart on my shoulders. I have to be careful with him.

"You did, and I can't begin to tell you how much that meant to me."

"So what happened?"

This is the hard part. The part where I still want to run and hide. But I won't. I have to trust Niko with this. Otherwise, we have no hope of ever having a real chance at a relationship. We can't build a future on lies. Not when that future is what I want more than anything.

"He showed up."

"Who?"

I give Niko a beat to let it sink it. After a moment, his eyes go wide, and his mouth drops slightly open. "Malcolm is your ex? I knew I hated that guy. I'm going to throw him out. How dare he show up here. He should have left the moment he saw you."

I think I love you, Niko. I don't say it out loud, because we aren't ready for that even if my heart is.

"Ana said you would do that," I say instead, smiling. "It felt too scary. I didn't trust that I was worth that sort of help. I should have known you cared enough. I should have known you would protect me. But he got in my head. He told me the board would never pick my little agency over his firm. He made big, empty promises about getting me my old job back. I never believed he would. I know he's never going to get me a spot at the firm and admit his mistakes. What I did believe was that no one would ever choose me. I didn't think I would survive that. But then, by leaving, I realized that what I was really doing was taking the chance away from myself. That the only way I could know if you picked me, or if the board picked me, was if I actually tried."

My hands are trembling. I inhale a deep breath, encouraging myself to keep going. "So I'm back. I'm asking you to forgive me. I'm not asking you to be with me because I know I broke your trust in so many ways, but I am asking you to let me pitch to the board. Because Malcolm does not have your best interests in mind. He will not take care of your hotel the way Aspen Sky will, whether I still have a job with Amber or not. I know you know that, and I'm asking you to let me help you convince your dad."

Niko steps toward me and takes my hands in his. I can't decipher his face, but I prepare myself for the worst. "I'm so sorry that happened to you. No man should ever treat you that way. I want you to know that."

I nod.

"And thank you for telling me. It's a lot to take in, but I really appreciate you trusting me enough with your life."

I nod again. All of this is great, but none of it is an answer to my question about whether he'll forgive me. His thumbs gently rub the back of my hands as he scans my face. I don't know what he's looking for, but I try to project every ounce of my heart for him to see. I am laying all of it bare. No more hiding.

"I just have one question," Niko says. I blink, waiting. "After all of this, will you stay? Not forever; I'm not asking for a commitment. But for a week, maybe? I want time with you. The time we lost and then some."

I let out a huge sigh, tears brimming on my eyelashes. I blink a couple times so the mascara doesn't smudge. "Yes, yes, of course. I mean, I'll have to run it by Amber, but yes, I would like that very much."

"I lied. I have two questions."

"Okay …"

"Can I kiss you, again?"

Instead of answering, I reach up and take his gorgeous face in both of my hands. He smiles against my lips. The kiss is fast, passionate, nothing like the one on the boat that was full of excitement and lust. This kiss sinks deep into my soul, carrying with it all the vulnerability and trust we're rebuilding. Niko's hands run into my hair, pulling me closer to him and I move my hands to his back, feeling flexed muscles through his light-weight dress shirt. Niko puts a hand on my waist, inside of my blazer, pulling me taut against his body. "I missed you," he whispers in my ear.

Someone clears their throat. "Okay, this makes me *so* happy, but Alexander just texted that they are getting antsy downstairs."

I jump back at the sound of Ana's voice. We must have

missed when she opened the door. I put a hand over my mouth and she looks us both up and down. "Niko, go wipe the lipstick off your mouth, and Jenni, let me smooth your hair."

She squeals quietly as soon as Niko steps into the bathroom. "I love this, I love this, I love this!" She runs her fingers through my hair, tucking one side behind my ear.

Niko emerges from the bathroom. "Are you ready?"

"Let's go."

I grab my computer and the three of us make our way down to the conference room. "The board consists of my dad, Dimitri; Ana's father, Andreas; two financiers; and an actor, who joins on video from California. You might recognize him from some TV sitcoms. But don't worry about it. I honestly think he mutes us until his assistant tells him it's time to chime in. He's a distant cousin who likes to put his name on things."

"That doesn't sound terrifying at all."

"It won't be. Just pretend it's you and me. No one else."

Knowing that Niko is going to be in there, rooting for me, helps. But it is still intimidating.

"Don't forget me! I'm coming in," Ana declares. We both turn to look at her. "What? I'm the new events and hospitality manager; I need to know about our marketing strategy as much as anyone else."

"That is a very good point," Niko says, winking at me. "Then you've got both of us in your corner. You were slated to present first, and I never updated the agenda, so they are probably still expecting you. Malcolm will come in for his portion afterward."

Good. I don't want to have to do this with him in the room. I would prefer not to have to see him ever again. I probably won't be that lucky, however.

Ana grunts. "I wanted to see the look on his face when she strolls in to take over." She's wearing a smirk that only a woman on a revenge mission could wear. She might be enjoying this a little too much.

When we reach the conference room doors, Niko enters first. "I'm sorry for the delay. I hope you've enjoyed the additional refreshments."

Ana and I enter the room behind him.

On the other side of the long oval table, Malcolm stands before the group, the Prewitt Luxury logo spinning on a large screen behind him. When he looks over and sees me, his eyes bulge out of their sockets. I hear Ana snicker behind me, but I'm frozen, transported back to the last time Malcolm and I were in the same room with a client.

"WHAT THE HELL WAS THAT?" *the client spits out, pointing toward me. "Is she calling me sexist? Trying to force some political agenda on my festival? Why is she even talking right now? Whiny cow."*

Is he serious? I was just trying to help. All I did was point out that an advertisement telling men to "leave the women and children at home" for the heavy metal portion of the festival might incur some criticism. It's a valid point, and he is going to feel pretty stupid when Malcolm agrees with me.

I stand my ground.

Except Malcolm doesn't agree with me. He takes the client's side. My boss—my boyfriend—is taking sides with a man who just spewed misogynistic hatred at me.

"I'm so sorry, Mr. McCarthy," Malcolm says, his hands up in the air, feigning innocence.

My stomach drops. What is he doing? We talked about this before we left the office. Malcolm agreed that the billboard was insensitive and a bad look for the festival. He had commended me for picking up on it and gave me the go-ahead to address it during our meeting. Why is he doing this?

Malcolm glares at me and then continues. "Miss Swanson is completely out of line. We would never question your judgment."

I stare at Malcolm, waiting for the catch. He has to have an angle. He wouldn't throw me under the bus like this. It would make the whole firm look bad. But he refuses to make eye contact.

"Get her out of here," McCarthy says, his voice filled with vitriol. "There's nothing I hate more than a woman who constantly plays victim. It's a billboard, not a royal decree. It's not that serious."

"Jenni," Malcolm addresses me. "I think you should go. I'll take the meeting from here."

My hands shake as I gather my things and stand, staring at Malcolm, wanting to believe this isn't happening. It's some cruel joke.

He never stops me. I walk the twenty blocks back to our office and don't hear a single word from him.

Chapter 32

I stare at Malcolm as his shock fades into a smirk. Meanwhile, my mouth is ajar and I'm still frozen in place. He knows me well enough that I'm sure he can see the uncertainty written on my face. He thinks it means he is still in control. His words ring in my head. *"I think it's time for you to leave."*

But I try to remember what Piper said. I am the only person who can stand in my way. I can't give up now. I can't let Malcolm control or define my life anymore. I have to keep going, even if he's going to stand here the entire time. I have to live my life without worrying about his approval or disapproval.

I muster all the strength I can and take a step forward and address the table. "I'm so sorry I'm late. There was a miscommunication, but I believe I have the first slot on the agenda, and I would love to tell you all about what makes Aspen Sky Marketing perfect for this hotel."

My stomach clenches as I wait for an answer. Dimitri looks at the man sitting next to him, who looks like he could be a professional wrestler. Other than the stark difference in body composition, both men share Niko's eyes, which leaves me to assume he must be Nikos's uncle, Andreas. Then the man on his other side catches my eye.

Barnaby! What are the chances? He winks at me and then gives Dimitri an encouraging nod.

Dimitri faces me. "You are quite late, Miss …"

"Swanson. Jenni Swanson." I silently beg the room to allow me to speak. I might lose my nerve if I have to wait and go after Malcolm. "Again, I'm terribly sorry. I would never waste your time. I will be very direct and quick with my presentation to make up for—"

"I've already set up my presentation. This is highly unprofessional."

Niko steps forward to join me. The stare he gives Malcolm is chilling. "She was talking. Don't interrupt her again."

Niko puts a hand in the center of my back. It's a private show of reassurance even while he's going to bat for me out loud.

"Niko, I'm sure it was an honest mistake," Dimitri says.

"I don't think so, Dad. Women are interrupted thirty-three percent more often than men in corporate meetings. That's not okay."

My heart flutters as Niko defends me.

Dimitri glances back and forth between the two younger men, his eyebrows knit together. Niko and Malcolm are locked in a standstill. The air in the room thickens with tension.

"Okay," Malcolm finally answers, rolling his eyes and throwing his hands up in the air. "I apologize for interrupting. When you didn't show up and Niko disappeared, I offered to go ahead with my pitch. And I would appreciate the professional courtesy to continue."

"Oh yeah? Like you gave her the professional courtesy of—"

"Stop." I set my hand on Niko's arm to calm him, even as my own pulse is racing. I don't need him to cause a scene on my behalf. Not yet anyway. I want the chance to give my presentation, whether it's before or after Malcolm. I need to prove to myself I can do it even if more than half the people in the room don't believe in me. "It's okay. I can wait." Turning to Malcolm I say, "I'm sorry, Mr. Prewitt. You're absolutely right. Go ahead."

Niko, Ana, and I take seats at the table and watch as Malcolm, clearly flustered, attempts to regain his composure. "As I was saying, I represent a luxury brand marketing firm out of Chicago. Prewitt Luxury has worked with some of the largest hotel and hospitality brands in the world, including the world's leading five-star hotel, and of course, Psomas wine brands and vineyards."

Niko leans over to whisper, "What is your plan?"

"I believe in my message. I don't want the board to pick me just because of who Malcolm is. I want them to pick me because of what Aspen Sky has to offer."

Malcolm continues with his presentation, focusing on massive campaigns, primetime television ads, and full-spread magazine features—all the things they excel at. There's one thing he's forgetting to keep in mind, though. He is treating the Omorfiá like it's the JW Marriott and his presentation is full of stock photos of people in ball gowns and luxury cars. He clearly hasn't done a single ounce of research on the hotel or their target demographic. It's honestly laughable, at least where Niko is concerned. I don't know whether his dad recognizes this or not. Maybe he wants the Omorfiá to cater to such high-end clientele.

I lean over toward Ana. "You never told me your dad was Dwayne 'The Rock' Johnson."

"Hardly," she whispers back. "Don't let him hear you say that, or it will go straight to his head."

Malcolm flips the slide and yet another diamond-studded model in a sleek hotel lobby fills the screen.

Niko whispers in my ear. "If he says the word 'upscale' one more time, I'm going to throw an apricot at him."

I snort. And then have to pretend to be stifling a sneeze when Andreas glances over at us.

"And that is why I think you'll be amazed by what Prewitt Luxury can do for your upscale hotel."

I bump Niko with my knee in silent warning not to actually chuck a small fruit across the room.

"Thank you, Mr. Prewitt," Dimitri says when it's clear Malcolm has finished.

"Since we are in the unique situation of having both parties here at the same time, why don't we have Miss Swanson give her presentation and save all questions for the end when we have a better grasp on both agencies?"

The men around the table nod in agreement and Dimitri gestures for me to take the floor.

Niko squeezes my thigh under the table. My chest feels tight with nerves, but his touch gives me the strength I need to stand.

"Thank you," I say, and plug my laptop into the presentation screen. "My name is Jenni Swanson, and I represent Aspen Sky Marketing. We are a small, female-owned agency specializing in marketing independent hotels and resorts around the world. We think every property is unique and needs a tailor-made marketing plan to reflect that."

I pull up the first slide of my presentation. A chart plotting the ROI of all the campaigns we ran in the first quarter of the year. Once I'm talking, the tightness in my chest starts to ease. I'm confident in my proposal.

"As you can see, we work with properties that do under ten million in revenue each year, not twenty-five billion like most worldwide luxury brands. Clientele in this bracket need different strategies and tools than the major industry leaders.

As an agency, we have made it our goal to identify the best ways to be successful in this bracket.

"Let me show you a ranch in Durango, Colorado. The property has twenty cabins and a total of eighty beds. The site includes a working horse stable, blacksmith workshops, and a community garden open to the public. Last year, we ran a digital ad campaign targeting couples in their thirties whose online activity suggests an interest in homesteading, western romance novels, and traveling with friends. In addition, we created a featured guest campaign, where we produced high-quality videos interviewing real guests about their stay. We used those videos on social media and as ads on video-sharing platforms."

"Hey, I think I've been there. I filmed a movie somewhere in that area once."

We all look around the room, confused.

"It's me, over here on the computer." I forgot about the actor cousin on video.

"Oh, hi! Then you know how unique it is."

"Yep, it's dope. Sorry for the interruption."

I make eye contact with Niko, who is covering his mouth. No doubt because he's trying not to laugh. Ana sits with rapt attention on me, and the rest of the men in the room shift in their seats, waiting for me to continue.

"The ranch saw an eighteen percent increase in winter bookings and a record twelve percent year-over-year increase this past spring, which was already their second-busiest season. We have seen similar success with a dozen properties in the same revenue range."

I flip to the next slide and a photo of the Omorfiá fills the screen.

"After spending time here, I have seen that the Omorfiá Hotel is unique in its emphasis on lifting the community in which it sits. If I was running your marketing, I would emphasize the opportunity for guests to purchase local art in the on-site gallery, the chance to eat produce grown on the rooftop, and the walkability to all of Mykonos's best spots. Today's travelers are eco-conscious and self-aware, and will jump at the opportunity to support businesses that share their values."

I flip through sample campaigns and comparative clients, showcasing how well we work in this sector of the market.

"But most of all, what makes Aspen Sky different from larger firms is that we know how to get the most out of a tighter budget. TV commercials and fancy magazine spreads might create brand awareness, but they cost a lot of money for unrealized sales. By targeting specific audiences, we can get the most return out of a smaller budget and reach the people who are ready to book their next Greek getaway."

Niko smiles and I know I've nailed it. Not even Dimitri can argue with that logic.

When I'm done, Malcolm stands to join me. One of the financiers asks Malcolm a question about the cost of his flashy campaigns. He answers with the same charisma and finesse he's always had, without ever really answering the question.

"Mr. Prewitt, what do *you* see as the key selling point of the Omorfiá?" Barnaby asks, giving me a knowing glance. Dimitri leans forward in his chair, his gaze fixed on Malcolm.

With this back and forth, I start to feel a bit shaky. Presenting prepared material is one thing, but answering direct questions with Malcolm standing next to me is another.

"That's a great question," Malcolm starts. "The key selling point of this fine hotel is its location. Look around you. This island is magnificent. The beaches, the architecture, the culture —who wouldn't want a piece of all of this luxury?"

He raises his hands as if revealing text in the sky before continuing. "Imagine sinking your toes in the golden sand of Santorini, a luxury cabana stocked with Greece's finest wines—"

Everyone in the room turns as we hear chaotic laughter erupt from the computer monitor. "Dog, are you serious right now? I've never even set foot at the Omorfiá Hotel and even I know it isn't on Santorini. You get lost?"

Our actor friend has grabbed his own device and is laughing while spinning around in his chair, making me dizzy the longer I watch the screen.

I glance over at Niko and Ana, who are both trying to hide gleeful, almost-maniacal, smiles. Dimitri is running his hands through his hair. His knight in shining armor is suddenly looking rusty.

Hope blossoms in my chest. This is my chance to show I'm much more prepared than Malcolm. "If I may, the thing that makes the Omorfiá great isn't its location on Mykonos. There are hundreds of resorts on this island, all with the same access to the ocean and flavors of Greece." I use air quotes on that last phrase, and Andreas snickers—exactly what I was going for.

"Okay, okay, it was a simple mistake," Malcolm says, a fake smile plastered across his face. "I'll own that. But it doesn't change the fact that we have decades of experience marketing top-end luxury hotels just like yours."

I step forward, reasserting myself to finish my statement. "As I was saying, the location isn't what makes the Omorfiá special. The Omorfiá bridges the gap between luxury and mid-range hotels. At the Omorfiá, you can feel a touch of luxury in rooms to die for while still being able to rent a bike to take a picnic lunch from Yia-Yia's to a remote beach for the afternoon. The Omorfiá feels like coming home. It feels like family. It doesn't matter who you are or where you come from, you can enjoy your stay."

Dimitri looks like he is contemplating what I've said. He leans over to Andreas and whispers something.

"It's like a premium wine—all the flavor of luxury wine,

but more accessible and better-selling," Dimitri says to the room.

I don't know much about wine, but I think he understands the point I'm trying to make. "Precisely. You aren't losing any of the value, but you're gaining so much more."

"I like it," Andreas said with a nod. "Dimitri, our vineyards are exclusive and top-of-the-line. The Omorfiá doesn't need to be. I think Miss Swanson on to something. We can't compete with all those waterfront resorts. We need to find our own place in the market."

Dimitri nods.

"Wait, hold on. You can't be serious." Malcolm points a finger at Dimitri. "You brought me here. You said it was as good as done." Malcolm is starting to lose his composure, his blonde hair slipping out of place. He's pacing.

Dimitri clears his throat. "It's business. You know how it goes."

"I have a question for Mr. Prewitt," Ana jumps in. "What made you want to work with our small boutique hotel? From your presentation, it's clear that you typically work with such grand entities."

"I'm glad someone is still taking this seriously. I see a ton of potential with this hotel. I would love to see the Omorfiá expand throughout the Mediterranean, onto other Greek islands, Malta, and even up into Italy. This property won't stay small forever. If Niko Psomas is anything like his father, I'm sure the brand will take off, and I want Prewitt Luxury to be right there with it."

He gives me a pointed look. That was definitely an attack on my presentation.

"So it didn't have anything to do with the fact that you knew Jenni was here and wanted to undercut her, yet again?"

Malcolm takes a step back. "I don't know what you're

talking about. I came here as a favor to Dimitri and my father. And because this is a fantastic opportunity, of course."

I stand, dumbfounded, but also loving the fact that Malcolm is getting put in the hot seat while not being the one lighting the fire.

"So you didn't fire her from her job without cause *while* you were dating, creep on her social media, see she was here, look up the hotel, and *then* ask Daddy Prewitt if you could come check us out as a client?"

Had Ana listened at the door earlier? Because I'm pretty sure I only told those things to Niko. She is firing on all cylinders. Malcolm is starting to look terrified. His pupils are dilated and his brow is starting to sweat. But like any animal backed into a corner, he intends to go down fighting.

"No, that's not it at all. If she's been telling you lies, I wouldn't be surprised. She lost her job because she was incompetent and argued with clients. I had nothing to do with it. And I'll say it again: I'm here because I believe in the long-term potential of this property."

Dimitri stands abruptly, placing his hands on the table in front of him. "I do not appreciate being used as a pawn in your personal matters. I have worked with your father for a long time and, if this is true, he is not going to happy hearing about this little move of yours."

This is getting ugly. I should intervene. As much as I appreciate what Ana is trying to do, I don't need to turn this into a court of personal affairs.

"I think we're all getting a little out of bounds here," I say. "Can we stay focused on the hotel and what is most important here?"

Dimitri nods at me, reluctantly. Malcolm, on the other hand, isn't ready to let it go.

"Mr. Psomas, trust me—it's all lies. That's what she does. She's a lying little witch." His lip twitches and I can tell he's past the point of calming down. Despite the fact that he just called me a witch, I'm kind of enjoying this. No one, and I mean no one, ever makes Malcolm lose his cool.

"Watch your mouth," Niko's voice is stern and steady. "Do not talk about her that way again. I know you used to push her around, but not anymore. Nobody talks to her like that if I have anything to do with it."

My throat constricts. Is he doing what I think he's doing? I am not ready to talk about this with everyone in this room. They are all going to know I'm weak.

"What does that mean?" Andreas stands. He's even more intimidating standing up.

"What does what mean?" Malcolm says.

"That you pushed her around."

Malcolm rolls his eyes. "What happened between Jenni and I isn't anyone's business but ours. She's clearly been telling Niko lies."

"Papa, he was just like Callie's boyfriend."

Before anyone can respond, Andreas lunges at Malcolm, putting all his weight behind a stiff punch to Malcolm's jaw. Malcolm falls to the ground, grabbing his face, while Andreas looms over him. Dimitri grabs his brother at the same time that Niko jumps around the table to stand as a buffer between his uncle and Malcolm.

All the air whooshes out of my lungs. When I breathe again, however, it feels like a fresh start. I didn't realize how much I wanted to see Malcolm finally get his due. I didn't know much I needed someone to stand up and defend me. I'm not weak. There's nothing wrong with me. He is the one who is wrong. I don't condone violence, but seeing Malcolm lying on the ground releases all of the power he has held over me. A weight falls from my shoulder.

"That was for my daughter. She lost her life because of a man like you."

But it was also for me, even if Andreas never realizes the gift he's given me.

Niko puts both of his hands on his uncle's chest. "Okay, I think he's got the idea. Why don't you go take a walk?"

Ana takes her father's hand and escorts him out of the conference room. I hope they're able to have a real conversation about Callie and how much they both miss her.

Niko reaches a hand down to Malcolm, but he brushes it off and picks himself up off the ground. "You're going to be lucky if I don't press charges. I was just assaulted on your property."

"Young man, I think you're going to be lucky if I don't drop your firm from all Psomas wine brands. You played me, treated my son with disrespect, and I just don't like you. So I would rethink that threat unless you want to deal with your father."

Malcolm grunts and dusts off his suit. He gathers his things and heads to the door. "You know what? Good luck and good riddance."

"Feel free to find a new hotel to stay at tonight," Niko adds as Malcolm exits the room.

"Can someone tell me what just happened?" A voice rings out from the laptop on the table. "This is the most exciting board meeting I've ever attended. I need to start showing up in person."

Barnaby grabs the laptop. "We're going to convene this session. We'll let you know when we reschedule."

With that, he closes the laptop and heads toward the door, grabbing the other financier on his way. "We'll let the three of you talk. Niko, you have our support with Aspen Sky Marketing."

When it's just Niko, his dad, and I, we all take a seat at the table. Every bit of tension has left my body, leaving me exhausted.

"I'm so sorry, Mr. Psomas," I say to Dimitri. "I never meant for any of that to get personal. I promise that if you choose to work with my agency, nothing like this will ever happen again."

"Miss Swanson, you made some really good points in your presentation—things I hadn't thought about. I don't like to admit that I'm old or stuck in my ways, but there's a possibility I wasn't seeing the whole picture. Aspen Sky is a perfect match for the Omorfiá."

It takes a second for his words to sink in. When they do, a burning sensation flutters in my chest. I did it. I really did it.

"I appreciate that, sir."

"And I haven't seen my son so passionate about anything in a long time. I won't pretend to have been a very involved parent, but I would have to be an idiot not to see how much he cares about you."

Niko and I lock eyes. Clearly, we weren't hiding it as much as we thought we were in that meeting. "Dad, I—"

"No, no. It's okay. Have your fun. If the two of you think you can work together even with this budding romance, you have my blessing. Just don't make me regret it."

Once he leaves the room, Niko pulls me into an embrace. I lean my head against his chest.

"Are you okay?" He asks, stroking my hair.

"I think so." I nod and squeeze my arms around his middle. "We did it."

He kisses my forehead.

"So what's next?"

Chapter 33

Niko and I escape to his room, since I no longer have one, and collapse on the bed. His room is slightly larger than mine was but not the giant suite I had been imagining. There are little touches everywhere that are just so Niko it makes me smile—a stack of books on the nightstand, a collection of shells on the desk, a picture of him and his mom in California.

"Thank you for letting me collapse here. I don't think I've ever been this tired."

"Where did you go last night?" He rolls onto his side and tucks my hair behind my ear.

"That is a very long story involving an airplane, a bus, a ferry, and jumping in a stranger's car when the taxi line was way too long."

"It sounds like an adventure. I kind of wish I could have been there."

"If you had been, I wouldn't have had to race across the island!"

"Well, I'm glad you did." He takes my hand. "I wish I had known everything you were going through. I would have done so many things differently. I made everything about me once

Dad brought in another firm. I didn't even pick up on any of it. I'm so sorry."

I smile up at him. "Don't apologize for other people's mistakes. You had no idea, and I refused to tell you because I was scared you would look at me differently."

"Never." His face is so sincere. "You, and all women like you, are so strong. I would never think otherwise."

"Well, I know that *now*." I might be ready to talk about it, but I'm still not super comfortable with such open vulnerability and declarations. Something to work on, I guess.

Then, over his shoulder, I see two mosaic art pieces on his night stand. "Our mosaics! You picked them up!"

"I did. I stopped by yesterday morning. I was going to bring yours to you after the party."

I pick up my sunburst and a smile spreads across my cheeks. It's even more meaningful now that I've finally accepted the path my life has taken. The sun is shining and I couldn't be happier.

"Thank you! I love it. They both look so good."

Niko leans in and kisses me tenderly. I close my eyes and take it all in: the soft touch of his lips, the salty pine smell of him, the warmth of the bed beneath me. I could stay here forever.

And then my stomach growls and it's quite possibly the loudest, most unattractive noise that has ever come from my body.

My cheeks flush and I try to pretend like nothing happened, pulling Niko closer into the kiss.

Still, he pushes me away. "You must be starving. You didn't touch the refreshments in the meeting. When was the last time you ate?"

"I had a sandwich on the boat, but yeah, that's about it for the last twenty-four hours."

Niko jumps up from the bed and reaches for his suit coat

and wallet. "Well, that is unacceptable. You stay here. Get in the bed. Rest. I will get us food."

"No, I couldn't. Please don't leave."

He leans down and kisses me one more time. "I will be back soon. I promise. You can't survive on a breakfast sandwich."

When Niko leaves the room, the silence finally gives me a minute to process everything from the last few hours. I don't want to go back to Chicago. I don't even want a corporate job. Without realizing it, I had been trying to make myself fit into a box that wasn't right for me. I had been so focused on squeezing into it that I never stopped to evaluate. Meanwhile, in the last six months my life has been building up around me into something I really enjoy. I just had to let go of that box. I had to accept that my dreams have changed.

I snuggle into the pillows. I don't know how I'll ever be able to stay awake until Niko gets back. The bed is so cozy, and I'm feeling stress-free for the first time in years.

A knock on the door pulls me from the bed. Is Niko back with food already?

When I open the door, Alexander is there with my suitcase. "Mr. Psomas asked me to bring these up to his room," he says with a wink.

I blush. "Oh, thank you, Alexander. I … we just came up here to relax since I don't have a room anymore."

He gives me a sly grin. "I could find you a new room, if that's what you would prefer, Miss Swanson."

I think about it for a second. I'm done shying away from the things and people I want. I'm sure Niko and I will talk about it later, but until then, I'm not going to run away just because I don't know what he wants.

"Nope, this is good for now." I reach out and take the handle of my bag. "Thank you, Alexander. I'm sorry I disappeared from your birthday party. I hope it was a good time."

"Don't apologize. It was very special. I'll let you rest, but please let me know if there is anything else I can do."

He stops and considers something for a moment. He breaks character and gives me a hug. "I'm so glad you came back."

"Me too."

He leaves, closing the door behind him, leaving me in Niko's hotel room with all of my things. I look around the space and catch my reflection in the mirror. Despite all of Ana's efforts earlier, I could still use a shower. So I lug my suitcase into the bathroom and lock the door. Steam from the shower fills the bathroom and I disrobe. I let the hot water pour over my body. Never have I appreciated a shower more than I do right now, not even after week-long backpacking trips. I wash every morsel of dirt and grime from a day's back-and-forth travel from my body and lather my hair in conditioner.

I cry into the water, releasing all the pent-up emotion from the last few days. I can really let it out now that I'm on the other side. It's not sorrowful tears so much as cathartic ones, mourning the years I spent trapped in shame and guilt created by one man who never deserved an ounce of my energy.

When I step out of the shower, I check my phone. I have a message from Piper. I had sent her a quick thumbs up emoji when Niko and I left the meeting, letting her know everything went well. I was planning to call her later and give her the entire play-by-play.

> Piper: I hope that means you nailed it! The presentation ... or Niko ;) Amber was confused but relieved that you're okay and still there. She wants you to call her after the presentation. I told her it might take a little longer to buy you some time, but you know her. The sooner the better.

Jenni: Thanks, you're the best. I'll call her. Cliff notes: Everything went well. Nailed the presentation. Malcolm got pummeled by Niko's uncle. Made up with Niko, but haven't nailed him.

Jenni: Yet.

Piper: Yesssss. Slay, queen!

I quickly dress and brush my hair. I consider finding a blow-dryer, but I'd rather just let my natural waves have their moment today. Once I'm dressed in a pair of jean shorts and a plain white top, I sit at Niko's desk and send Amber a text. I know she'll see that before an email, and I don't want to keep her waiting any longer now that I have good news.

Amber: Give me three minutes and I'll call you.

When my phone rings, it's a video call. My first instinct is to decline and call her back with audio only—my hair is still wet and I'm not wearing any makeup—but after a second, I realize Amber is not the type to even notice, let alone care. She just wants to hear the news.

When the picture comes to life, I'm looking at an image of Amber in a hospital bed.

"Jenni, hi! How are you?"

She is in a blissful mood, considering everything that has happened out of her control the last couple days.

"I'm great. But how are you? Are you at the hospital? We can do this later."

"No, no! Let's talk now. I need to know how it went. And yes, I'm at the hospital, but it's fine. I already had the baby. He's sleeping in the bassinet."

At that, she flips the camera around and shows me a little wrapped-up burrito of a baby with her husband sleeping on a recliner in the background. Of course, Amber would be taking calls from her hospital bed while everyone else sleeps.

"Oh my goodness! Amber! He's adorable! Congratulations."

"Isn't he? But we can talk about him later. What happened at the meeting? I'm dying to know!"

I laugh. I'm so relieved I don't have to tell her I failed as she sits there recovering from childbirth.

"The good news is that we got the client." I can't stop from grinning as I tell her. "We are going to finalize the paperwork tomorrow, but the presentation went well and they are really excited to work with us."

I hear a small cry and see a nurse place Amber's baby in her arms.

"And the bad news?" Amber croons in a baby voice.

"What?"

"Usually when someone says 'the good news is,' they follow it up with bad news."

While Amber is making faces at her baby, the door to the hotel room opens and Niko comes back in, holding two greasy brown bags of food. I gesture to the phone, so he knows to be quiet. I was hoping not to have this conversation in front of him, but I can't ask him to leave his own room. He sits down on a chair next to the desk.

"Oh! No, Amber, there's no bad news." I say her name in the hopes that Niko will understand what conversation I'm having.

"Okay, tell me everything anyway. What happened at the meeting?"

Niko sets down a bag and pulls out a couple of loukoumades, dripping with honey. He makes a dramatic show of placing one of the fried balls in his mouth and then licking the honey off his fingers. He is trying to make me laugh, and it's almost working.

"The director of the board brought in his own marketing team. He had wanted to work with a more traditional firm, one he had worked with before. So we ended up having to duke it out a bit."

Niko, now with a chin covered in honey, whispers, "Tell her it was my fault."

"No!" I mouth back.

"I missed that. What did you say?" Amber asks. She's now breastfeeding, and I'm starting to picture how all our meetings will go for the next year.

"Nothing. I was just saying that there was some internal drama and miscommunication on the board. I thought I wasn't going to be able to give my presentation, but we got it all worked out in the end."

Amber is crooning at her baby again. Meanwhile, Niko is dangling another fried dough ball in front of me to tempt me into hanging up the phone.

"Well, you're lucky I am full of hormones and high on baby smell or I would ask you a dozen more questions. For now, I'll just take the good news and not worry about anything else."

I make eye contact with Niko. I have one more thing I need to discuss.

"Amber? While I have you on the phone, I was hoping I could extend my trip? Not a vacation—I'm happy to continue working remotely—but I wanted to check if it would be okay to be on weird hours for a while longer? There are a number of things I still want to see and do here on the island."

I never ask for time off or extensions or anything that could possibly be seen as me not being at her beck and call so I'm holding my breath to see how she'll respond.

"That's fine. As long as you meet your deliverables, I don't have a problem. I won't be online anytime soon if this little guy has his way. When you're back, I want you to take over my client load while I'm on leave. I've already sent you a hand-off document of what needs to be done over the next few weeks. Once I'm back to work, we'll get you your own clients. Welcome to life as an associate—as long as you help me find a replacement assistant."

Did she just say what I think she said? My body buzzes with excitement.

"Yes! Of course," I say, trying not to squeal until I'm off the phone. "Wow, thank you. I won't let you down."

"I know you won't. Enjoy the rest of your stay." Amber hangs up just as her baby starts to cry again, and I put my phone down.

"I brought food," Niko says. "If you couldn't tell."

"I got a promotion!" I squeal and bounce in my seat.

"In that case ... I brought food to celebrate!"

I grab the bag of loukoumades and inhale the fresh aroma. "How did you know I've been dreaming about this food since the other night?"

My heart melts into a puddle of joy at Niko's smile.

"Lucky guess," he says. "Come out to the balcony and eat with me."

There's a small table on the balcony, and Niko brings both chairs to one side of the table, so we can sit together and watch the ocean. A pair of seagulls fly in front of us, and I watch them circle and head down to the beach in the distance. Niko takes my hand in his, but we eat in peaceful silence.

I don't want this moment to end. In the back of my mind, there's a long list of things I need to do: talk to Niko about the contract, change my flights, call Piper and thank her from the bottom of my heart, apologize to pretty much everyone, tell my parents I'm staying longer, and figure out what our working relationship will be going forward. But the only thing that matters right now is sitting here with my hand in Niko's, listening to the crashing of the waves and breathing in the salty air. For once, I'm not hiding anything or pretending to be someone I'm not, and it's refreshing.

Eventually, Niko cleans up our late lunch and takes everything inside. When he comes back out onto the balcony, he pulls me up from my chair and wraps his arms around my waist, pulling me against him as he leans against the stone balcony railing.

"Well, your boss said yes. Does that mean you'll stay with me for a while longer?" Niko leans down and kisses my cheek, edging closer to my jawbone.

"I'm considering it."

He moves to my mouth, and I sigh. "What can I do to convince you?"

My knees buckle. "That's working," I say against his lips. I want nothing more than to keep kissing him, but I need to talk to him first. We need some boundaries. I gently pull away, putting some space between us. "First, can we talk? I've been thinking a lot about what your dad said about us working together."

Niko's smile drops. "Okay …"

"No, it's not bad. I promise. I was thinking, I'm not the only employee at Aspen Sky. It might be best, for us, if someone else handles the account. That way, we can focus on each other, without the pressure of work. Do you think that's okay?"

He pulls me closer to him and nuzzles his face in my hair. My whole body is electrified, responding to each and every touch. "I like the sound of focusing on each other. I can focus here—" He kisses my temple. "—and here." He kisses my neck.

"Good … great." I'm starting to lose my breath. "I'll make sure the account gets assigned to someone."

"Good, because I am not giving you up. Not when we're just getting started."

I lean into him, kissing him passionately to show him how much that means to me.

He picks me up, wrapping my legs around his waist. "I'm going to carry you inside and do what I have wanted to do since the moment you climbed on the back of my scooter at the beach. As long as that's okay with you?"

"Yes, please."

Chapter 34

Ten days later, I am sitting in the kitchen of the Omorfiá Hotel with my laptop open on the stainless-steel workspace. It's after hours, but Niko and I are making a cake, and I'm catching up on some admin work for Amber while he mixes.

"You can't leave tomorrow without a taste of my grandma's portokalopita. It's a must."

I believe it. I'm pretty sure I've gained ten pounds since I arrived in Greece almost three weeks ago. And every single ounce was worth it.

"I can't believe you're smart, generous, sexy, *and* you can cook. I mean, give the men of the world a break, won't you? They'll never be able to keep up." I wink at him over my laptop screen.

"I never said I was a good cook. I said I would try to make it. I make no promises it will turn out."

I finish the last of my notes for next week's staff meeting and close the computer. I stand and go to join Niko, where he has just pulled a tray out of the oven with shredded phyllo dough on it.

"Isn't this supposed to be like a crust or wrap? It's the same thing as the baklava, right?"

Niko bops my nose with a flour-dusted finger. "Very clever, young padawan. But in this recipe, you shred it and bake it into the batter. It adds texture to the cake."

"What's a padawan?"

"Are you serious?" Niko eyes me. "*Star Wars*? Yoda? None of that rings a bell?"

I laugh. He can't be that serious. "No. I don't remember the last time I watched a *Star Wars* movie. Maybe never?"

Niko clutches his chest as if I've stabbed him. "This is a tragedy. I'm just now finding this out? How has this not come up in all this time we have been connected at the hip?"

It's true. Niko hasn't let me out of his sight since the board meeting. Each day, we've spent a few hours doing the bare minimum of our respective work—Niko pulled an extra desk into his office for me—and then exploring the island, eating at all the best restaurants, and spending our nights together. It's been one of the most exhilarating times of my entire life.

"I don't know," I say. "Maybe because we were having too much fun having a life?"

I stick my tongue out at him. His jaw drops clear to the floor. "How dare you make fun of *Star Wars*."

Niko lunges toward me and I run to escape his grasp because I know what's coming. I'm too late, though. His hands wrap around my waist, tickling me. He won't stop until I give in or distract him with a kiss. I choose the second option.

His mouth tastes like oranges, citrusy and sweet. "You were sneaking orange slices from the cake, were you?"

"I plead the fifth." He kisses me again. "Are you done with work? Want to help with the rest of the cake?"

"Put me in, coach!" We move as one back to the cooking space.

"Will you make the syrup?" he asks, before handing me the recipe.

That I can handle.

"I forgot how much I enjoy cooking," I say, as I pour sugar into a simmer pot. "I used to cook a lot with my mom." I smile, remembering all the times we made peach cobbler after visiting a u-pick farm in Palisades.

Niko is cutting oranges and removing the seeds before tossing them in the food processor. "Oh, yeah? Why'd you stop?"

I don't want to think about it too hard, but if I were to guess, Malcolm said something at one time or another that made me feel it was an undesirable hobby. He would only ever want to eat out at the hippest places.

"Who knows? It doesn't matter now."

A few nights ago, I called my parents to check on them after their camping trip. My mom got teary when I told her everything that had transpired on the trip—the important things about getting the job and that met someone. When I asked her what was wrong, she smiled and said, "I am just so proud of you. I have always been afraid I gave you too much of my worry gene and that it was going to keep you from being happy. It just makes me so happy to see you so confident. My old Jenni is back."

The admission had shocked me. I didn't know she felt that way. But maybe we can both work on worrying a bit less and trusting a bit more. I told her I loved her and that I couldn't wait to catch up when I get home.

Niko brings my attention back to the kitchen. He's chopping pistachios and almonds into tiny pieces.

"What are you working on over there?"

"This is my *yia-yia's* special ingredient. Most portokalopita cakes just have orange slices on top, but we always add nuts for a bit of salt and texture."

Sounds delicious.

"And don't think you're safe from the *Star Wars* conversation. I've decided this will be what keeps us busy until we see each other again. We'll watch the whole catalog start to finish and discuss."

"I'd like that." My heart warms at making plans for the future with Niko. As I look around the kitchen, with a new job, and a future with this man I have fallen for, I am unabashedly happy.

But getting the promotion isn't the happy ending. Niko isn't either, no matter where our relationship goes. How I feel—at home in my own skin—is the happy ending. It doesn't change anything that Malcolm did to me, but I know I can mourn what happened to me while also celebrating the new life I have in front of me.

Who I was then doesn't have to be who I always am. He doesn't get to hold that control over me anymore. I get to decide what I want for my life. I'm not going to let anyone take that away from me again.

I finish with the syrup and set it aside to cool.

Niko pours the cake batter into a round pan. "Want to do the honors?" he asks, holding out the plate of orange slices.

"I do!" I smile. He brings them over and stands behind me, hands on my hips. "You want to lay the slices around the pan, however you want. They are supposed to add a bit of tanginess, but are mostly decorative."

"So here?" I say, placing a half slice at the edge of the cake, gently dropping it onto the batter.

"Yes, and the next one can go here." He guides my hand and places the next slice. We lay all of the slices on the cake and then put it in the oven.

Niko pulls me into the restaurant and onto his lap at one of the tables.

"Well, now that we are going all-in on the new changes to the hotel, what other ideas do you have?"

"That's what you want to talk about? Now?" I lean in for a kiss, not wanting to spend my last night with him talking about work.

He eases me back. "I do. I think your ideas are incredible, and I want to hear them. Once you leave, I'm going to need a passion project to keep me from crawling to Colorado to see you before Christmas."

Niko has already booked a flight to visit me in Colorado for Christmas. Piper and Sarah are hoping to have the inn reopened by then and have promised to let us be their first guests. I have already started looking for apartments I can rent in Pineview Springs or maybe the next town down the mountain. It's the first step to taking control of this new life.

"Well, off the top of my head, I can think of one or two things for you to do."

"I knew you would." Niko squeezes my thigh.

"In addition to your garden on the rooftop, you could put in a bee colony and plant native wildflowers around the entire property for pollination. The bees would help the island ecosystem and you could sell the honey in local markets and as souvenirs at some point. You could partner with a local beekeeper."

He laughs and nuzzles my shoulder.

"What's so funny?"

"I'm just imagining Alexander in one of those beekeeping uniforms. What are they called?"

"A bee suit?"

"Huh." He shakes his head. "They should really have a fun name for those. Bee suit is very anticlimactic."

"Oh, my gosh, you are so ridiculous sometimes. Focus!"

"Yes, ma'am." I drape my arm over his shoulder, running

my fingers through the hair at the back of his head as we lock eyes. "What else?"

"Well, I would love to talk to Ana about hosting community events like open mic nights or cooking classes."

"She would love that," Niko says.

Niko and I continue to talk about our plans for the next few months while we wait. We both want to soak up as much of each other as possible. This week has been one of the best of my life and even though we're going to be apart, I'm not worried. I know that we both have really exciting things happening in our lives, and we will be there to support each other. I'm not worried about the next life goal or whether someone approves of my choices. For the first time—possibly ever—I feel comfortable with where my life is rather than racing to the next accomplishment to prove myself.

We hear the oven timer ding and head back into the kitchen. Niko pulls the cake out of the oven and sets it on a cooling rack. "Grab that syrup. We're going to pour it over the cake, so it soaks into the sponge."

I gently pour the syrup from the pot, trying to make sure I cover it evenly. "Like that?"

"Perfect. Now grab those plates and silverware."

Niko leads me through the back of the kitchen to an outdoor, private dining area with a view of the ocean where someone has set up a candlelit table. The table is set for two with champagne and a vase full of white roses. It's completely breathtaking.

"Niko, this is too much."

He sets the cake down and grabs a lighter out of his pocket to light the candles. Once everything is ready, he pulls out my chair. Niko cuts a slice of the still-warm cake and puts it in front of me.

"Well, you haven't tasted the cake yet. It could all be a disaster."

I highly doubt that. I take a bite to prove to him that it's incredible. The warm spongy cake melts in my mouth. The orange and nutty flavors marry beautifully. And the syrup—it's almost sickeningly sweet, but the tartness of the orange slices balances it out.

"That might just be the best thing I've eaten this entire trip. You're spoiling me!"

He grabs my hand and pulls it toward him, placing a gentle kiss just above my knuckles.

"Everyone deserves a partner who treats them like the most important person in the room. That's who you are to me, and I'm going to keep spoiling you until you believe you deserve it."

He places another kiss farther up on the inside of my arm. "And then I'm going to spoil you even more."

Bonus Scene

Did you fall in love with Niko? Scan the QR code below to read a bonus scene of Jenni's arrival at the Omorfiá Hotel from Niko's point of view!

Leave a Review

Wow! I can't believe I live in a world where you just read my book! I hope you loved it. Thank you from the bottom of my heart. If you enjoyed the book, please consider leaving a review on Goodreads, StoryGraph or Amazon! Reviews help spread the word and are essential for indie authors. It also brings a bit of sunshine to my day anytime my book is shared!

Acknowledgments

This book has been a long-standing dream. In practice, it has been three years in the making. So many people helped along the way.

To my husband, Jon: I owe you the world. Thank you for always being my biggest supporter and my own personal golden retriever MMC. You fill my heart with sunshine. Adventures with you are my favorite! I hope this book reminds you of the week we spent on Mykonos 11 years ago!

To my children: Thank you for endless patience and forgiveness when I spent hours on my laptop. Thank you for always going with me to the park and letting me write while you played. Thank you for filling me with hope for the future.

To Sarah: Thank you for being my ride or die bestie for the last fifteen years. Three years ago, I sent you an unhinged Marco Polo about finally having "the idea" for the book I've always wanted to write. You were the first person to hype me up, and you are still hyping me up after all this time!

To the Pirate Queens (a.k.a. the best critique group): Thank for reading every version of this book and listening to my rambling, my frustrations, my fears and my tears. You are all amazing and I can't wait for our very own accidental getaway someday! Because you know we are all just as clumsy and awkward as Jenni!

To Rachel, Emily & the Tenacious Writing community: I could have never done this without the classes, workshops, moral support and feedback. I have never found a more inclusive, supportive and uplifting group!

To all the indie authors who came before me: Bravo to you! Thank you for paving the way and making it a little less scary to embark on this journey.

About the Author

Molly Gray has traveled the world, but still feels most at home inside a good rom-com. A former journalist, Molly now spends her time being a mom to her three kids and writing romance books with an adventurous streak. On her desk, you can almost always find chips and salsa. She also loves hiking, crocheting, coaching her kids' sports teams, and reading...of course.

Website: http://www.mollygraybooks.com
Instagram and TikTok: @mollygraywrites